Goldsmith Jones

Sam Taylor-Pye

Clink Street

London | New York

Part 1

San Francisco 1863

Chapter 1

Joe goes missing

Joe and me did such fine work of hiding on board the steamboat, that when she docked up at St. Frankie's Bay, and we walked off the deck, no one was the wiser. He gave me half the winnings, just in case one of us got robbed, and we headed up Jefferson Hill, and carried on until we got to Union Square.

It was hot, and it was crowded. All the stores, the hotel, the gold mint, and the jailhouse had stars and stripes banners hanging from their faces. Either side of the boardwalk, there was people. Men, the few women there were in this city, and their children were waving little union flags above their heads.

We asked a seller how much for one and he said fifty cents.

"Fifty cents?" said Joe. "Mister, this is robbery."

"No, Mister," he said, "this is San Francisco. Now you going to buy or continue wasting my time?"

There was some sick folk resting in carts and wheelbarrows they'd been carried in. One of them wasn't long for the grave by the sound of his coughing. Had a flag laying down dead on his chest as if preparing for the coming.

"Mister," I said to him, "want me to wave your flag for you?"

He said yes.

I took it from him and started shaking it above his head.

I turned to Joe and gave him a wink, and he gave me a sly one in return.

Down the center of the square comes a great procession. A small army of well-fed school children marched by, singing "Battle Cry of Freedom," completely out of tune. But, their clothes were sure dandy. Not raggedy like mine.

Joe put his hand on my shoulder and said, "See, what I tell you? Soon you'll be nagging me you're too fat to button up your waistband. Won't be needing that rope on your waist for nothing but selling."

"If it's fifty cents for a flag," I said. "I reckon I got a few nickels' worth tied up now."

"Well there's a smart fella, hang on to what you got, just in case."

Next comes the benevolent society: the Sons of Jesus. The reformers, the do-gooders, and the unions: the bakers, the fishermen, the pipe makers and what seemed to be hundreds more, all took their time, marching down Clay Street in the sun.

Joe tapped me on the arm.

I turned and saw his brow was sweating. And his fingers were shaky.

"Boy," he said, "I reckon it's time I started looking."

"But Joe," I said, "don't go just yet. The best show ain't arrived. They got the navy coming by, and everything."

"Ah, let it be, will you?" he said, shaking me off.

"Oh, but Joe. What about eats?"

"Ah, all's you think about is your belly," he said. "And what about me? Hell, I ain't asking you to come."

"Well I ain't asking you to go."

I could see he was itching to run, so I pulled hard on his sleeve to make him stay. "Look, Joe," I said, "don't get mad, will you?"

"I ain't getting mad," he said. "And I don't need to be nagged at by a low-down whore-child. I only said for you to wait here while I go a-looking is all I was saying to you if you'd cared to listen to me for once in your born days."

"I know it was," I said.

"I mean I brought you here didn't I? Now stay and watch the show. I'll be back in a jiffy."

So I surrendered.

Before he turned to go, I took hold of his hand, one last time and said, "Joe, what if that Devil comes calling you again? Then what am I going to do?"

"Now looky here," he said, turning friendly. "What I tell you about nagging me so? The truth of it is, I got a good angel on my side today. That Devil comes a-knocking, he'll chase him back down to Hell, don't you worry none. Now be a good boy and keep an eye on the clock face till I get back."

I marked out my bearings. The clock tower was in the center of the square, next to the gold mint, the bank and a hotel, which was back of me. The jailhouse was there too, hiding in the corner like a thief.

"I'll be back within the hour to fetch you," he said. "Oh, and keep your hat on tight."

The Society of California Pioneers caught my eye. They were coming down the road carrying a wagon full of digging devices.

"Did you hear me?" said Joe, making me jump. "I said keep your hat on tight."

I put my hand on my head and made sure my cap was still on. The Pioneers come marching down the road. I did like everyone else: waved my flag in the air like a crazy-man and whistled as they come by. They were putting on one hell of a show. Had some fella with a shakier hand than Joe's holding onto a bottle yelling, "Run for cover: it's nitroglycerin, it's going to explode!" Everybody was laughing. I turned to Joe to laugh along with him. But he'd already gone.

Time had passed. I checked on the clock face. It was three on the hour. At half past, the military come. Army first. Then, the one I'd been waiting for: the navy. Marching to a drum, six in a row. A sea of dark blue: with a gold stripe going down the leg and two around the cap. They looked comely in their attire. I imagined myself being dressed up just like them, and marching on so. One navy stood out among the rest. He was like the angel Gabriel might be, when he comes down from heaven to walk with the living.

He caught me spying on him. Kept his eyes stuck fast on mine and would not let go. My heart went running rabbits. My face was burning hot. They began marching downhill so he couldn't look at me no more. And I was thankful for it. For, I could breathe again.

The parade finally ended, and everyone decided to leave at the same time. Dust was getting chucked up everywhere. An omnibus, two man buggies, and horse riders elbowed for position to get down the river-wide Clay Street. There I was in the middle of it all, getting pushed and shoved and stepped on from every direction.

I decided to wait for Joe on the porch outside the hotel. But it was fancy, and they did not appreciate my raggedy kind on their property. It was no surprise then, when I got chased.

I climbed up onto a part of the roof, where I could get a good lookout for Joe, and waited there instead. Eventually, the square cleared.

I kept a keen eye on the clock tower. The hour had well passed, for it was a quarter past four. I looked out for Joe but could see him nowhere. By six on the clock, I began to fret.

I climbed back down off the roof, eagle eyed a friendly looking sort wearing a crumpled suit, and asked him where the boarding house was. His Spanish was worse than Joe's. He told me I needed to head back down Jefferson anyhow. So I did.

I hurried down the long hill. When I got dockside, I asked a man wearing rag-boots like mine where the cheapest board for rent was. He only had gums so could hardly speak without slobbering. But he could point all right, to a gray painted house nearby.

I saw it.

Outside, folks armed with sticks made war with a bunch of hungry seagulls over an upturned cart of oranges. I stole in amongst the fray of hungry drifters and grabbed two for Joe and me. I stuffed them in my pockets, walked up to a finely dressed preacher on the boarding house door, and said, "Sir, you seen a fella come by wanting board for his boy and him?"

He said no, and asked me if I was a degenerate.

I told him, "Nossir, I ain't nothing like that."

"Well," he said, "I don't see no fully paid grown-up alongside you, so it means that you are one, now git."

I cursed to myself and spat on my own shoes. Nonetheless, Preacher chased me off of the premises and back onto the road. I stood on the dock by myself flag in hand, with my two oranges stuffed in my pants pockets, and half our life savings living in my shirt. I checked on those precious dollars every moment I remembered which seemed all the time.

There were plenty of regular sailors about. Joe said for me never to talk to them, but needs must and I did. I spotted one who looked friendly. I went up and said, "Hey mister, can you help me? I'm looking for my Pa."

Before Sailor had a chance to say nothing, some older boys with pipes hanging from their mouths came from out of nowhere. They pushed me out of Sailor's way and gathered around me like a cage. The boss of them all said, "Hey, son-of-a-bitch, this is our part of town. Get to your own side or I'll give you trouble." He showed me a fist full of nasty knuckles and a knife in the other and told me to get walking. So I did. And I kept on walking. Eventually, I ran. Until, I got further down the Dock Road, to Washington, where they stopped following me and headed back the way they came.

Time goes moving on. My feet were dragging and my belly was sore. A fella was cooking mussels. It was one dollar a batch, but you needed to have your own bowl. I carried on to the next. Cheap dried fish was on offer: twenty-five cents a bag. But they smelled all wrong. I was too sleepy to eat anyhow. Soon I found a hut full of barrels smelling of low tide. I snuck inside and curled up to bed.

I must have slept a couple of hours. Woke up, and heard seagulls dancing on the roof. Then, a great bang comes that made my living soul nearly shoot out of my body. Next, I hear folks right outside of me, yelling and firing off guns. Another God almighty bang comes, shaking off the roof.

I listened up. It sounded like cannon fire, but not exactly.

My body was quaking. I swallowed dry courage and took a peek outside.

The night was falling, and smoke was rising. The smell of powder shot burned my nose.

Another explosion comes. I covered my ears.

I looked up from the crack in the hut door and saw red, white, and blue stars come falling from the sky along with gold dust from a heavenly pan on high. Another blast shook the planks above my head. More brightly colored stars showered down from the Lord above. I stopped being fearful and smiled up at the pretty wonder exploding before my weary eyes.

When the war with the sky was over, I come out from the shed.

It was nearly dark. The heavens had turned the color of a fresh skinned rabbit. I looked around for Joe, but I could see nothing, except for the fog that began creeping and twisting around my feet like a snake.

Boats were creaking and the sea was lapping. Soon it was dark. And I was blind.

Over by a lamplight hanging from a post, there was a shadow-man, who kept staring at me. He gestured with his head for me to come to him. At first, I thought he was Joe, but the bend of his back was all wrong, as was the shape of his hat. He kept on motioning for me to come to him, which got me thinking he was a new friend of Joe's. And maybe Joe had asked him to keep a look out for me. Which made a whole lick of sense.

I went up and asked him if this was the case. He said it was and that Joe had told him to give me this fifty-cent piece of silver, which he showed. And I could tell it'd just been minted, on account of it being so shiny.

I put the eagle in my top pocket and followed on behind.

The fella had a lamp of his own. With the fog becoming so thick all's I could see was his hand swinging with the glow. When we got to an alleyway that stunk of everything that smelled bad, he stopped and blew the light out.

I said, "Mister, why'd you go and blow the lantern out for? Now we can't see nothing."

"Well," he said, "I prefer it that way." Then, without a word, he put his hand on me and tried to kiss me: stinking of liquor.

I pulled away and said, "No Mister, I think you got this all wrong. I'm looking for my Pa."

"Don't Pa never kiss you?" he said.

"Not on the mouth like that," I said. "He kisses the top of my head sometimes, that's all mister, that's all he ever does."

So Mister started kissing the top of my head, and playing with my hair.

"Mister," I said, trying to keep his hands off, "I only come here thinking you were Joe."

"I'll be Joe," he said. "I'll be anybody, just let me kiss you darling."

And he started up again.

"No, Mister," I said, "I don't want you being nobody. I don't want you being nothing."

Next, he tried undoing my rope and putting his hand down my waistband. I protested, so he let it be. He got hold of my hand instead and put it down the front of his waistband. Right then, I knew he were no angel. And Joe always said, "If ever a body bigger than you tries getting you to touch their nakedness, you tell that body to go on back to Hell where they belong. Then say a prayer to Jesus, and ask him to take the sin away." Which he always would, seeing as he loved me so. But I could not say nothing, nor remove my hand. For Mister had such a grip on it, and was working it in such a manner, that my face turned hot crab and my heart went running wild rabbits. A strange weariness comes over me. And soon I was too tired to do anything, other than let him do all the doing.

When he finally done and spewed, I said, "Mister, please, can you take me to back to Joe now."

But Mister said nothing. Next, I heard footsteps running away. I put my hand out to touch him, but that Devil was gone. So was my cap. And there I was, on my own in the darkness and the blinding fog.

Chapter 2
I am found

I heard voices all around me, and bodies rustling; grunting and squealing like hungry hogs.

I couldn't help it. I started to cry.

I wanted to run but I didn't know where.

I edged my way out the alleyway, toward the firefly glow of a lantern hanging high. Someone tapped me on the shoulder. I hit my back on the wall. The stranger held up a light to my face.

I could see him clear. It was an older boy, smoking a pipe of horse-shit and something else. He was wearing a friendly smile.

"Howdy," he said. "My name's Juan, what's yours?"

I caught my breath, and said it was, "Jones."

"Howdy Jones," he said. "Are you all right? You look shaky."

"I'm fine," I said. "I think I just got robbed is all."

"Anything of value?"

I told him, "My cap. Figure it was probably worth an eagle around here."

He passed me his smoke and said, "Maybe. But I doubt it unless it was spanking new. Was it spanking new?"

I said nothing, only took his smoke and played like I had a drag.

"So you ain't from around here?" he said.

"No," I said, coughing. "Me and Pa just come off the boat and into town. He went looking for a board. But he ain't showed yet."

"And he was meeting you here?" he said, looking shifty.

"No," I said, "up Union Square."

"This ain't Union," he said, "this is Washington."

"No, I know it is, but I got chased. I was up Union. Then I was on Jefferson."

"Jefferson?" he said. "Hell, you're lucky to be alive if you made it past Jefferson. Sydney Ducks run that part of town. They'll kill a kid if they don't like him. All their folks are convicts from Demon's land."

"Oh," I said, shaking so that I could hardly stand.

"Are you sure you all right?" he said, giving a hand to my elbow.

"I'm fine," I said, checking on my money, my flag, and my oranges.

They're a couple of scrawny dogs come chasing after a runaway rat. Juan pulled out a pistol from his waistband and took a shot at it in the foggy dark. Some other boys come out the creeping wet shadow, and I heard more shots fired. A dog began to howl and whine.

Juan said to his friends, "Shit, don't leave it lying there. Put the devil to rest will you?" And when no one was heard to do nothing he handed me his pipe, loaded up a shot, disappeared into the fog and I heard a bang, and no more howling comes.

He moseyed back and stood close by my side. "So, what's your plan now?" he said, taking back his pipe, striking up a match and puffing.

I looked at him close. The glow of fired-up tobacco shone on his face. My heart went running rabbits.

"I don't know," I said shaking. "I guess, maybe head back to Union or something, and wait it all out."

"Risky," he said, leaning his arm against the wall above my head. "Especially now the Ducks have marked you out."

"Marked out?" I said, holding on to myself. "Why? I ain't even done nothing."

"Well, they ain't too fond of nancies," he said, passing me his pipe, "only girly girls."

"Nancy?" I said. "Mister, my name ain't Nancy. It's Jones. Goldsmith Jones."

"Well," he said, "you sure had me fooled. Say, you can share a board with me tonight if you want. I got a fresh hunk of cheese, salami, and real whiskey."

The mention of free food got my belly going mad-dog. But then I comes to my senses. I remember what I been told about something for nothing. And how there's always some Devil's price to pay, in the world of mortal men.

I shook my head and said, "No, I got to find my Pa. He'll be looking for me right now. Probably going crazy. Besides, I ain't for drinking no liquor, or being with nobody who's liquored up anyhow."

"Jesus Christ," he said laughing, "are you trying for being one of them preachers?"

"No," I said. "I just know it does me no good when I hang with the liquored up kind. Only bad things come from that company, I know."

"All right," he said with smiling eyes, "I won't get liquored up, I promise. But, it's fourth of July and I'll bet a million, your old man's well oiled by now. Probably whored up someplace getting robbed blind as usual, am I right?"

I shrugged and felt my lips quiver. Tears come falling.

"See," he said, putting his arm around my neck, and stroking my cheek. "I knew it. I knew your old man would be a drunkard. I say your safe bet's to come with me. Get some hot eats. We can look for that old son-of-a-bitch in the morning. How's that?"

Heavy guns were firing off in the distance, and the sound of angry men. I checked on my money, my oranges, and my flag. I pulled myself to one piece and wiped my eyes. I looked into Juan's eyes and said, "All right."

And so, that's how I first got to being at The Shades. It was a rickety old building that creaked and moaned and threatened to fall down on top of you with every step you took in it.

Juan led me to a room, cloudy with smoke smelling of horse-shit and strange weeds. There was another thing that got my belly howling. Over by a fired-up Billy stove, some boys were poking at the flames with chunks of baker's bread and greasy yellow cheese. As we got close by they all turned, and stared at me. Their dark faces glowing with sharp tongues of fire dancing in their eyes.

He took me to a shady corner and sat me down on a bench. Cleared the tangles in my hair with his fingers while drinking from a jug. He passed it to me.

I took a swig and it nearly burned my lips off. "Thought you said no liquor," I said getting sore.

He laughed and said it was all but water. And what about me? Being such a greenhorn. Ain't used to proper whiskey at my age.

I told him I weren't as young as he thought. Only it gives pleasure to some to think it otherwise. And so I kept myself appearing so. For better my fortune be, when playing the child. Singing songs from before the war. When all young men were but children. Before judgment day comes along, like it has. Bringing Armageddon to the whole of the world. And I told him how Joe said it were a-coming, "For he'd seen it in a dream," I said, "and now there ain't no time for digging graves before them horses come a-killing and muskets come a-blowing the whole of life to smithereens."

"Well, ain't you a shrewd horse to have in the barn yard," he said. Got me clean water to drink. Cooked himself up some cheese bread but instead of eating it himself, gave me some. Made a child's game of us taking turns blowing on it to cool it down. And I decided that I liked Juan. For he was kind, and he was friendly, and he was handsome as you'd ever want to be.

After we had been done eating, he took me to a place out back where horses lived. It was packed tight with hay. We both climbed on top of one stack, and he told all about how his Pa was a drunkard. And beat him until he was broke. And one day he saw his relations coming out the general store and waved

14

at his Ma. But she made like she didn't know him. And when his little brother turned to wave goodbye, she made him stop and act like he was a stranger too. When I told Juan I'd be his brother, he smiled at me, and my heart went running rabbits. Soon he was courting me with pretty kisses and precious words. He was older than me by a few years with a body working like a man. When he stared into my face with kind eyes, it gave me such pleasure, for I was sure I was ugly as a stray dog. And when he was done doing himself, I felt melancholy and started crying. And he did not get angry. Instead, he held me in his arms. Where I cried until I slept.

Next morning I woke up smiling to the smell of horses. I watched them chewing: as I lay, comfy-cozy in the warm yellow hay.

All but for my back, and the cold, empty space beside. For Juan was gone. And so were my two oranges.

I checked all my pockets. My money was still there and so was my flag.

I slid down from the hay taking most of it with me. I brushed myself off and went a-looking. I climbed through a broken-down window, and snuck inside the Shades: past the Billy stove room, into another room, stinking of liquor and piss.

It was stacked high to the sky with bunked up boards. And there was Juan, with another body with a belly full of child.

I shook Juan, lying there, wrapped up in his comfy blanket, and said, "Where are my oranges?"

He told me to pipe down and said he didn't know nothing about no goddamn oranges. Then his belly-girl woke up and told me to get lost.

I told her I wasn't speaking to her, I was talking to him.

She spat ugly words at me.

I persevered with Juan. He turned back to sleep and kept his eyes closed.

Tears come to mine. "You said you'd help me find Joe," I said to him.

He said he didn't know nothing about no Joe, and I said he did, and that was the Pa I was talking of.

She kicked at me and told me to go back to whatever shit hole I come from.

I told her to go back herself, "To the Devil," I said, "where you belong."

Juan pulled the blanket off of his head and swore at the ceiling boards.

She told him not to even think about going nowhere.

He told her to belt up or else.

She paid no heed.

He pulled on his shirt, his braces, and his boots. All the while she protested, pecking at him like an angry crow.

He grabbed a hunk of day-old from his bag of treasure and tore at it like a dog. I pleaded, and he gave me some too.

I followed him to the Billy stove room.

He found my two oranges under the bench we'd been sitting. I said they weren't for eating; they were for Joe and me.

He swore at the sky and gave them back.

We headed down the hall to the front door. He unlocked the latch and kicked it open. Outside the Shades, down the steps, near the barn, there was a water barrel. He ducked his head inside, lifted it out shaking it and spraying me with clean water. He wiped his face with the end of a horse blanket and said to me, "Come on, if you're coming."

I ran after him and followed him straight down the hill to Washington Dock.

It was a gloomy-looking morning, and the wind was blowing a gale. Tall ships were banging into each other while seagulls circled over making loud screechy cries. I saw the steamboat me and Joe had come by had gone. In its place was an ironclad full of navies sleeping it off on deck. Except for a couple of black boys was tying ropes, and sweeping up the dirt, hiding out under their whitey-Joe feet.

Down by the edge of the bay, some men stood like a gang of ruffled crows, pecking at the sand with sticks and dark umbrellas.

"Wait here," said Juan.

So I did. I ducked next to a horse-drawn cart and watched him go see what was happening.

He was trying to get a look-see, but with all the crazy high hats they wore around these parts, everyone seemed to be six feet tall, so he could see nothing.

Eventually, I saw him get swallowed up by a bunch of black coats. Soon they made a parting, and out he comes like Moses from the Deadly Sea. A man was with him: a lawman by the look of his badge.

Juan and Sheriff stood toe-to-toe talking, looking at me, nodding, then talking again.

Juan gestured for me to come.

I stood up from my hiding place.

Sheriff had his coat undone. Had his hand in his pocket showing off his gun.

I felt my knees go shaky. I put my hand on the cart-horse to keep myself steady.

Juan left Sheriff's side, comes to me, takes my elbow, pulls me up, and starts leading me to him.

My hair was blowing long and crazy in the wind, for I had no cap to keep it covered. As we got closer, all the high hats were staring at me. Just like Joe said they would.

I turned to Juan. "Why you taking me to Sheriff for?" I said. "I ain't done nothing."

"It's OK," he said, "you ain't in trouble with the law."

"I am, I am," I said, digging my heels in the sand, and pulling him back with me.

"Look," he said, "they might have found your Pa, or whatever you call him by. You got to say if it's him or not, now just come on."

I looked at the plain-faced high-hats in front of me. Then at the beach and I could see nothing.

"It ain't him," I said. "He ain't there. He won't come down the waterside. He don't like it. We only come by boat because I wanted." I pulled away and ran back to the horse cart, and hid back behind the wheel.

Juan lifted his hat to rub his head and went back to Sheriff's side.

I sat there shaking in the spitting wind.

I patted my pocket.

My money was still there.

I checked on my oranges.

Still in my two pockets. I tried pushing my flag down into my rag boots, and out of their strangers' eyes.

Juan comes back to me looking weary. He bends down to where I was crouching at the wheel.

"Just go see what they got," he said, "then you can tell them what you want for yourself, all right?"

I looked at the crowd of crow-men and their poking sticks. Seagulls were trying to get a look-see, diving down from above their high heads. They tried chasing them off, but those sea vultures were determined. A fella pulled a gun and shot at one and missed. Then another tried seeing if he could do better. Then it was Sheriff's turn, and that seagull made a fool of him, making like it was a goner. Then went flying over his head screeching in the angry sky.

Gun smoke was blowing over and stinging my nose. My head was aching and making me see stars. I dug my heels in and shook my head. I told Juan, "I ain't going no place."

Juan put his arm around me. "Jones," he said, "they ain't going to shoot you. Come on, I'll go with you. I'll make sure they don't."

Chapter 3
Joe's return

The beach stunk of rot. Sheriff led me through the crowd of black coats and stood me next to a large gray thing, swollen up like a dead seal, except for it had limbs and a boot still on one.

"Recognize this body?" Sheriff said.

The limb without the boot showed a brown mark shaped like a bean. Joe had one just like it. That's when I saw it was him.

I pushed Sheriff out of my way. I got down on my knees and lay my body on top of Joe's. I put his hand to my cheek. It was frozen as the lake in winter and blue as the mountain in spring.

I looked at his face, not thin like it ought to be. His eyes half closed just as if he was sleeping. I tried waking him by shaking him and yelling at him, and calling him names not fit for righteous ears, but regular to ours.

The first thing I done when I stopped wailing was checks his pockets. The money was spent, so I knew he'd been robbed. I looked around for a villain. There were too many faces looking down at me. Any one of them could have been that Devil.

A doc put his hand on my shoulder.

I pulled away saying, "Get your hands off of me."

A one-eyed preacher rattled words from the Bible.

I told him to, "Shut the Hell up."

I turned to Sheriff. "What you standing there for?" I said. "Do something for Jesus Christ's sake." But he didn't do nothing. And that preacher just stood there, tut-tutting at my fitting choice of words.

I clung to Joe's clothes and hollered in his chest. My eyes were running, my nose was running, my heart was bursting inside my ribs.

Someone pulled me off of him.

It was Sheriff. He starts carrying me away.

I turned my head to see Joe. And he weren't looking at nothing. He couldn't see anything at all. I twist my head all around, back and forth, looking for Juan, but he was plain out of sight.

I watched as Doc laid a worthless old sack over Joe's face.

My knees give way. Sheriff let go of me and I fell to the ground.

A bunch of strangers carried me off someplace I'd never been afore.

My legs start working. I was kicking and yelling and biting at their hands. Seagulls were screeching. Hangmen were hollering. They took me inside a building.

A bunch of clerks was in there. They all stared at me like I was a killer and went running for their lives straight out the front door.

I heard the lock behind me get fastened tight. I looked around to see where I was. A dark prison of a place: with ink-blotched desks and papers smelling of iron death. Sheriff's men tried pushing me into a chair that went creaking and screaming every time I touched the seat. I refused being forced into its arms with all my might.

A union flag was falling down off the wall. Someone slapped me hard in the face just for looking at it. Another had a jug of liquor and tried pouring it down my throat. I choked as hell-fire ran down into my belly, burning my soul while I was still alive.

I spread my eyes around the room. It was full of stranger Joes. Not one of who looked friendly. They told me this was the customs house. Began asking me a bunch of stupid questions like, "Where you hail from? How you get here? Where's your ticket? Where you get all your money from?"

They run their hands up and down my body and deep inside my pockets. They took all my treasure from me. Robbed me blind and lay all my gold worth in a box. Then set it down on a desk that was plenty out of my reach.

They kept on saying to me, "Who's the fella? How you know him? Why you keep calling him 'Pa' for, he ain't your Pa. He your boss, is that it?"

They tried a thousand different ways of asking me the same questions and I told them nothing. I figured they gone and killed Joe, stole his money, and now had me trapped there for killing too.

I was crying. I could not get the sight of Joe out my head. I could only think of him dying. I thought of that time *she* tries drowning me. Dunking my head inside a barrel of water, telling me to, "Thank the Lord," for I was being baptized: being cleansed all of my sins. Telling me I was a wicked child, a Devil's child, who lies day and night. "Not a word of truth comes from your lying lips," she said. And while she buried my head down in that water they all stood around gawping, and doing nothing, not even Joe. I was bursting for breath. She tore me out by the roots of my hair baring all my face to shame. Before I got to fill my lungs afresh, she held my head down under again. And I breathed water. The pain of it burned my ribs and made my eyes bleed. And that's how it was for Joe. That's how he went. Like I suffered right then. Only longer than me.

I puked up and Sheriff's men gave me water and a piece of rag to dry myself off. Then left me alone while they stood in the corner conspiring.

They didn't know it, but I was sat there the whole time planning my escape. They had the door and the window covered by a couple of mean looking fellas with their sleeves turned up and their muscles on show.

It was gloomy outside so it was dark inside. But it was hot, and I was baking. I was next to a table. They had a lantern lit, stinking of old whale oil. Beside that was the jug of liquor they tried to poison me with.

I heard them talking. When I heard the word "jailhouse" I knew it was time to make my getaway.

I took the jug of liquor off the table and makes like I was going to start drinking.

They took one look at me swigging and turned the other way.

I had my rag in my hand. I kept tight hold of it. I filled liquor in my cheeks three times, and each time I put the cloth to my burning mouth and soaked it with the contents. When the cloth was drenched, I lay it on the table next to the lantern.

Their talk was coming to a close, so I knew I had to work fast.

I moved quick, like a snake.

First, I bent over the table. Made like I was praying. When I was sure they weren't looking, I turns viper.

With one hand on my whiskey rag, I opened up the lamp and stuffed the cloth deep inside.

I watched as it caught up ablaze. A wild dragon growing in front of my eyes, living and breathing nasty hell fire.

Soon the lantern was rattling and shaking.

I ducked under the table. Put my fingers in my ears and waited for her to blow.

Then she did!

The room around me was black with smoke.

Fire was spitting from the table legs, and crawling on the floor. Men were yelling, "Fire, fire!" I watched their cowardly boots go running out the customs house door.

The fire was hopping mad. My raggedy clothes were burning hot. I was getting choked with deadly smoke. I covered my nose and mouth with my sleeve and made my getaway fast.

Ducking low under the black cloud, I held my breath, dodging fire and running out the door, and under cover.

I hid out behind a heap of barrels down dockside, coughing out my lungs and trying to be quiet about it. I turned back to look at the customs house. Flames were leaping like jackrabbits from between the plank walls. Loud, angry bells start clanging. Horses comes a-thundering. The firefighters were a-coming!

Men were running to the dragon fire with buckets of seawater. The whole of the dock was swarming with folks carrying buckets, or just staring and pointing like fools at the house of flames. Washington Dock was now filled with people gawking at the fire and black snake smoke.

I stared at the direction of the beach where Joe was. I watched them haul him off the sand and put him in a wheelbarrow, then ride him over to the carthorse I'd been hiding behind. Men lifted him onto it, and laid a shovel next to Joe's stiff body.

There I watched them ride off, in the direction of the graveyard.

Chapter 4
A critter befriends me

I hid up a tree and watched, while men shoveled dirt on top of the box they'd put Joe in. When they'd done patting down the soil, they left without a prayer.

I climbed down from the branches and talked to Joe a while. At first, I was mad and beat on his grave with my feet. Then my tears fell. I fixed some stones around his grave, took the flag out my rag-boots and placed it where his heart might be. Told him I'd come find him tomorrow if I could remember how to find the place. I straightened myself out. Combed my hair with my fingers, and headed back to the city. To find a board. And get my money back.

Every body around me was looking. Sometimes they were whispering. Then pointing in my direction. I figured I ought to lie low for a few days, so I hid out. I found an old place that at one time, before the war, and before tobacco was a state offense, appeared to have sold plenty of it. Now, the place was all boarded up and closed down. At first, when I climbed through some broken planks in the wall, I thought it might be full of gold leaf treasure. Each time I opened up a dusty drawer, I reckoned I'd find a mother lode of real tobacco worth a fortune inside. But, as it turned out, the whole place had been robbed. Drawers that had once been filled with those precious leaves from Virginia were clean. All but for a few scraps tucked inside the seams of the wood. I gathered at much as my fingernails could dig out and kept for selling.

The first night I lost Joe, I spent in there, hiding behind the counter, wrapped up in nothing but my arms. I had no food, no lantern, no nothing. Next morning, after crying over my misfortune, I polished up my brave heart with my sleeve. Snuck out, and went to see what was left of the customs house, and my money.

I could smell Washington Dock before I saw it. All charred wood and low tide. I hid behind some barrels and took a good look at what I'd done. Most of the customs house was burned out. What was left looked like a bunch of blown out safety matches.

The desk where they had my oranges and money was still alive. Smoke or steam was blowing from its seams.

I was thinking of making a run for it, to see if my treasure was still there, but every time I went to try, some lowdown Joe got in my way. There was one right in front of me standing there gawping. He began talking to another who'd come up besides. I crept up behind a set of crates smelling of soap and listened in on the conversation.

It turns out two somebodies had stolen their way into the Free State. Evidently one was "a degenerate drunkard," who "would probably kill himself if he weren't already dead." And a smart one, "a long-haired, sly-eyed trickster." Seems they'd had him cornered, but he played with his dark arts, summoned the Devil, and escaped clean out of their sight.

"Figure he be the one behind the gold house getting blown up?" said the other fella. Which I took to mean the customs house, since they probably had a whole hoard of gold stashed in a safe box someplace hidden away from everybody who needed it.

"I figure so," said the man with all the know-how, "which is a felony," he added, "attempted murder on all counts of the law. They'll hang him when they get him. And what a show that'll be."

I was busy thinking what the hell to do now I was an outlaw when I saw there was somebody sat next to me.

It was a kid, about my age.

"Goddam," he said, looking at the burnt out building. "I wish I'd stayed around to see this going up. I'm Raccoon by the way."

I took stock of him. His face was sugar brown but overly round. He had a thing of squinting his eyes too tight for what was natural.

"So," he said, "you think this outlaw's still in town? Hiding out someplace? I bet he's a real killer too. Did I hear that fella say there were two of them? I heard they're checking all the boats coming in now. Figure Confeds are going to come sneaking on board. Start the war up here. They got sympathizers everywhere, evidently. What do you think?"

I reckoned it was a time I skedaddled. So I did, onto the nearest roof out of there. I climbed up onto the cedar planks and balanced my arms so that I could run, and then jump over onto the next building.

I heard thumping feet on the rooftop behind me.

"Hey, hold on!"

It was that kid, Raccoon. Still following me. Next thing he was on my side.

The wood clanked beneath our feet. I got to the end of the rooftop and saw there was nowhere to jump but down. And nothing below to break my fall, so, I turned back and started running back the way I came.

He was tailing me behind, saying: "Hey, wait up!"

Seeing as I couldn't outrun him, I stopped, out of breath, and sat down behind a chimney.

He joined me.

Clouds were holding the sun prisoner. It blinded my eyes just looking at it. All's I could see in front of me was black-blue spots and shiny red and white daggers. My ribs hurt from all's the running. I was tired and growing melancholy. I pulled my knees to my chest and hung on tight.

"You weren't running away from me, were you?" he said.

I buried my head in my arms so as not to look at him. My shirt was dirty and stunk of everything bad.

"Are you hiding out?" he said, blinking hard.

I said nothing.

"Are you trying to hide out being a girl?"

I turned my face to his and gave him snake eyes to look at.

"Well," he said, "I just thought you might be because you got hair like one. And you look girly like they do too, so I reckon you could pull it off. Only, looking girly's going to get you lots of attention around here. You'll probably get fellas turning sweetheart on you in no time. Which I suppose is all right. Make lots of money at being a cocksucker too. Are you one?"

I told him to go away.

He said he didn't mind if I was, for most of his friends made their living just so. Except for him who figured it weren't his line of business. Finding no pleasure in such a thing, as he kept on saying to the sky.

I watched him out the sides of my eyes. He was squinting hard and fast while eating a ripe red apple.

I asked him where he got it.

He fed me a story.

"So the truth of it is," I said, "you stole it."

He shrugged. "I wouldn't call it stealing," he said. "All in all, it was payment for listening to a crazy-headed story for an hour of my time. Sometimes all people want is to be heard out."

"Well, in my book, taking coin from a toothless gutter-hog, too lame on the liquor to stand, then running off with it, is called stealing"

"Oh, it wasn't like that," he said, laughing.

"Now looky here," I told him. "I ain't no thief, and by the way, I ain't called Nancy or that word you said back there. My name is Jones. Goldsmith Jones. That's the only name I got and the only one I answer to."

"All right," he said, shrugging, blinking, and making my skin crawl.

He tempted my forgiveness with a bite of his apple. It was red and round and clean, with no sign of worms tunneling through it or nothing. I surrendered and dug my teeth into its pure flesh. It was sweet as a melon and juicy as one too. We took turns crunching, peeling off the red skin and making patches on our faces like it was war paint. When we'd done, Raccoon tore off some bark from a cedar plank, split the sheet in half and rolled each one into a peashooter. Then we had a spitting contest, to see who could fire out apple seeds the furthest.

I won.

The sun beat off the clouds and I felt brighter.

Soon I was telling Raccoon all about Joe, and the money Sheriff stole from me.

The clouds soon got revenge and made the light fade.

After I'd made done with shedding tears, stamping my feet and flinging curses in every direction, he said, "Jonesy, want to get your dollars back?"

I looked at him, with sore eyes and said, "I do."

He dug up a misfired seed hiding between the roofs. Blinked hard a few times, and shot it back at me. I picked it off my shirt and returned fire.

"OK," he said, "let's go get it." And off we went, to reclaim my fortune.

We travelled over some rooftops to where Raccoon showed me a building that was much like a longhouse. We crawled over to the next roof and lowered ourselves down.

We stayed out of sight, behind some barrels. I saw some four-eyed clerks with stripy shirts and braces going inside carrying boxes of papers that looked burnt. We got up from our hiding place, and with our heads low, and our hands in our pockets we strolled up to the window. We squatted on our heels and taking cover beneath the pane, I stole a look in and hid back down.

"I can't see my oranges," I said.

Raccoon took a peek. "Yeah, but I can see money chests."

"Where?" I said and lifted up my head to take a look-see. He was right. There were two iron safes in there.

"Jones," he said, "is that your money?"

I looked over at where his eyes were pointing and saw a pile of green notes sitting on a desk. Those dumb-ass clerks had gone and left my genuine Union dollars unattended. But where had gone my silver eagle, and my oranges?

Raccoon went to leave. I grabbed hold of his sleeve and said, "Where you going?"

"To get your money."

"What are you out of your mind?" I said. "You're just going in, just like that?"

"Look, I know what I'm doing."

"Well, you ain't doing it with me around. They'll catch you. Then they'll throw me behind bars. Then they'll hang me."

"You?" he said.

"Yeah, me," I said. "The truth of it is, I'm wanted. It's *me* them fellas back down Washington were talking about. Joe was one and me, well…"

"You blew up the bank in San Marco?"

I said, "What?"

"I heard the Suarez brothers done it, to get back the money the government stole from them. They got the money hid someplace no one's going find it. Trust me," he said, "I'll have your whole stash of dollars in my hand easy."

"What about my eagle?" I said. "I had three dollars, a solid silver four-bit coin, and two oranges."

"Forget about your oranges," he said, "we can get them anyplace. I'll see what I can do about the rest."

"Hold on a tick," I said making a prisoner of his arm. "What's the deal here? I mean, you ain't risking your neck for nothing so what's in it for you?"

"I don't know," he said. "How about fifty-fifty?"

"Fifty-fifty? That's all my money sitting in there. What I earned fair and square. I ain't robbed it or nothing. The truth of it is, I ain't never stole a thing in my whole life."

"OK," he said. "How about, fifty-fifty, and we can be honest friends."

"Honest friends?"

"Sure," he says. " I mean, you're new in town. I reckon you need an honest friend more than the money probably. A lot of swindlers around. Anybody else might rob you of the rest in no time. And you said it. I'm the one taking the risk. If I get caught, well, it's the rope ain't it?"

I took another look at my money, lying there naked. I thought how Juan had to give me free food and board for nothing. And this ordinary boy was going to take half my treasure and force me into a bond for all my fine work. I looked at my dollars again, and figured what choice did I have? "All right," I said, "you got a deal."

And off he went to work.

I could see inside. There were two clerks busy talking. And I don't know how he did it, but Raccoon got behind them unnoticed. Within a few ticks of the clock, he was back out again and by my side.

"C'mon," he said, "We got to move fast."

I didn't ask why. I just started walking with him, away from the dock, and up the hill into town.

Finally, I said, "Well, what happened? Did you get it?"

He gestured for me to be quiet then led me behind another building. Opened up his jacket and showed me a whole stash of green cash stuffed into his shirt pocket.

"Oh Jesus Christ!" I said, smiling, and looking all around to make sure we weren't being spied on. "You play crazy wild cards, do you know that?"

He smiled and beckoned me to carry on walking, away from the dock and up the hill toward town.

"Is that all my money?" I said.

"I counted five dollars," he said.

We were trying our best not to look suspicious, but fear of getting locked up in Sheriff's prison got me itchy, so kept checking behind and looking back dockside. We passed by the grain store and admired some of the horses hitched outside. A fella with one leg hiding by the door hollered, "You there, boy."

Raccoon and me flung a look at each other.

"Ain't you the one they had held up in the custom's house yesterday?"

"Oh shit," I whispered, "they're on to me."

Raccoon sprang into a run, grabbing me by the arm and making me go with him.

"I told you I was wanted," I said, panting like a dog.

"C'mon," he said, pulling me down to the ground, "we'll hide out here." There was a stack of crates against a building wall. He pulled one aside.

There was a hole broke through the wood. He told me to climb through first then pulled the crate back to keep us hidden.

We were underground. I could smell dirt and rat's piss.

"There're critters living here," I said. "They ain't going to like us breaking into their property."

"Don't worry," he said. "They're night-time fellas. They sleep it off all day. Just stay close behind."

And so I did, crawling like a crab with my hands on the cold dirt beneath me. Forgetting to duck and banging my head on the floorboards of the building above. Catching my pant leg on a nail, thinking it was rat's teeth. And nearly crawling over Raccoon to get away from it.

Soon I saw the light. Next thing we were standing in the center of crowded Union Square. We dusted ourselves off. Found shady refuge under the roof of the junk shop where you could buy nearly everything for a penny. We stood amongst a group of lowdowns, looking in the window to see what worthless pieces of shit could be bought with an empty pocket. A spoon with the handle gone missing might still be useful. A lot of mugs with rusty holes in them.

"Suppose you could melt the tin down and make something worthwhile," said Raccoon.

I put my mouth to his ear. "Where's my money?" I said. "Half of five dollars is two dollars fifty cents. We shook on it. So half of that's mine."

"Well, actually we didn't shake on it," he said. "But don't worry, I'm going to honor it anyhow. Come on!" he said, out loud. "Let's get some eats."

We ran down and alley to a place called Roma Joe's. Hanging in the window were rings of sausage and balls of golden cheese as big as your head.

After spending half our winnings on meat, cheese, and a hunk of rye, we found an unhitched horse cart with a wooden roof. We climbed in and sat on a pile of hay and got busy eating. Acting like a couple of tomfools, we pretended we were critters: biting off the meat with our teeth and taking little nibbles out of the bread and cheese. Finally, we stuffed as much as we could into our mouths, nearly choking on it. After drinking from a barrel of water, we headed on back to that rickety old house all the kids called the Shades.

Along the way back Raccoon picked up two oranges free from a cart selling them for five cents apiece. He tossed me one while we carried on walking. He dug his thumb down the center of it and showed me how to drink the juice out of it. Which was like how I imagined water to taste if you were living in heaven.

"How long you known him?" he said about Joe.

I shrugged.

"What happened to your Pa?"

"Hell knows, I guess. The truth of it is," I said, "my real daddy was a Richie-Joe. And I don't know why, but I got living with some lowdown relation by mistake. Then this Joe comes. He was her fella. Rest his spirit."

"Going to go looking for your Pa now?"

I shook my head.

"How about your Ma?"

I said, "Gone. Truth of it is, I ain't got nobody left in the world to look for."

"Nobody?" he said.

"Nobody at all."

We walked along a boardwalk and stopped outside the general store. It was full of hundreds of useful buying things like kettles, and scissors, and devices you could only guess the purpose of.

"Contagion come and took both of mine," he told me, giving me a torn piece of pocket to dry my eyes with. "Pa's daddy was an Ohlone chief and Ma's grandma was a Salish princess from way up north. Pa went first. Then Ma took up with a son-of-a-bitch Frenchie bastard. Contagion comes a knocking. Took her with it. Left me behind with that crazy-headed lowdown. I waited till he was liquored up one night then cleaned him out good and proper. Been on the run ever since. So, what are you going to do now? Get retribution?"

"Well," I said, spotting a fine looking musket, "that'd be the right thing to do I figure. I mean the law's all always shooting off people just for looking the wrong way. Truth of it is, though, I'm just too tired to even think about it right now." And I began weeping again.

The owner of the store came out and told us to skedaddle by throwing a bucket of dirty water at us. With our clothes soaked and smelling of sour ditches, we carried on walking, with our hands in our pockets, kicking at stray stones.

"I tell you what," said Raccoon. "I got a plan. Started my own treasure already. Nine paper dollars stashed. You put your two dollars in with mine, and we'll have enough to get started on an adventure someplace the hell out of here."

I took a sidelong look at him, wondering if I had just gone and bound myself to him, for two dollars fifty.

"Well, I just got here from somewhere else," I said. "And let me tell you, there ain't nothing out there but miles of desert death going one way, and ocean going the other. And I ain't sailing off to China to get myself killed. No, what I need to do is lie low. Get a job I suppose. Get my own board. We probably ought to part ways. Like you said, we didn't shake on no deal."

He looked at me like I was speaking Portuguese. "All right," he shrugged, "if you really want to go it alone."

And we didn't say nothing more the rest of the way.

We walked up the steps leading to the front door of the Shades. Before we went in, he tossed me a silver coin.

I caught it and looked at him.

"Your eagle," he said, "I forgot to tell you, I got that too." Then he touched his cap and climbed up onto the roof and toward the top of the building, where he disappeared behind a chimneystack.

Chapter 5
Every man's a merchant

When I got through the front door, I was collared right away. A girl called Alley Mac dressed up in man's attire said I had to pay a month in advance right now. She told me to remove all my money and sent me to the Billy stove room. Told a bunch grog-eyed boys to shuffle out of our way, and then sat me down on the bench. Passed me a tin cup and a jug of my own, which she said was mine to keep.

"Three dollars buys you a clean sleeping board for a month," she said, striking a match against her heel, "and that includes half a loaf a day, some cheese, and real whiskey. Also, you get a blanket for the whole time your living here. Suarez brothers own the place. You run into trouble; they bail you out. It's best goddam deal a kid can find around this part of town, trust me, I tried them all."

She took a long drag and passed it to me.

I smoked up and tried not to cough.

"Alley Mac," I said, "what do I do when the month's up, and I don't have another three dollars?"

"Well, there's two kinds of work that make an easy buck. First is trawling drunks. But, get caught, and it's jail. Maybe even hanging depending on how drunk the judge is that day.

Second is dirty work down Dead Man's Alley. Two bits a customer. You only need doing some a day to cover your board. A couple of rules: Boss don't allow working on a church day, that means Sundays are free. Second, Ma Wong don't like our boys muscling in on her business, so the rule is: fella wants to poke you send him down her way, Chinese Town, where all the Girly Boys are. Dead Man's strictly regular frigging, and other pleasuring of the like. You do know what that is, don't you?"

I shrugged.

"Stick you hand down a Dead Eye's waistband; tug on his rooster like this until he's done spewing?"

"I know all about it," I said. "Fella gave me a solid eagle for it yesterday."

"A solid eagle you say? You still got it?" she said, wearing a frown.

"Yes," I said, frowning back.

"Can I take a look?"

I gambled my lot and showed her.

She bit into it. "I knew it," she said. "It's tin." She showed me the outside of the coin. "See that: silver on the outside, and underneath, cheap metal not worth half a bent cent. Think you'd know that fella again if you saw him?"

"No," I said, thinking how I was going to collar that kid Raccoon when I saw him. "He blew the goddamn light out to make me blind."

"Bastard son of a bitch."

"Yeah," I said, looking down at my feet.

She put her hands on mine. "You see that villain again," she said, "you come and tell me right away. I'll make a point of telling Boss. And I'll set the dogs on him real fast."

"Ain't you the Boss?" I said, taking my hands back to myself.

"No. Saul's the Boss."

"Saul?"

"Yeah," she said. "Saul Suarez. Don't worry. If you ain't seen him yet, you'll know it when you do."

A weight fell heavy on my soul just then. There were too

many names and too many faces. I held my head in my hands and started rocking back and forth like a loon.

"Look," she said giving me a pat, "forget about that old swindling Dead Eye. Your lucky ship's come in to dock. You got real friends sailing on your side now."

I rubbed my eyes dry.

"Come on," she said, passing me a hankie that I got to keep for nothing. "Let's get you set up for working."

We stood by a big cupboard in the main hall.

"When the South Americas dock into Washington," she said, handing me a couple of hats to try on, "or the Chinas, you're busy down the Dead Man. On other days, there'll be nothing."

It was a felt preacher and an old navy. I chose the preacher. I like the way it held my hair and hung over my eyes.

"All in all, it's pretty good business. You should make enough to pay for the poor days as well as entertainment and the like."

"Entertainment?" I said.

She tossed out some boots for me to try.

"Sure, we got all kinds of pleasure going on here. Bear baiting on a Monday; comedy at the Music Hall on a Thursday. But best of all is the Frenchie girls they got showing at Ricardo's Palace on a Saturday. Now here's a secret." She put her arm around me and looked shady. "They charge a double eagle for the whole show, but when they put their legs out like this, it ain't nothing but pink ribbon sewn on the underneath. Now, I'm friendly with a girl who'll let a fella see the whole of Kansas for a song. But that's on account of me being in a position of authority. I could probably arrange for her to show you it for say, four-bits?"

She showed me a photographic likeness of the girl she had in mind.

"What happened to her other leg?" I said.

"Critter trap. Oh, it's a hell of a story. I'll get her to tell it you as part of the deal. What do you reckon on that? She takes your fancy?"

"No thank you."

She showed me another. "I bet you'll like this one. Four-bits. How's that? Take your fancy does she?"

I turned the likeness around, trying to figure out what I was looking at.

She hung her head over my shoulder and pointed. "It's the curiosity of it that makes her special."

"Oh," I said, nodding. "Well, thanks, but no, I figure I ought to save it up for something useful. Like a gun."

"A gun?" she said, lighting her cigar again. "How much you got left?"

I showed her a plug of pure Virginia I had tucked in my back pocket.

"You got twenty-five dollars to add?"

I forgo the gun and we shook on a knife. Handed over my prize tobacco. She gave me a rusty piece of shit, with a blade that would barely leave a dent in my finger in return. Then turned back to the cupboard saying:

"Now then, dirty work," and began pulling things out. "You can take this can of shoe shine and whatnot." She passed me a tin and some rags. "Make out you're shining shoes so as not to get chased off by the lawmen. They don't like kids hustling; think Punks are nothing but a bunch of cutthroat thieves. And Nancies, like yourself, only confuse the hell out of them, which makes them miserable, and liable to violence. Just remember, it's all about your regulars. They're walking gold mines. Just love dishing out the treasure. See these cufflinks?" I looked and saw a fine pair of navy anchors shining on her sleeves.

"Pure silver," she said. "I got a top hat: pure beaver. Same fella. Over the years, I've won pearls, perfume, all kinds of Yankee knick-knacks, most of which I turned over for a fast profit. Just remember, I'm your banker. You pass all fine merchandise over to me for trade, nobody else, get it?"

"I get it," I said. And put on a new jacket that smelled cleaner than anything I'd ever worn in my entire life.

"So, it can be a lucrative business if you use your hand right or your licker. Most of the time they just want someplace to polish their rooster. If I were you, I'd tell them I prefer under the arm like so. It's just easier to deal with afterward. Quick wipe with your handkerchief, and you're done, get it?"

"Yeah I do, but Alley, my name ain't Nancy, It's Jones if you please."

She looked me over like she was buying a saddle. "Look, kid, with that hair and those looks, Nancy Boy's what your name's going to be around here. If you want to be getting called Punk, you need to get a shortcut and a few scars. Lose the girly looks. See what happens after your balls fill the bag. I reckon in time, the way you're going, you'll polish up pretty dandy, Mister Jones. You could be worth a gold fortune, in the right part of town."

"A gold fortune?" I said. "You reckon so?"

"Yeah," she said nodding, "C'mon, let's find a board for you to sleep on."

Chapter 6
David and two Goliaths

The board I slept on with Juan the night before was taken up by a couple of somebody else's playing cards. Juan's fat bellied girl gave me daggers every time I looked in his direction, so I had to take up sleeping back in the Billy stove room instead of the room with all the bunks.

For nights I lived there, in that dark place, stinking of liquor and piss. All the Punk boys in their man age jackets and big shit cigars, coming back from a night's work, with little whore girls hanging around their necks for paper money, throwing loaded dice and playing cheating cards.

There were thieving and fighting and unfriendly fucking. Beatings for robbers, dirty favors for winners. I stayed out of the fray. Hidden like a critter behind a broken down chair. A blue long-backed beauty it was, with shiny gold running ragged through its veins. At one time or another, it had been a fancy thing. Now it was an ugly thing, a broken down thing. With rats feasting on its belly, stealing all the insides for their greedy little nests, hidden beneath the floorboards, someplace dirty undergrounAt that time, I suffered bad with losing Joe to the grave. Crying long until my eyes could not open up to see. One morning I went outside to get fresh air in my lungs so I could breathe better. I went to the hay barn and stroked a pretty horse. A fine chestnut with white socks and gold threaded mane.

Juan met me. I could smell something tasty.

"Want some salami?" he said.

I said, "Thank you," took what he had, and got busy eating.

"Sorry about your friend dying," he said.

I didn't say nothing, only kept on chewing.

"I come looking for you," he said. "But, you'd gone. I was scared maybe you'd got caught up in the fire or something."

"I didn't see you," I said. "I was there the whole time. Looked out for you everywhere but you'd cut and run is what happened."

"Well," he said, rubbing his hands on his shirt, "I try not to steer too close to the law when I can. Never know what they're going to pull you in for nothing. And with Rowena and the baby and all…"

I'd heard enough. I took my salami and climbed up onto the haystack where we'd been together a couple of nights before. I looked down at him. He was rubbing his head with one hand and doing nothing with the other.

He took a slow turn and looked up at me with comely black eyes.

I stopped eating. My belly was full, but a new hunger tore at my guts and made them go mad dog. My blood turned to fire. My heart went running rabbits.

He took his hand off his head and come running up the haystack to me.

He tried to kiss me. I turned away saying, "No."

"What if I was to say 'please'?" he said, wrestling the salami out of my hands.

I said, "The answer's still 'no'."

He was breathing fast. He put his hands together like he was praying. "I beg you," he said, "I'm lost."

"Lost?" I said. "How you are lost? You sitting right here."

"I'm lost without you," he said.

I wanted to kiss him but didn't know where to start.

Then he took hold of me and pressed me to his chest. The

smell of him made my head go giddy. He rubbed his tongue on the back of my neck. Before I knew it, a strange sickness comes. My thing was aching. I grew tired and crazy headed at the same time.

Soon we were kissing on the lips. He put his tongue in my mouth and I let him. I felt like I was going to die and be released into heaven. Only I started thinking of Joe on account of it.

Tears come to my eyes.

He stopped kissing. "Why are you doing that for?" he said.

"I don't know," I said, water raining down my eyes, and my chest shaking, lips trembling.

"Well, can you stop?" he said, holding my wrists tight and getting edgy.

"No," I said, "I can't."

He let out a big sigh and tore his hands away from me. I reached out to pull them back and wrap him around me again. I made him hold me, and I held tight to his neck and tried to stop sobbing.

He surrendered.

"I didn't mean to get mad," he said.

"I know you didn't," I said.

"It's just people crying makes me angry. Because what am I supposed to do about it?"

"Nothing," I said. "It weren't your doing."

"I lost my family too you know," he said.

"I know," I said.

"And I ain't crying about it. If I did people would go heckling me and beating the shit out of me."

I agreed. They probably would. Then looking at the size of him, and the muscles on his arms they might think twice for fear of dying first.

"Want me to teach you something?" he said into my ear, pecking it with kisses.

I wiped my eyes with my sleeve and said, "What?"

He undid his belt and unbuttoned his waistband. And pulled his thing out, which was long and mean-looking.

"Do you like it?" he said.

I said I did.

"Want me to show you how to tug them off, as we do down the Dead Man, to get them spewing fast?"

I told him that I didn't know.

"Well," he said, "you want to make a fortune out there, don't you?"

I said, "Yes."

"Some fellas wait in a line making bets on how fast you can get the other done see. So, it's more money if you beat them at it, get me?"

I did. And that night in the barn with Juan, I learned all about working down the Dead Man. And how to make all the money you'd ever need to stay alive around here. Watching him spewing up like a whale, sending seed flying up in the air, and it did make me smile. We laughed long about it after. Soon I fell sleepy in the hay, and with my head on his beating heart I looked up and watched him dreaming. His black whiskers poking through his top lip and on his chin. All in all, he was handsome as a boy could ever hope to be. Or hope to be with.

Next morning, I opened my eyes and saw his Belly-girl looking up, staring at me. Before I could do nothing, she had me by the feet and was dragging me down off the hay. She pushed me out of the barn and into the street and began to beat me. First with her fists. Then with a jug of liquor; I could smell she'd not been long drinking.

I made my getaway fast. I pushed her down and ran up the muddy steps, sliding through the door, into the Shades, and banged my way into the Billy stove room.

She followed, close on my tail, calling me all kinds of names and curses from behind.

There was nobody in the room, so I got behind her back, and punched her one low, saying, "It ain't got nothing to do with you. It's private business between one man and another. So you keep your nose out of it."

She got hold of me and pushed me against the bench, so I fell and hurt my spine.

"Man?" she said. "You ain't no goddamn man. And you ain't got balls ever to be one neither."

I got up and got ready to knock her one for good, and then I did.

Right on the nose.

She put her hand to it. Blood ran through her fingers and dripped down to the floor. She started squealing like a cut pig.

When I saw what I had done, I covered my ears and went to make my escape. I turned to the door and saw Juan had woke up.

I looked at him.

He was looking at her.

She was crying and bleeding.

He grabbed me heavy by the arm. Swore at me with unkind words and got ready to clobber me one with his fist.

I twisted out of his grip. I ran back toward the benches. Only Belly-girl tripped me up, and I went flying on the Billy room floor.

Juan stood over me.

"Stand up," he said.

So I did.

"Get ready for a fight," he said.

Before I could say nothing, he had his shirt stripped off and got his fists ready for punching.

Belly-girl stopped crying and started smiling. She went running out the room yelling, "Fight, fight! Everybody. Juan's going fight that new little cocksucker. C'mon. I got five dollars says it'll be all over in five ticks of the clock."

Next thing, the whole place was up. Boys come piling in the room, climbing on benches and sitting on tables. Soon the place was stinking of old liquor, ugly sleep and horseshit cigars.

"Who's fighting who again?" said one kid, yawning and rubbing his head.

"Juan," said Belly-girl. "Juan's going fight that girly little shit over there." And they all looked at me.

"What?" said the kid. "That Nancy? Hell, that ain't no contest. He'll knock him out cold in two minutes."

"I say he'll do it in one," said his friend next to him.

"Nope," said another one from behind, "it'll be over in thirty ticks on the clock. No question about it."

I could only stand watching Juan warming up: jumping up and down one moment, crouched over the next, beating up the air with his fists like he was fast punching a lame dog.

Alley Mac came barging into the room with two of her Bully Boys fast on her heel. "What's going on here?" she said. When she was told, she came up to me and looked me in the eye. Told me there was to be a fight, and I was in it.

Once she explained the rules she opened up a pocket watch. She put her head on mine and said, "Kid, you ought to know, Juan's been trained. He's a regular down Union on a Monday. Which means, you ain't got a chance in Hell, so I say count five and go down."

"Five minutes?" I said.

"No," she said, "ticks on the clock." Then snapped her pocket watch shut and blew a whistle to say all bets were on.

"Alley Mac," I said, trembling. My eyes sprouted tears. "The truth of it is, I can kill a body if I got to. I can and I will."

But, she was deaf to my words. Everyone was shouting and passing coin while she got busy calling odds.

"Kill a body?" said Belly-girl to the back of my head. "Nancy figures she's got bull in her blood, does she?"

I turned.

Her nose was caked red. She glared back at me with snake eyes. "Listen here bitch boy," she said. "When the wolves have done running the hens to death like they ought to, and all that's left is the rooster: that's the only killing you'll be doing. Be wringing that cock's neck all day long down the Dead Man. Paying for the pleasure, I'll bet too."

I wiped away my tears and lifted up my chin. "I don't know what schooling you got," I said, "but where I come from it's the foxes catch the chickens, not the wolves. And as for the roosters, well you only show them the cage when it's time for bringing on the young. The rest of the time the hens leave the goddamn rooster be. So you ought to take a feather out of their book afore you go spouting off your fat belly mouth. Seen whales with smaller blow holes than that noise maker you got spread all over your face."

She took a breath, spat at me and said she'd never seen such an ugly faced Nancy in the whole of her life.

I said, "My name ain't Nancy. It's Jones. Goldsmith Jones. And you ain't never going to forget it by the time I'm done with you." Then I pushed her down on the floor, and I got ready to boot her one.

I was about to, then thought better of it.

But she played smart and made like I had. She lay there, white-eyed, like a dying horse; holding onto her belly, crying out for Juan.

Someone told him what was going on. He stops jumping and comes a-running. He went down to her then turned toward to me, saying, "Now you're going to die."

And then he was a-coming, with his fists full of killing.

I ran behind him.

Kids were yelling. Kids were booing. Coin was jingling. Coin was flying up through the air and over to Alley holding bets.

"Come on you cock-sucking coward," one says. "Do your business and go down!"

"Punch him low," said a body back to me. "Get him in the balls. Do it. Do it now!"

But I didn't do nothing. For Juan was too fast for me.

He threw a punch to the side of my head. I ducked, but I was slow. He caught the side of my eye. I staggered around like a drunkard holding onto it.

The skin below was broke. I was bleeding. I was going deaf with the noise of kids screaming down my earhole.

Juan swung at the air.

I dropped down.

I tried hiding in the crowd, but they pushed me back into the circle. I was dozy. My head was sweating. Hair clung to my face, stinking of iron blood.

Juan was coming for me again. I had no time to think. Then, when I figured all was lost, Joe come a-rising from the grave and jumped inside my head.

"Start jigging boy," he says. " You can dodge that Devil. Then get him when he's unawares."

So I did just that, ducking and diving to Juan's crazy man swings.

I was dancing. I stumbled over my feet and fell onto my side.

Faces started laughing.

Juan forged a smile and made it solid. I watched him standing over me with his pals cheering him on from behind.

I stood up for my life.

He got ready to put me in my grave.

I dodged the first swing coming at my head.

Then the second.

On the third, I saw something.

A long black snake hit the straw, and there was a smack on the ground, like a clap of thunder, and I jumped. Another big snake—flashes come. Blowing straw up off the ground and making dust clouds rise.

Everyone stopped silent.

They were all looking at the door back of me.

I turned my head. And that's when I saw him. The Boss. Saul Suarez.

A tall, handsome body dressed in black leather, with a fine Spanish hat covering his eyes. His hands were black. He held a long-tailed horsewhip in his fist.

I realized my eye was off the game. I turned to see if Juan was coming for me. But his eyes were fixed on Saul.

Right, then I knew this was my moment. I did just like Joe said. I clenched my fist, pulled back my good arm. Then, let it go. Square into Juan's face.

He thought blood was spewing from his mouth. So, while he was busy checking on it, I took a few steps back. Made myself turn bull. Put my head down low, brought my shoulders to the front, and with my hair hanging down and my face burning hot, I charged at his stomach, with all I had.

Juan went down, down, down onto the ground.

He grabbed his belly and gasped for air.

Everyone's heads turned to him, lying on the floor.

At first, there was silence. Except for Juan's moaning. Then the clapping comes. A single pair of hands.

A regular sound. Like the slow beat of a drum.

Everyone saw Saul, leaning against the doorway, one toe leaning against the other. Smiling wide as he clapped for me.

A couple of fancy dressed ladies were hanging by his side. They joined in. Then everyone started clapping.

Only Belly-girl, on her feet now, kept still and silent.

Alley counted up the numbers. All the punks sang time with her.

I stood over Juan, curled up, rolling either side like a baby, with Alley counting, me winning, and money jingling, everywhere.

I went up to Belly-girl. Her mouth was hanging open like a broken trap.

I stuck my face in hers and said, "Who's the man now, huh? I say. Who's the man now?"

"Shouldn't count your chicks before they're laid," she replied.

I said, "What?"

Then she hit me. Hard over the head with her fist. Knocking me out cold, for the rest of the count.

Chapter 7
A friendly offering from above

Next day I was getting ready to lay my head down on my coat and try and get some shuteye when Raccoon poked his head through the broken legs of my chair.

"Congratulations on your victory," he said. "Too bad Alley Mac didn't class it as a win."

"Well," I said, crawling out from underneath, "I'm starting to learn nothing around here is fair."

"Ain't that the truth," he said.

We went outside to sit on the hallway stairs. We poured a bucket of water over some puke, dried it off with some straw and sat down.

"Say," I said, "Did you watch the whole fight?"

"I did," he said, lighting up.

"What did you think?"

"Well," he said, "I thought your Bull Run was sure something."

"That's an old trick of mine," I said, stuffing straw into my pipe. "I only use it now and then. Can kill a man with it, if you ain't careful."

"Well, that's mighty handy," he said. "Although, I figure Juan will want revenge on you for it. For honor and all."

"It ain't him wanting honor and revenge," I said. "It's his old lady that's got it in for me. She doesn't like him and me being friends, that's what it is." And I blew out some smoke rings thinking on it.

"I told Violet about you," he said. "Reckoned you and me would make for good friends."

"Violet?" I said. "What, are you shacked up with a girl already. How old are you, ten?"

"Hell no," he said. "I'm fourteen years living."

"Bullshit," I said. "I could be years older than you."

"Reckon?" he said, spitting out weeds. "I'd say, you could be years younger."

I gave him snake eyes to look at.

He hit my arm with a soft punch, and we laughed about it.

"The thing about Violet, " he says, "is, well, she ain't like any regular person you probably know."

"Why?" I said. " Is she crazy headed too? I tell you if she's old enough to bleed, I don't want to be around. So, thank you, but, no thank you."

"No, look," he said, opening up his bag of smoke for me to pinch. "Violet ain't nothing like Juan's business. For a start, she's been living twenty years. And don't act like a punk or nothing at all. In fact, Violet might be like the Ma you always wanted but never had."

"I doubt that very much," I say, taking a light from his sparked up offering.

"We're living good," he said, shaking out the match. "Got our own stove, food, and everything. Look, it won't hurt any for you to pay just one visit," he said.

After talk of sweet food and Chinese tea got me thinking. I said, "All right. I guess I'll come with you."

When we got to the top of the roof, we climbed down into a hole that had broken through. We crawled through a space between the boards and stopped at a part where the light was shining. Raccoon gave a series of knocks that sounded like a code of sorts. When he got a similar reply, he told me to back up, then lifted up the board beneath where our feet had been. I lifted myself down through the hatch.

Daylight blinded my eyes. I squinted and saw the place, and it was all right. There was a table of sorts. A fired up Billy, a bucket for washing and another for doing your business. There was an old bench and better-looking blankets that Raccoon said was his bed. By the window stood a board with a comfy looking mattress and a fine looking quilt. And there sat Violet: a long and slender body, with skin like a dove, wearing a bright purple robe with gold dragons down the front.

"How you do," she said, hanging down a hand for me to shake or kiss or what I did not know.

When I did nothing, she took mine and shook it for me.

I touched my hat and said, "Hello."

From somewhere in his jacket, Raccoon took out a small box wrapped in brown paper.

Violet's eyes lit up like the stars.

Raccoon handed it over to her.

Paper and string went flying everywhere.

Finally, the box was open. It looked like tobacco but smelled like a skunk.

"Tea?" said Violet. "All the way from China?"

"Sure," said Raccoon, shrugging.

Raccoon pulled up a bucket of rainwater that was hanging out the window and filled up the copper.

Violet turned to me and said, "Young person, would you do me the honor of laying out the table for our little feast."

Right away I knew her voice was strange. It was a kind of South and Red Coat English. But talk of real food and plenty of it got my mouth dripping like a dog.

She unfolded a tablecloth, and together we hung it on a board sitting on two orange crates. Then, pulled out a box from underneath the comfy bed. One by one, I was handed cups and plates so fine that when you held them up against the daylight, you could see right through them.

She hummed a tune so sweet that soon, Raccoon and me

were humming along too: our heads swaying back and forth, fingers snapping, and feet tapping.

She took out three sweet buns from a tin. Picked off the ants, and stuck them in a jar. Climbed to the window and released them back into the wood where she said they belonged.

The window was but a beaten up hole in the wall. A piece of smoky lace hung from a nail on the side, and a spider kept a tidy web in the corner. Violet explained that just like Noah's ark, the spider and the ants never declared war on one another, which was a lesson from God to all men, to reject such carnal desire for killing everything they could set their hands to.

It started raining, making a racket on the tin roof. While we waited for the kettle to whistle, Raccoon and me put our heads through the window and looked down below. The road was turning into a muddy river. Folks were holding onto their crazy high-hats running scared from the pissing down rain. And we laughed our heads off, crying, watching them slipping and sliding in the shit.

"Hey Jonesy," he said, "lie on your back like this."

I turned on my back and faced the gray sky, and smiled as the rain beat my face up with sweet drops of clean water.

"This is what it must have been like for that Frenchie traitor Robespierre when Madame Guillotine cut his neck off him."

"Madame who?" I said, "Cut his what?"

"Madame Guillotine. That's how Robespierre's enemies got their vengeance on him. See that piece of roof hanging above?"

I looked up and saw a length of wood swinging slowly in the wind.

"Well, imagine that's her. Just one big razor sharp blade. They made him look up at it, so when they let go of the trigger, he could see it coming for him all the way down."

I put my hand to my neck and felt my heart beating through my fingers.

"Want to know something else? Something that'll gets your heebie-jeebies going?"

"Sure," I said.

"Before they caught up with him, fella turned yellow belly.

Dumbass tried shooting himself in the head but done it all wrong. Blew his chin straight off his face. So he had his whole jaw hanging off when they done it to him. Now just imagine that. Having your own jaw hanging there like that, looking up at the thing coming to cut your head off for good."

I drew a picture of it in my head then spent the next few ticks praying to the Lord, to make it go away. When I opened my eyes again, I saw angry clouds lording over seagulls the size of vultures. They circled up above caring less for nothing: not blades, not drowning, not dying, not nothing.

With my hair hanging down, blowing in the wind, I looked up at the dark heavens above and tried thinking what it felt like for angels when they fly.

The kettle sang.

"C'mon boys," said Violet. "Stop playing tomfools now, it's time to go and get our tea. It comes all the way from China. So has taken too long and hard a journey for us all to neglect and waste for nothing."

While we were getting down, I took the opportunity to ask Raccoon, "What kind of talk is it she's making?"

"Demon's land," he said. "Violet used to be a Sydney Duck."

"What, that raggedy gang of nasty Joes from Jefferson?"

He nodded. "There used to be a whole family of them at one time. They crossed three oceans to get here. Ran the whole of town before Saul's daddy took the bosses out. Now they're just a bunch of lowdowns mostly. Always stealing Spanish cocksuckers like slaves or worse. Sometimes they sell them off to Ma Wong's down Chinese Town. That's why Saul takes them in. To stop them getting sold, or killed off."

"Well, ain't Violet got Sydney Town friends?" I said. "Ain't they going to come looking for her?"

"Yeah," he said. "That's why Saul keeps the door locked up so tight."

I looked to where he was pointing. There was a screen, with a one-eyed crane killing a fish painted on it. We stole over to it and looked behind.

The door had a keyhole.

It smelled of rusty nails and rotting wood.

I bent down and put my eye against the iron. I saw nothing but darkness.

I stood back and looked up above the door.

A wooden cross was hanging. It was the Lord Jesus, bare-naked. Looking like he'd been got at by a six-shooter. Blood was pouring out of everywhere,

I backed away, holding onto my heart.

"Don't let that scare you," says Raccoon. " I got the genuine ear of the Spirit Wolf on me."

He had a cord around his neck with a scrap of a dead dog tied to it.

"My Grand-daddy gave it to me," he said. "It's always kept the bad luck away. I'll make one for you to wear if you like."

I looked at it. The skin was old and yellow. The fur was white and mangy.

"No thank you," I said.

Raccoon and I knelt beside her. I waited for it, as Violet poured hot tea into my fancy cup. When she'd done, I drank up. It tasted like I was drinking from a puddle. But I did not complain. I let it be. I snatched my bun off the plate and tore into it with my teeth like a dog. She scolded me in no time.

"Young person," she said. "That is not how gentlefolk eat at this table. Now, please put the bun down. We have not yet thanked the Lord for giving us our daily bread."

When we were done crossing ourselves and saying, "Amen," I made a run for my bun again, but she got to it first and cut it in two with a deadly looking knife.

"Now," she said, "you cannot possibly eat your bun until it's buttered on both sides."

So I let her do it. But it was taking forever for it to get done, so I called to Heaven, saying, "Jesus Christ. I'm going to starve to death by the time she's done doing."

She stopped doing and said, "You are the most uncivilized

young person I've ever met, and I will clean your dirty speaking mouth out with soap if I hear you use the precious Lord's name in vain again."

It was then I decided that I did not like the name "Violet" at all.

I borrowed Raccoon's ear. "A Joe should have a man's name if he ain't a girl, and he ain't a liar. And how long's it take to butter a goddamn bun?"

Violet heard me and told me to stop talking whispers. "Only cheaters and spies talk in shadows," she said.

A critter comes out of a hole. Raccoon and me set to work catching it sending boxes and paper, and dust flying everywhere. Violet took pity on it and hollered for us to leave it be. She buttered tiny pieces of bun faster than my eyes could follow. Then set about calling the critter by a precious name, and setting food out for it right away to eat.

I could only stare at that little rat, filling its fat belly on what was mine.

She ordered me to sit down and pray forgiveness for being wicked, which I had done, a thousand times already. My belly was aching sore, so I begged fast and finally, I was allowed to eat.

After my third cup of horseshit tea, I found myself feeling like a cloud might if it could be a human being. I moved to the nearest thing, the floor, to lie down.

I was breezy like the sky.

I looked up at the rafters. Dirty cobwebs were everywhere. There was a nest up there in the tangle of boards, but no birds around anyplace, except for outside, squawking.

The weather inside my head changed. Rainbows were dancing. Real ones. Lots of them. Rainbows on the nest, rainbows on the spider strings, on the secret hatch Raccoon and me had climbed out from. They were flickering before my eyes going from one place to another, moving by themselves. Or somebody was doing the moving for them.

I turned my head to the window.

It was Violet.

Dangling a string of cut up glass in front of the prodigal sun returned.

Raccoon come and lay down next to me. "Ain't that tea something?" he said.

I looked at him. Plain as potato pie. My eyes fell on Violet. Comely as the devil. Sitting on the comfy bed, playing with her tricky glass.

"It ain't actually from China," he said, "it's only something I pick up along the deer track off Pacific. I mix it up with horse backie. It don't cost nothing at all. And sells for a dollar a bag. I got me a real economy going with it."

I kept my eyes on Violet and her rainbow maker.

The cloud in my head suddenly lifted.

I sat upright.

"Why's they call themself Violet for," I said, trying to keep it low.

"Don't talk behind my back," she says, hearing everything. "It's neither ladylike or gentlemanly." She wrapped the glass up and hid it under the covers like a spy. "If you must know," she said, " it's because I got eyes the color of those flowers they got outside the town hall."

"They're called violets," said Raccoon.

I had to take a look-see at this for myself.

I stood up.

I was dizzy and nearly fell down again.

When I was steady, I straightened out my back and walked up to her.

I stood well out of arm's reach and took a good long look at that face. "Your eyes ain't like violets," I said. "They're blue, like a wolf's eyes."

"No," she said. "No, I tell you, if you come closer and take a look, you'll see violets in there someplace."

I swung a quick look back at Raccoon.

He shrugged and complained he was hungry.

I turned back to Violet. Her hair was curled up and powder white like her skin. It was tied back with a scarf like an old-timer, only she was young.

I lifted my chin and walked up closer still. I smelled soap and something else that I could tell cost money. I looked around her neck for trinkets. It was as I thought. She had idols everywhere.

"What are you so shy of?" she says, playing with a gold Jesus dying around her neck.

"I ain't shy of nothing," I said, and I told her how I won the fight with Juan.

She pointed to my cheek and said, "You're going to have a scar there if it ain't looked at. Want me to sew it up for you?"

I said, "No," and held my hand to face. I touched the wound with my fingers. It felt big and hot, ugly and raw. I looked around for a reflection.

"There," said Violet, "on top of the dresser."

I went to the table.

It was nothing but a bunch of old boxes with a sheet lying on top.

There was a looking glass. I only ever saw myself in water, or inside a windowpane. My hand shook as I held the reflection up to my eyes. And now I saw all of me, clear as day. With an ugly wound, I would have forever, thanks to Juan's angry hand.

I put the mirror back down. I'd done with staring at my face, which looked nothing like I thought it did. The truth of it was, I figured I was far more comely than I happened to be. And now all I saw was a disappointment. I sat down on the comfy bed next to Violet and stared at the floor. Which had no rug, and was dirty.

Violet soaked the end of her scarf with some whiskey and told me it was going to sting when she cleaned my wound, which it did. Like the devil.

She told Raccoon to light a taper then get a box that had sewing things in it. Violet got a needle and held it over the flame. It went red hot, like a poker. When it cooled black, she pushed some blue cotton thread through it. Then squeezed my cheek, where the cut was. It was bruised sore. I put my hand up to stop her tailoring my face. She told me to stop fussing like an infant.

Raccoon was stood by the cupboard. I shot him a sharp eye to see if he heard me howl. He was busy amusing himself by watching me, so I shut up fast.

I grabbed a tight hold of the patchwork quilt. Each time that needle went digging into my skin; I squeezed my fists until my knuckles burned hot like the fire.

As she patched me up, she told me a story. About falling sweet on boys that were nearly men, and how it was asking for trouble. "Because what a man wants, ain't right for a boy as delicate as you," she said. "Some won't reign in their horse for nothing. They'll hurt a boy like you for the pleasure of it. Leave you cut to pieces in the end. Poor little doll."

The needle poked me and I hollered. I tore myself away from her and took hold of the looking glass. My cheek was red and it was throbbing. I looked into my own gaze. She'd sewn me up like a goddam scarecrow.

"Want to see some of my scars?" said Raccoon, lifting up his shirt. He showed me every mark he could find. Each one had a story more ridiculous than the one before. "My granddaddy was a chief also. Of the Ohlone Tribe," he said.

"I know," I says, "you told me already, a thousand times."

"I reckon it was only the once, I told you."

"No," I says, "It's the third time I've heard you talk about your granddaddy today."

"That's a lie," he said.

"It ain't a lie," I said, "I ain't never lie."

"You boys stop quarreling," said Violet. "Now, you two tidy. I got to get myself made up for meeting my gentleman."

"Gentleman?" I said to Raccoon. "What gentleman?"

"My own navy gentleman," she said, spying again.

"It's Captain Nelson," said Raccoon. "He's a legendary warrior of the sea."

"Now young man," she said. "We've had this conversation before. You know my navy gentleman ain't no legendary warrior; he's too much an angel for such unnecessary violence. Although he has sailed everywhere there is to go in the world of wonders, which, I suppose, makes him an adventurer of sorts. Tonight we are going to the theater to visit Our American Cousin, who I have not seen in ages."

I helped Raccoon put the cups away. Every time I put one back, Violet took it out again, checking it to make sure it weren't chipped. I nearly dropped one, worrying about it.

She fired me off of that work and ordered me to do another. Made me pull a trunk out from under the comfy bed. When I was done, I was told to step away, for my clothes were dirty. I watched her unpack a man's fine dark blue evening suit with thin stripes running down and a boiled white shirt. She bent over the bed and pulled out a hatbox. Inside was a topper to match, with a shiny silk ribbon horse glued tight to the base.

"I need to look my very best for my one and only," she said. "Last thing I want to do is bring shame upon his good name. Unlike that other person he had the misfortunes to become associated with." And gave me a sly look for nothing.

She called for Raccoon. "Dear," she said to him, "Be a fine gentleman won't you, and fetch my toiletries?"

Raccoon did everything he was bid.

I stood in the corner, cloaked in shadow. I watched as Raccoon began humming along to another of Violet's tiresome tunes. Tapping his heels to the beat. Smiling. Eating from a jar of sugar she offered him but refused me. Raccoon held out a piece for me to take but I declined, saying, "I don't fancy growing black teeth stinking of rot."

I kept my arms folded tight against myself and started thinking of ways to leave.

Raccoon set up the looking glass on the table so it wouldn't fall. Then, put some steaming water into a bowl and set it alongside.

Violet thanked him, calling him, "an angel," and a "gentlemen," and a "regular sir". She opened up the bag and took out a razor blade, some white soap, and a bottle of cologne with gold letters on it that meant it was expensive.

She lathered up the brush, and began doing her cheeks with it and her chin. She then done Raccoon's face: singing and smiling and fussing over him like he was a pup.

I sat there watching in torment for I was not a liar. The truth of it was Raccoon would not shut up about his grandpa, and it smarted me like that goddamn needle had, running like the Devil under my skin.

"I need to be going," I said.

"You're leaving?" said Raccoon.

"I got things I got to do," I said.

"Like what?" he said.

"Well, be sure and come again soon," said Violet without even looking at me.

"Sure," I said, not looking at her, but searching for that hatch in the roof.

"The easiest way out of here is probably out the hole in the wall," she said.

I said thank you and good-bye to all then went to make my way out.

"Mind you don't harm my spider-friend with your dirty feet," said Violet.

I held my tongue. Climbed out the hole and onto the roof.

It was pissing down rain again.

I turned to check on the web, to see if it was still in one piece.

And of course, it was.

Chapter 8
Fair-haired devils

Alley Mac moved me to a bunk belonging to a freckled faced boy who pissed himself every night. Every day I woke up in the cool of dawn, with my Johnnies stinking and my legs stinging, only to turn around and find Freckle boy snuggled up in my blanket.

Once, I woke up, stole it back off of him and went to sleep the rest of the morning off in the barn.

The air was damp and warm. The horses welcomed me with a nudge. Began talking to one another in that language all their own, through blowing lips and stomping hooves. Pretty chestnut with the white socks was a real darling. Her lashes hung long and low over her black eyes, and she smelled as sweet as new cut hay.

I was holding onto her, pressing my nose against her neck, to breathe her in, when I heard a noise. It was an older boy, making sounds. Strange sounds. Hurting sounds. A cold bolt of lightning ran up from my toes and out my head making my hair feel like it was standing on end.

I let go of my darlin' horse. I stood solid, with my feet nailed to the floor listening out for more of what sounded like danger. When, to my wide-open ears, comes a familiar voice, saying words I'd heard said to me before. Precious words, the kind of words that comes along with pretty kisses, and broken down hearts.

My stomach twisted and turned upside down. My face was on fire. I held my breath and made myself move so I could see what I was hearing.

And there he was. Juan. With another boy. A blonde haired devil. More his age than mine. I knew who he was right away. Everyone called him pretty, and comely, in a way that I was not.

My eyes, seeing what they did, didn't know what was what. For they had never seen such a thing to know how to think it. And therefore, could not figure on how or why or nothing. I only knew of women doing such a thing, for they got a hole made for happening. And I was a dumbass. I just did not know nothing. Only thing I could think of was impossible. All of what Alley Mac had told me that time, first time, before she robbed me blind, comes run, run, rushing through my empty head. I could only try and hold near forgotten words. Like catching fish jumping in a river, with wet hands. I watched, and I watched, and I hated that white haired devil for living where I used to be. For my home was Juan's arms before Belly-girl comes along, cursing me. Making him think he sees the devil in me. When the real devil was right here all along—lying blue eyed and butt naked in the hay.

I heard him saying to Juan in his sleepy voice, "What's that? You hear something?"

Juan got off of him, and stood with his back to me. He buttoned up his waistband and pulled his suspenders back over them. I watched his shoulder blades moving up and down, making the muscles on his back move with them. The whole of heaven comes shining through the plank barn walls, pouring gold sun onto his whole body. Making him like a winged-up spirit. Like Angel Gabriel comes judgment day.

I ducked and hid low in the dusty shade, behind Darlin's heavy hooves.

I heard Juan's footsteps shuffling coming my way through the hay.

I shut my eyes to make him begone.

But he would not disappear. And his blinding glow kept coming for me.

Darlin' blew her lips, snorted, and started stepping without moving any place. I kept behind her. Hiding out in her gloomy horse shadow.

Then comes Juan. Dark without the sun.

I could smell him, and that blue-eyed devil on him. I opened my eyes. I wanted to tear at his legs with my teeth like a dog. But I stayed still.

"Shit," I heard him say, low, under his breath.

I opened my eyes. Saw him looking down in my direction. His chest still heaving, his hair in disarray and his dark face screwed up like ripples on a dead man's beach.

"Who is it?" said the blue-eyed devil, his shirt held up tight to his chin, covering up his scrawny chest.

The sound of his voice drove me mad-dog. Made me itchy for some kind of weapon, like a gun.

While I sat, crouched at the horse's feet, staring over at him, I had a waking dream. That I had such a gun. A pretty Colt with an ivory handle. I saw myself stand straight and tall. Taller than that blue-eyed Devil. And more a man between my thighs than he could ever hope to possess.

I aimed straight between his ribs counting each bone as I did so. My finger was hot on the trigger, my body bursting with desire to let it all blow. Then I did. Pulled that pretty trigger and felt good when it all comes undone. Dust and hay blowed all around a golden bullet. I saw it travel through the air real slow. Barely moving at all. As if there were hardly such a thing as locomotion. It kissed that Devil's skin, then ripped the flesh apart like it were only paper. Thick red blood runs iron-smelling rivers over the pale yellow hay. Deep, deep, deep it flows, beneath the dirty ground below.

All the while, my heart: cold and heavy as lead death, sits, unmoving behind my slim bones.

I swallowed bile. It went burning hell-fire down into my choking lungs.

"What are you doing here?" said Juan to me.

As soon as I heard him, I jumped out of my dream and lost my balance. I fell; turned over on the dirty ground, and held my hands over my face like a scared critter.

Juan was staring down at me with angry fists.

I feared, for no reason, other than my own thoughts telling me so, that he had the knack of reading minds. And I reckon he'd caught me red-handed thinking killing.

I put my arm over my face in fear of him kicking me one in the head for revenge.

"Go on," he said, making me jitter, "there ain't nothing here for you to see."

"Who is it?" said the blue-eyed devil to him, in his voice as sweet like sugar pie.

"Nobody," Juan said back to him. "Just the horses. Don't worry so. I'll sort them out." Then he began fussing with my Darlin' horse. The one with the white socks and the pretty eyes.

He stroked her head, and she was liking it better than me; nibbling on his hair and blowing in his ear like he was everything in the world and I was nothing. He was smiling back and kissing her forehead in return. Then he slid his eyes on me. His stare was narrow and hard. "Go on," he said keeping it low, "Git."

My lip was going. I started crying.

"Goddamit," he says, "I told you to git." Then gave a mean kick in front of my body making the hay fly in my face.

I turned over in a hurry and scurried on out of there like a runaway rat.

Out of the barn gate, I flew.

I stumbled on my boots, scraped my knee, and it bled. I saw a tin piss bucket sitting out for doing laundry. I grabbed hold of the handle, and with it sloshing and spilling, I twisted my body, giving it all I had, and chucked it at the plank barn wall.

Stinking water went splashing everywhere.

I waited for Juan to come rushing out to beat me one, and got my fists ready for the game.

But he did not come.

Darlin' comes to the barn gate instead. Started grunting mean and stamping her hooves at me with crazy man eyes.

"Stop it," I said to her, beating my foot on the dirt.

She looked up at me, her lashes long. Black eyes shining.

I was sobbing. "I'm sorry," I said, wiping my nose with my sleeve. "I wouldn't do nothing to hurt you, I swear, I'd never hurt you. Of all people, it'd never be you. Unless you made me. And then it'd only be self-defense."

She blew out a noise through her lips, which I took to mean, "All right. Just don't be doing it again."

I lowered my head in shame. Then nodded back at her, in the manner horses do. She stood solid and stared me out. The other horses come and joined up with her. They stood side by side. Keeping a watchful eye on me.

"All right, all right I'm going," I said to her and her friends. "Consider me gone, you hear. Consider me gone forever." Then I climbed onto the barn roof and hid from the world a while, until the long dark night comes a-calling and I went running back, looking for the light.

Chapter 9
I start working

There was only one other time Juan comes, chasing me into the barn with pretty kisses and precious words. Only, this time, he got me to do a thing you do down the Dead Man. Only when I went to spit it all out he told me to swallow all of it, so I did. But I become pained with worry for days after. For I'd heard a couple of girls talking. One had done the same for some Joe and she figured he'd filled her belly with child by doing it. Her friend said it might just so happen that way, and told her to drink vinegar to stop it from coming true.

I didn't know what was what so I was terrified. For how's a boy to live if he gets filled with child? So I drank vinegar too. Only I puked it up straight after.

I was so cursed with fear I dreamed I had a critter growing inside my belly gnawing my insides to come out. Next morning, I went to Alley Mac for I was sure she'd know what to do about it. When I saw her, I said to her, "What happens if a body swallows the seed."

She said, "Why do some of you boys play the part of child around here when you ain't one? Stop being such a greenhorn dumbass. Fellas ain't got nothing of the like to worry about, only girls the ones that got to live life being terrified. If you ain't figured that out by now, you ain't got no chance."

I said, "Is that why you dress like a boy instead? Because it makes it kind of like you are one?"

She looked at me with her eyebrows hitched, lit a match to her pipe and said, "Ain't you got something to do? That ain't being stupid."

"Only, Juan said there was a law trying to come in, saying females ain't allowed to dress up like fellas no more or else."

"Which ain't nothing to do with you."

"No, I know it ain't, but I just wondered what you'd do is all. But, for what it's worth, I think you make a better looking man than most fellas."

"Why thank you, Mr. Jones," she said raising a smile. Then reached in her pocket and flicked me a shiny nickel for keeps for the kindness.

I caught Juan and Whitey being friendly bedfellows one more time, in the barn, only I left right away and went back to my empty board where I cried and cried until I puked. I was trying to cover it up with straw when a bald headed kid come up to me tapped me on the shoulder saying, "Alley Mac wants to see you."

Its seems my paid up board had run out, and I was to start working down the Dead Man's Alley for real.

She set me up on Washington Street a block away from the Shades. I was made to stand on top of a crate yelling, "Shoe shine, get your shoe shines," five cents for the regular, two bits for the presidential service—which meant frigging or sucking on a Dead Eye's thing.

Alley Mac had a fella set up for me already, and said she was sticking around to make sure I done the job well.

I took a long look at that Joe. He was clean, but old, around thirty years living. His ears were overly large. Had red marks on his face that she said was due to him not caring much for fruit or vegetation, and not the clap like everyone was saying.

She went to him and they talked in private.

He swung a look at me and smiled.

He seemed friendly.

Alley Mac comes back to me saying, "Why didn't you smile back? You got to smile back when they smile at you. Polish your teeth with your sleeve."

So I did.

She ordered me to get down off the crate and tuck my shoeshine things away before they get stole. Then with me carrying my crate, Alley Mac, me, and Dead Eye headed down Dead Man's Alley.

Men and boys were hidden in shadow. Some were standing toe to toe smoking pipes and talking. I saw a couple of Dead Eyes standing unmoving and erect like stone statues, each with a boy close up to them. One punk was moving his hand, frigging back and forth, the other had his face pressed against Dead Eye's open waistbands. Another boy had done doing his and was spitting the job out into the dirt. The strong smell of liquor was offending my nose. I felt like I couldn't breathe. My heart was running, I was panting hard like a hunted down critter. I wanted to turn back and fly, but my feet were stuck fast to the ground like Jesus nailed to the board.

I thought, for a moment, I caught sight of Juan. I swallowed courage and looked closer still, to see if Whitey blue-eyes were with him. But they weren't there. And the thought of them, maybe being together, someplace else, lying butt naked in the hay, made my eyes fill with tears.

"Don't start crying," said Alley Mac. "Dead Eyes don't like it, and the kind that does, you don't want to know."

I wiped my tears away, apologized and told her I didn't feel well, and how I ought to go back and try again tomorrow.

But she had her mule ears on. "Now look at your man and give him a smile," she said.

I looked at the fella. And his contagious looking skin. Strange ears that didn't seem to belong to his head. Had his hands in his pockets and was staring at me with crazy owl eyes.

I bit my lip to stop my tears from spewing down my cheeks. I swallowed hard and tried on a smile.

He smiled back and gave me a little wave.

"So, you know what to do?" she said.

I nodded.

"All right," she said. "I'll be waiting around the corner for when you're done. And don't worry, he's nice. Just be nice back. Make him feel, you know, welcome. Keep smiling at him. Look interested. And, before he tells you what he wants, get in first with your own order. Ask him if you can tug on his rooster. Tell him it turns your fancy. That way you'll be running the show, not him."

"What about asking for money," I said.

"No, I already took care of that, all's you got to do is your job."

"All right," I says, "but, do I got to call it 'rooster,' can I call it something else?"

"Call it what you will," she said, "just make sure he understands what you're getting at. Some of them have a way of taking their own meaning and you don't want that. They get all kinds of strange ideas. So be clear, all right."

"Yessir," I said. And I did all right. So I was hired on a regular basis.

He helped me be canny. Gave me two kinds of treasure. A cheap trinket to sell on to Alley Mac, and a thing of value for me to keep in my tin box I kept buried under the floor boards, behind the old blue chair with the raggedy gold veins.

After a couple of days of Alley Mac setting up work, I become independent. A real Dead Man-boy, I was, hustling for my own treasure.

And I soon learned I hated it.

If a Dead Eye weren't trying to take hold of my precious thing, squeezing it and pinching it until my eyes were watered, they were ordering me about. Complaining all the while saying, "What the hell you doing? You ain't never chewed the bone before?"

"Oh c'mon mister," I said to this one, one time. "If you only pay me another two bits, I swear I'll have you done. I reckon you were nearly there, as sure as anything."

"Another two bits, eh?" he said. "I see how your sly hand works. Tricks of the trade. Draw the whole business out, so you can get your greedy fingers into more of my hard earned coin, is that it?" Then he went on kicking at me.

I was alone. It was dark save for my own lantern sitting by my side. I went falling ass first into the ground when he kicked me; one hand clinging to the wall, another trying to keep his angry boot from making enemy with my face.

I steadied the lantern to stop it blowing out. "Now mister," I said pleading with him, "there ain't no need for cheating talk. It ain't my fault you ain't spewed up in time."

"Well, whose fault is it, might I ask? It sure as hell ain't mine."

I saw the glow of Alley's lantern at the start of the road. She was walking the dogs. Her Bully Boys with her: two dark angels with pipe smoke for halos. Together they were doing the rounds and checking up on us Dead Man boys. Making sure we working all right.

Dead Eye and me waited for her to pass. As soon as they'd gone, he started frigging off his own thing, to see if he could get it working. He was huffing and puffing. His hand going like a piston and getting no place fast.

"I don't know whose fault it is," I said mumbling low unto myself. "Why don't you blame it on all that liquor you been drinking. Or how about the goddam war you never shut up about for two minutes. Or the cost of living in this shit hole like you kept saying. One thing's for sure, it ain't me that's the problem." And it was true. Afore he comes along, a fella with a cock the size of a young bull paid twice as much for the same thing as I was done right here, and that fella spewed up in the air like a whale. And that was in no time at all.

I figured my words were tucked tight to my lips, but he was a hog who'd heard the trough corn filling: all ears, wide open like the plain. He stopped doing his own thing and corded up his waistband. He checked to see if he were done up all right and then he went for me. Reached out with his arms to grab me, but I got out of his way and backed myself against the wall.

I went for my knife. I flicked the switch and opened up the rusty blade. I pointed it at him and stabbed at the air saying, "It'll gut you. I swear I will. If you come near me, one-inch, I'll do it. I'll cut you dead."

But he was no greenhorn. He played high stakes and raised me with a gun. Held it in the air swearing loyalty to the Devil, and threatened to blow my head off to kingdom come.

I said, "Go ahead. Let it blow. Let the whole world know your dirty business while you're at it."

"You're an ugly Nancy ain't you," he said, squeezing both my cheeks with his fingers to make me stop talking.

I tore my face away and spat at his. "My name ain't Nancy," I said, "My name's Jones, Goldsmith Jones."

I saw the glow of Alley Mac's lantern again, and the sound of restless dogs.

"All's well down here?" she said, sounding manly.

The Dead Eye took a prisoner of my arm, pushed the cold end of his pistol into my cheek. I could smell it wasn't loaded. But it was a killer all the same. One mighty bash of that against my skull, and I'd be spewing blood and brains just the same.

"All's well," he said to her, sounding like a kid. I could see him smiling. He weren't old, but most of his teeth were gone as if he was.

Alley Mac carried on walking, and her heavenly glow followed on behind. I looked to my own little flame flickering to death in my lantern. He saw me looking and kicked it out cold. Then he dug the pistol in so deep that it was cutting into my skin. I reckon he must have sawed off the end of it and it was all the rough metal that was tearing into me like a broken jar. He told me to get back to what I was doing, and do it right this time or else.

I must have made a crying critter sound with all hurting to my head.

Alley's hounds started barking at it.

I saw her glow coming. She and her boys turned back to where I was and began walking down the Dead Man toward us.

She held her lamp up. It took a place of where her head was. So all's I saw was a headless body coming my way.

The hounds were barking, getting loud. They snapped and growled while pulling hard on the leash.

I turned to salt. I tried calling out to her, but my voice had lost its will to be heard.

"Hey you there," she said into the dark.

I saw the light of the world sway to and fro, blinding mine with its brightness. And for a time, I could not see. I heard the sweet clicking of guns come from her direction.

Dead Eye took his gun from my torn cheek and fumbled around trying to load up. I told myself, "Run," but I heard the dogs beat me to it. Panting and running, fast paws racing loud over the ground. I turned my face to the wall and felt around for a way to scramble up the building before her hounds of Hell come to kill me. Gnashing their teeth and biting at my flesh, tearing me to pieces while I'm still alive. I might have cried out but I don't recall. For in my head, I was screaming deaf, and could hear nothing. Only when Dead Eye says, "Oh shit," did my ears start working.

I saw him stuff his gun down his waistband, and run off like a yellow-belly coward into the darkness. With Alley Mac's devil dogs following on behind.

When she caught up with me again, she said, "Did you get the money?"

My hands were shaky. I fumbled around my pocket and showed her a two-bit piece. Before I knew what was what she had it from me. And stole it away in her top pocket. "From now on," she said, looking nasty, "you work daylight hours, get it?"

I did. And I was thankful for it too. It meant less coin but at least I wouldn't be caught out blind again, for a time.

Chapter 10
Deadly butterfly

My legs were getting burned raw from Freckles pissing every night. I figured my only hope was to see if Raccoon would take me back as a friend. One rainy day, I climbed up to the top of the roof and squatted outside the hole in Violet's wall, waiting to see if they'd invite me in. I saw them together. Violet was wearing her purple gold crane robe and her George Washington wig. She was teaching Raccoon steps to a strange dance along to a tune she was humming. I watched the show from the spider's web, leaning my arm so that I didn't tear it all apart.

It was a fairly simple dance. Two steps forward, turn, left foot back and then lift, do the same again then do it the other way around.

Raccoon was getting it all wrong. I was trying to get his attention to tell him to twirl the other way and nearly crashed into the hole and onto Violet's comfy bed.

"Jonesy!" he said, breaking free of her and coming to me, smiling.

I looked at her to see if it was all right for me to enter. She had her hand on her chest and was making a meal of catching her breath. She fumbled her way to the bed and lay prone while gasping like a gold fish.

"It's all right," Raccoon said to her, "it's just Jonesy come to visit. You are coming to visit, ain't you?"

I climbed down.

"Mind your muddy boots on my quilt," she said, suddenly revived.

"I ain't gone nowhere near your quilt," I said low.

"Want some tea?" said Raccoon, "it's just stewing."

"All right, "I said, "but you got any food to go with it?"

"Oh plenty," he said. "Roma Joe gave me a job passing the word around saying two doors down's got maggots in his meat pies. I got a couple of day olds and some for reward."

"What about her?" I said to his ear. "We got to share?"

"A little," he said. "Saul sends his own food up for Violet, but she makes them take it away. Said she'd rather starve to death. But she takes my offering, only to keep the pangs away."

I looked at her. Her wrist was hairy and boney. Her cheeks hollow and shadowed beneath the powder wig white she had pressed all over her face.

"Rather starve to death, or what?" I said.

He shrugged.

"Saul ever comes up here by himself?" I say.

"Sometimes."

"What's he do?"

"I don't know," he said. "I scarper out of here. Don't fancy getting caught breaking in."

I thought about it. Then turned my mind's eye to Juan and that blue-eyed devil of his.

"Raccoon," I said in a whisper, "you know how a woman's got a hole?"

"Yeah," he said, blinking.

"Well, you know that Joe hangs around Juan of late: Whitey blue-eyes is what I call him."

"Simon Simon?"

"Is that his name? Well, that is ridiculous. But not surprising. There's something strange about him I tell you."

"Strange?" he said. "How so?"

"Well," I said, "I think he might have one. You know, a woman's hole."

Raccoon laughed until he cried. "He ain't," he said.

"He does, I tell you. I saw it with my own eyes."

"Saw it?" he said. "You mean a cooch? He ain't got a cooch, Jones."

"He does I tell you."

"Jones, he ain't. I saw him take a piss before. He's got a John Tom. It ain't much of one, but it's a one. I'd know if it were the other, trust me on that."

Then I told him what I saw that time—going down all dirty in the barn: sweating pigs and crazy wild horses. And I weren't angry telling it neither. I told it like it was and felt nothing about it.

"Oh," he said, squeezing his eyebrows back and forth. "You mean Simon Simon was getting fucked?"

"Fucked?" I said, getting close. "Fucked how? Fucked where?"

"In the behind, where else?" he said, pulling me closer away from Violet's line of sight. She was busy humming one of her sickly tunes, while painting her nails with squid ink.

"But how's that?" I said. "I got to know, I got to know everything what's going on around here, for its making me a dumbass for not knowing nothing."

"I don't know how?" he said, getting twitchy and pulling me down behind the crane screen. "Look, Jonesy, why you asking me for? I don't know nothing about nothing neither."

"I don't know," I said. "Sounds like you know something. More than me anyhow. But how's that, I ask you? How can that be? C'mon now, tell me all so I ain't a dumbass no more."

"I don't know," he said looking worried. He takes a couple of sneaky peeks at Violet, and then comes back to me. "C'mon, let's move, she's getting suspicious."

I let him go and stayed crouched down behind the crane, thinking.

"I get it," I says, joining him on the bed board, and talking whispers in his ear, "it's like when you're taking a shit and you make it go back home again afore it comes out. Except it ain't."

"I don't know," he says, rubbing his ear, "I ain't never tried to make my shit go back inside before."

"Well I ain't neither," I says, "it's just if you did that's what it'd be like, I'll bet."

"I don't know," he said, " I don't really want to talk about fucking no more."

"Well, all right," I say, my face burning red like a hot crab out the pan.

I let it lie, then fell into an even deeper whisper once more. "Listen friend," I said to him, linking his arm, "you won't tell nobody about it, will you?"

"Tell nobody about what?" he says.

"About me and Juan."

"What about you and Juan?"

"Nothing," I say, "only…"

"Only what?" he said. "Only what?"

"Nothing," I say, "only… nothing."

Two weeks I lived up there, in that attic with locked up Violet and Raccoon. I suffered many nights of loneliness from missing my own dear departed Joe and wanted nothing more than to be dead with him. But I was scared of dying. I worried that Devil might come to me in the dark, promising heaven, but dragging me down to Hell again. Sometimes, when I couldn't stop weeping, Violet would come kindly to me, wrap me in her arms, sway me gently, and hum a sweet tune in my ear until I fell to sleep. Every evening we took our China tea. One time Raccoon wore a smoking jacket and a top hat, and Violet gave me a gown she kept for special occasions. It was the color of lemons, and shiny and felt soft between my fingers. But it was itchy and uncomfortable and I didn't like wearing it. And wanted to take it off. Then she took some ringlets from her dressing box and fixed them to my hair, and showed me the looking glass. And I reckon I looked better than I ever did for a long time.

Almost every night, Violet would pretend to go uptown and meet her navy gentleman. Raccoon and me made out like we waited up for her return, playing dice, betting on sips of grog, and smoking horseshit and ragweed in our pipes. And she was all right, until one day she started going crazy-mad dog insane.

"My navy man and me are going abroad," she said one time while I was helping her sew buttons on a boiled shirt that must have cost a small fortune.

"Going to buy us an apartment in San Marco and live in peace is what we're going to do," she said. "Won't be long now."

"What about us?" I said, poking the needle through the buttonholes like she taught me.

"What about you?" she said. "You got your own lives to lead."

"We could come visit," said Raccoon, hanging from the rafters like a monkey and trying to light his pipe upside down.

I didn't say nothing. I waited for Violet to say something about the horseshit odor. But she seemed to have lost all sense of decency.

"Of course, you can come and pay a visit," she said to him while sewing curls up on her George Washington. "Only your friend here would need to apply deportment, and, that is a problem."

I looked up from my sewing. "Are you talking about me?" I said.

She bit on the loose thread hanging from a knot she'd made. It made a little snap when it broke. "Of course I'm talking about you," she said.

I dropped my needle on my lap. "Well, why's that a problem? What's 'deportment'?"

She rolled her eyes like she's been sick of hearing my voice even though I hardly said nothing.

"Something, I'm sorry to say, that you don't have."

"What do you mean I don't have it?" I said, jabbing the needle into the shirt.

"Watch what you're doing," she says, "you're putting holes in my finery." And snatched the shirt off of me and checked it for rips.

"Well, why don't you tell me what 'deportment' is," I said standing up, "and I'll tell you if I got it or not."

"There's no point," she said, folding out the creases. "You either got it or you don't, and you just don't got it."

I looked up at Raccoon. He started choking on his pipe and trying to lift himself back upright to climb down.

"Well, has Raccoon got it?" I said.

"Of course he's got it," she said, opening up the powder box and dusting her wig with it.

"Well, what the hell is it then?" I said.

"I said, watch your language."

"Well, tell me what it is then."

Raccoon was back down and waving his hands at me going, "Shhh."

I took no heed; made sure he wasn't looking, and stepped on Violet's long bare feet with the tip end of my boot.

"How dare you touch me," she said recoiling like a snake, raising her hands, and sending white powder flying all around. In a moment, she was up. After quickly wrapping her Chinese robe up tight around her body, she went fluttering to the other side of the room like a deadly butterfly. When she got where she wanted to be, she turned and pointed her whole arm at me.

I backed away to stop her from cursing me with her bony finger.

"That boy don't apply demands on me," she said to Raccoon, her eyes wild. "Who does that boy think he is making stipulations on me? Don't he know his place? Is he blind or just plain senseless?"

Raccoon was shaking his head and holding out his empty hands.

"He ought to be locked up in jail where all the likes of him belong," she said, wagging her finger at me.

"Likes of me?" I said, shaking my fists. "What are you talking about? Likes of me nothing, likes of you is what it is. Which is why you already are. Locked up that is. You crazy headed what-ever-it is, you are."

She started coming for me with her whacking hand ready for slapping.

Raccoon got in the firing line in front of me and held his hands up to her. "Violet, Violet," he said, "remember how you said violence makes you feel unwell. You get a headache and all sick in the belly. And how you get melancholy after."

"I don't recall saying any of that," she said.

"Well, Violet, you did say it," he said. "You told me plenty of times. Now, what Jonesy said ain't nothing to get fired up about. Just Jonesy don't hang with folks much. And says the wrong thing all the time. Ain't that right?" he said, turning to me, his arms out stretched like bleeding Jesus on the cross.

I didn't particularly feel like getting beat by her so I said yes.

"Now, Violet," he said, "why don't you just rest up a while. I mean you're looking tired. And Jonesy, why don't you and me play some cards?"

"No gambling, mind," she said holding out her finger at him.

"No gambling," he said giving up with his hands in the air.

"You're a good boy," she said to him. "You got a good soul."

Then gave me a look, like I was the Devil.

Raccoon and me sat down on our board, lit our pipes and started playing. I shuffled the pack and dealt. Just my luck, I had a straight run of nothing. Raccoon put down a seven and picked up a two. I picked up the seven and put down a four. He took that and put down another seven. I stopped playing. "We are playing Mexican bandit ain't we?" I said.

"Sure," he said.

"So, you're playing that other seven?"

He said, "Yeah."

I shrugged and took it up. It now appeared I was winning. Unless he was playing for a low run. I put down a nine just in case.

It was then Violet began talking overly loud about her navy. Going on how comely he was. How much deportment he had. And how if any boy so much as looked at him with lusty thoughts she would take a gun and blow his brains out.

We both held our cards to ours chests and looked up at her. Then at each other. "It's alright," Raccoon whispered to me, "just don't say nothing."

"What's that?" she said, spying.

"Nothing," he said.

She mumbled a string of words that made no sense, but sounded like they might be some kind of Catholic curse. She slumped back on her bed. Began playing with a string of trinket beads while Dead Jesus dangled heavy on the end.

Raccoon picked up my nine hearts from the pile, screwed his face up and shook his head. "Take no heed of all that, he said. Then, saying, "Bandit," lays his cards down, showing me his win.

"How the hell you do that?" I said. "You dropped two sevens in a row?"

He smiled and tapped on his dead dog necklace. "I told you it was good luck."

"Cheating, more like," I said.

He chuckled and handed me his bag of smelly weed to fill my pipe with.

Round two, and Raccoon was dealer. I looked at my cards. Put down a two and picked up a king. Which was exactly what I needed for a fast win.

I was one card shy when Violet called out, "Don't you be thinking about my navy. You stay away from him you hear. So much as lay an eye on him and I'll slit your throat. Make no mistake about it."

At first I though she had some fitful waking dream.

But when I looked at her, she was staring straight at me. Giving me snake eyes to boot.

"Yes, I'm talking to you," she said. "Who you think you are?"

I turned my cards faced down on the bed board and stared her out.

"You're one wicked little bitch-boy," she said to me, taking no heed.

I could only look on at her with my mouth wide open like a toad catching flies.

"Jones," said Raccoon, trying to hold me back even though I weren't even thinking of going nowhere. "Just take it easy, will you?"

"I tell it like it is," said Violet from her comfy bed. "Dirty Nancy is what you are. I know all about you, and that boy you gone chasing."

"Are you talking to me?" I said to her. "What'd you tell to her about me?" I said to Raccoon.

"I ain't said nothing," he said, holding up his hands in surrender.

"That poor girl's with child, don't you know it," she said, "and all she wants is some low down gutter hog like you making dirty with her man."

I looked at her with mean eyes. "I ain't no dirty," I said, "I ain't no gutter hog, and I ain't called Nancy."

"You're all of it and more," she said, "dirty little Nancy boy."

I loaded up a boodle of curses to fling back in return, but Raccoon covered my mouth with his hand to stop them firing out.

I wrestled with his arms, telling him to, "Go to hell," then jumped off the board on to the floor. I reached into my back pocket and pulled out my rusty knife to show her I meant business. "I don't know what you heard with your wide open ears," I said pointing the blade at her, "but it ain't no business of yours what I do and who I do what with, which ain't nothing anyhow. A man's business is his own business. Ain't nothing to do with nobody, especially the likes of you. Whatever it is you are."

She reached under her pillow slow, then stood up tall and straight looking manly for once wearing a nasty switchblade in her white hand, with cold blue veins running like rivers up her arm.

I took stock of the blade. Shiny, sharp and as long as my whole hand. With an ivory hilt and a wolf carved into the belly.

"You ought to be careful how you pick your words when you're talking to me," she said, pointing the knife straight at me.

Raccoon shot up and made a wall between us with his arms.

"Jonesy," he said, "why don't you go take a walk, while I talk to Violet, how about that?"

I looked at how she was holding onto the blade. Not a strong grip like I had on mine. With my knuckles turning white and my arm making tremors with effort. Hers looked like it was ready to fall out of her fingers on onto the floor.

"Talk to her?" I said. "Did you say talk to her? Because I don't know whether you noticed or not but she ain't a girl. She ain't got no hole like one, and sitting down to piss like one ain't gonna make her one neither. "

"How dare you," she said, raising the knife high above her head. Her eyes turned wild like a beat horse. She started gutting the air. Stabbing at it like she was cutting up a pig's belly.

I went running out of her killing arms' way. Pushing by Raccoon and nearly cutting him to pieces in the bargain. I took one mad-dog leap through the makeshift window, banging my head on the boards above.

"It's all right," Raccoon said first to Violet, then running over to me to say the same thing. "Why don't you all just put your weapons down? Let's all just be friendly and just talk it all over, shall we?"

I kept my eyes peeled. Raccoon had his palms laid flat for her to lay the knife down on them.

"I'd be careful if I were you," I said, "for she doesn't cut your hands off."

Raccoon flashed his eyes in my direction. "Just, go for a walk or something Jones," he said, "we'll talk later, just go on."

"Talk?" I said, showing him the tip of my rusty blade. "I think you done enough talking, Raccoon."

He turned from me and, holding out his hand to her, said, "Come on Violet. Give me the knife. I'll look after the Wolf for you, then I'll make some nice tea, how's that?"

"Deportment," I said out loud. "Only one body around

here that's got deportment and it's me. Unless deportment means crazy-headed lowdown, then it's both of you, you hear?" And with those final words I headed straight out of the hole in the wall, taking most of the spider web with me.

Chapter 11

I go see Joe

I was walking with angry footsteps down Washington Street: my hands in my pockets and my face getting sore from frowning. Raccoon comes running up from behind. He skidded to stop at my pace.

"She's alright," he said, like I should be relieved. "The spider's fine. Spin a new web in no time."

A whole boodle of curses was fighting to get out of my mouth. I kept it shut tight.

"Look," he said, "I never told Violet nothing about you and Juan."

"Well, how come she was talking like she was the goddam daily chronicle spewing out everybody's business for the whole of the world to hear if you didn't say nothing? Tell me that?"

"I don't know," he said, "I guess maybe she overheard…"

"It's called 'spying'," I said, cutting in. "Folk's swinging in the trees for lesser crimes."

"I wouldn't call it a crime," he said.

"Well, I call it a crime. Of the highest offense." I carried on walking straight, tall, and fast with my hands in my pockets, and my hat pulled low over my eyes.

"Where you headed," he said.

"I ain't decided yet," I said. Then stopped dead in my tracks. "Where's the graveyard from around here?"

"We got to go back up Washington," he said. "Turn first left, go to the end, then up Parliament, then about a hundred feet or so we…"

"Jesus Christ," I said, cutting him off again, "I don't need you to read out the whole goddam map, I just need to know which way to point the compass."

"Do you got a compass?" he said.

"I am my own goddam compass," I said, stabbing my chest with my finger. "My own goddam compass, you hear? I choose my own way. I mean why do you have to talk so much anyhow? I ain't had my ears burned off enough by that goddam crazy headed friend of yours now, have I? Give me precious liberty for Jesus Christ's sake."

"Alright, all right," he said, "you don't have to go all goddam Jessie on me every time I say something you don't like. I can just show you the way, how's that? Is that alright?"

I said yes.

It was up on a hill I hardly remembered climbing that time when I come to see them bury Joe. Some graves had tombstones on them, but most had done as I had, and placed rocks and shells and whatnot in various patterns to mark out the spot. I looked around for mine.

"It's got a union flag on it," I said to him, "a small one. And there was a tree stood straight over it."

A leafy birch was making shadow on the graveyard. One mound looked familiar.

I saw pebbles laid in way I might have done. "It's one of these," I said, looking at the little hills of dirt with rocks circled around. "I thinks it's this one, but, where's my flag? Someone stole my goddam flag."

"Might have been the birds," said Raccoon. "Probably stole it for their nest."

We looked up. The birch was all leafy and green. We searched for signs of red white and blue. Couldn't see nothing at all.

"I see a nest," said Raccoon, pointing up a tree.

We climbed up. Traversed over branches getting stung with their pointing ends along the way.

"Hey, I see it," he said.

I climbed over to where he was. Made a seat on the branch below. There was the nest above my head. I moved up ahead to the next branch. There was my flag, or what was left of it, sitting in a nest. "Thieves!" I said.

"Well," he said, "guess they needed it for bedding down the young."

We both made our way over and looked into the nest of tiny branches and straw. Little ones were living in it, sitting on my union flag. Ugly looking scrawny things with open beaks and long sharp tongues. I was getting ready to snatch it off them when Raccoon put his arm out to stop me.

"If the mother catches out the man scent, she kills them off."

"Why does that not surprise me," I said.

"Look," he said, "at least your flag's found a good home with the living. Want to go back down, and talk to your Joe or something?"

We got down and went over to Joe's grave.

"I'll go wait over here," said Raccoon, nodding to someplace else.

I said all right.

Then it was just Joe and me.

I looked down at the mound of dirt.

Got on my knees and fixed the stones to make a better line. "I should have brought some shells," I called over to Raccoon.

"Want me to find some?" he said.

"If you please," I said to him. I turned back to Joe. "Why didn't you teach me nothing Joe," I said. And felt stupid after saying it.

I looked around to see if Raccoon had been watching. He was busy collecting shells from the some other graves. I looked back down at Joe's dirt home and couldn't think of nothing else to utter.

I felt like a tear might come but it never.

Raccoon comes kneeling by my side with a horde of good-looking shells. We sat quiet, putting them around, making little spirals, and other forms of decoration. When we were done, he said, "You want some more?"

"Yeah, all right," I said. So we did that awhile. We put some sticks around, made it like a fort around the outsides. Constructed a doorway, paths leading to the entrance. Some cannon guarding the corners with stones and broken pieces of shell. When we done we stood up and looked at it.

"Goddam," said Raccoon, "if that ain't that's the best-looking grave I ever saw in my life."

And I smiled.

On the way back he said, "Fancy going fishing?"

I said not particularly.

We found a place by a run-off between the river and the sea, where Raccoon set up a fire. He went and showed off by catching a fish with his bare hands, then gutted it with his knife after killing it dead.

We sat around the fire eating it with our fingers and tasting pure sweet heaven on our tongues.

"You know Jones," he said when we were done, licking our hands, "I got this idea about fishing."

"Go on," I said.

"We start a business. We catch our own fish. Dry it out. And sell it. 100% profit. What do you reckon?"

"What about a fishing license?" I said.

"Don't need a fishing license."

"You do," I said.

"Yeah, but there's ways around that," he said, poking at the fire to keep it going. "Shouldn't have to be a license anyhow. Fish are growing wild. Don't belong to nobody."

"The free state of California would probably disagree with you there," I said while I snapped a few branches to add to the flames.

He shrugged, and set them right. "I suppose, but, good idea huh?"

I shrugged.

"We could be partners if you like," he said.

I gave him a good looking over. His squinting thing had turned to a moving eyebrow thing. He kept a never-ending circle of surprised and angry faces going all the while.

"Dried fish merchants?" I said.

"Yeah," he said, "Fine Dried Fish Merchants of San Francisco."

I pondered on the words. "Say, what's your last name?" I said.

He said, "Ricardo."

I held my hands out like I was showing off a sign, saying, "Jones and Ricardo: Fine Dried Fish Merchants of San Francisco."

"Or, 'Ricardo and Jones, Quality Dried Fish Sellers of San Francisco Bay'. Sounds better I think."

I watched his face twitching like a sick-in-the-head.

"Well, I don't know," I said. "The truth of it is, I like to go my own way."

"I know that," he said, "but, well, look at it this way, it'd be a way of you getting out of all that Dead-Man work."

"Getting out?" I said.

"Yeah, I mean, you don't really like working down there do you?"

And I thought about that. Most of the time I didn't, but sometimes I did depended on who they were, what they wanted, what they looked like, and how much gold worth I was of value to them. I was taking my time thinking on it all when he said, overly sharp:

"Jones, I got to ask you something. Kind of private."

"I'm all ears," I said.

"Well, you don't think I like you like that, do you?"

I looked over at him.

He was looking at a stick.

"Like what?" I said.

"Like Juan," he said so low that I had to ask him three times to say it again so I could hear.

"Do I think you like me like Juan? Well," I said, "the truth of it is, Juan's changed his mind on me so many times that…"

"Because I don't," he said, cutting in, talking to his shoes, and then looking at me without twitching.

I stared back at him the same.

He started playing with his fire stick. Poking at the charcoal and stabbing it to pieces.

"I just don't think of kissing folks, other than girls, " he went on to say. "And I get a real hard thing for Carla. Once I caught her taking a piss and when she lifted up her skirts I saw…"

I covered my ears quick to stop his voice from making pictures move inside my head.

"…So, I suppose I'll want to be marrying her," he says when I return my ears to freedom. "That's what you're meant to do if you want to get between a girl's legs, but I got to be eighteen first to get a license…"

While he carried on talking, a red-hot poker ran up and down my spine every time his mouth moved. Finally my lid blew clean of the pan. "Will you please just shut the hell up about goddam Carla or whatever her name is. My ears are being offended by your stupidity."

For a time we said nothing, only stared into the fire.

He sat there blinking, and twitching his eyebrows. Finally he said, "Why are you saying it's stupid? What, you think she can't like me?"

"I don't care a hoot if she likes you or no," I said, "and stop doing that crazy thing with your eyebrows, it's making my blood boil."

He took up a stick and started poking at the ashes. Huffing and puffing and twitching like a fool.

"Jones, look, I'm sorry," he said, saying it hard, like he wasn't. "I know you're peculiar and all that but the thing is, I'm just a regular fella, and…"

"Goddam—fella—regular what?" I say cutting him off dead at the line. "Jesus Christ, Raccoon. You ain't a regular nothing. And, by the way, my name ain't 'peculiar', it's Jones. Plain ole' regular Jones. And I warn you: you so much as call me low-down cocksucker again, I'll punch you out cold—like I did Juan, fair and square."

"I never called you a low-down cocksucker," he said.

"Yeah, you did so call me that."

"When?"

"That time on the roof before you robbed me blind, that's when."

"Robbed you blind? I goddam rescued your money."

"You rescued my money and stole half it for yourself and then passed me off with a junk coin to boot."

"Jesus Christ, you talk shit," he says, throwing the stick away.

I stood up, grabbed a stick of my own and starts beating a dead crab with it until it broke to pieces.

"Fine," he said, standing up, and dusting himself off with loud noises. He began stomping on the fire with his boot, to put the flames out. Sending sparks and pieces of fire going everywhere. Then walked off without me.

I brought my stick with me and followed him over the rocks and shells and driftwood beach. He was slumping along with hands in his pockets and head down, kicking innocent stones, and stepping over unfortunate branches with long strides.

He glanced over his shoulder once to see me, and when he saw I was tailing, he stopped, and waited for me to catch up.

We carried on together.

I was poking at the slimy red seaweed beneath my feet, and chucking it up in the air with my stick.

Waves were rolling in, leaving foaming dregs in their wake. An upturned crab, empty of all what made it living, went back into the swish-swash sea, then returned, to find a place of eternal peace amongst a dead head log. We shooed the seagulls away and Raccoon lay a driftwood atop its body, to make it so, and we walked on.

The sun was saying its last farewell. Making pretty colors in the clouds. Our eyes met by accident, and we quickly looked away.

We kept a-walking along listening to the music of the tide.

I nudged him with my shoulder.

He shot me a look.

I managed to forge a smile that was bent on refusal.

He looked at me again. "Sorry about Violet getting sore, and the things about you and Juan, and—I don't know what happened there—but, also, I never meant nothing by any names I ever said, even though I swear I don't remember ever saying them."

"I'm sorry too," I said, coughing it out, for I was choking on the words, "for going Jessie all the time even when you ain't thought you done nothing. On purpose, that is."

We shared another look. Then nudged. Started pushing each other into the foam. I threw my stick down and began a game of Gotcha with seaweed. Then I took to wearing it as a crazy wig, until salt water began burning my skin. I made a big deal out of it. And that made him laugh so.

As the sun went down, we headed back home to the Shades. All smiles again, for a time.

Chapter 12
Broken china

When we got back the attic room was in disarray. Violet was going mad dog crazy: wailing, flailing her arms just like I had done when I got the news of Joe dying. Raccoon got her to say what was wrong. She said a big commotion had gone down in the square. A big shootout between the Sydney Ducks, the Suarez brothers, and the brothel girls down Market Street. One of the bystanders was Violet's navy gentleman. It appeared he took a stray bullet in crossfire, and eventually dropped down dead on the spot.

She was beside herself. I even tried comforting her. I tried brushing her hair but she took the comb off me and threw it in the fire, saying it was the Devil's own instrument.

Raccoon made tea. We set the table. We picked the ants out the buns and stuck them in the jar for her save. Only this time, she threw the glass at the door and all the crawling critters ran up and down the walls not knowing where to go next. We handed her a cup of hot tea. She wouldn't take it. Wouldn't look at it. I tried putting it to her mouth to sip. She knocked it away, spilling it all over me, which burned my hand, and made all kinds of wicked curses fall out my mouth. "What are you doing, you crazy headed bitch," I said.

She replied by throwing up the tablecloth in my face and all the china went flying in the air before smashing down on top of me.

It was all going mad-dog, so I had to do something. I decided to try a thing that always worked with Joe. I picked up the mirror and held it to her face. She took one look at her reflection, and smashed her fist into the glass. And when I looked in it, all I saw was broken pieces of myself. Which only made me look even more ugly from then on.

She wrapped her bleeding hand in her handkerchief, and lay on her bed, curled up like a critter, and stayed like that for three days.

As the days went by, her whiskers grew. She started to smell bad. She refused to eat. She wouldn't drink. We were too scared to try and feed her.

Raccoon went and got Alley to come up and see what she could do.

She unlocked the door and tiptoed over to Violet. She took one look and said, "Oh, my Lord, I don't believe my eyes."

"What do we do?" I said.

"Shh! Be quiet," she said. "For god's sake, whatever you do, don't wake him up."

"Why the hell not?"

"Just, shh!" She said. "I got to run and tell the Boss. Little Brother's come a rising from the grave."

The wind was blowing, and whistling through the cracks in the wood. The dirty lace drape, hanging to the side, made the spider web shake. Raccoon and me sat huddled together on the bedboard, holding onto each other in the shadow. Watching the stranger on the comfy bed. Wondering what he'd done with Raccoon's precious Violet.

In through the hatch they came. Two Suarez brothers. First, a tall lanky fella called Gonz, followed by the almighty Saul. Wearing a handsome black suit, made to fit his body tight. A fine, waxed moustache covered his lip. His hair slicked back, and shining like crow's feathers. He hitched his black leather hands to his hips and walked up to the stranger. Clacking the floor boards with his boots spurs, as he did so. Saul studied him: the man who once was Violet, snoring and smelling bad, then spun around on his heels to face Gonz.

Gonz stood there with one hand in his pocket, and the other on the wall, killing ants with his thumb.

Saul spun back around, smoothed his moustache with his black-gloved hand and looked down at him lying on the comfy bed. Stringy hair sticking to his face. Days old beard: patchy and shabby as a drunkard's.

Saul put his hand on him and shook his shoulder fast.

Violet's other self grunted.

Saul shook him more.

The man turned, and not unlike a critter woke up from its winter slumber, held his hands up to his blinking eyes.

"What is it?" he said to Saul. "They on our tail already?"

"What?" said Saul. "No little brother, nobody's on our tail. You been gone. And now you're back. And ain't I happy to see you. Brother you been missed."

He lifted his head up high. Gave Saul a good looking over then smiled. Said his name.

Together they clasped hands. Saul, turned to Gonz, and Gonz smiled. He joined his brother in pulling Violet up onto his feet. When he was steady, they all put their arms around one another and hugged: with Saul kissing Violet's cheek like he was Jesus.

Little Brother, as Saul called him, began to come to his senses. He looked around to the unlocked door and said, "Where's the Jinx?"

"He had business to attend," said Saul, putting out his black-gloved hands in front of him, as to stop a horse getting ready to bolt.

"What kind of business?"

"The 'laying to rest' kind."

"A 'matter of retribution'?"

"I prefer to call it 'a matter of divine providence'."

"Divine providence?" he said. "Is that what you call it these days?"

Saul smiled and began twitching his eyes. I tore mine away, and swallowed shame on his behalf.

"My Colt?" said Little Brother, "the old man still got it?"

Gonz and Saul shared another look. Saul turned back to him, standing tall and still. Saul rubbed his chin and smoothed his moustache. "Well, uh, no, Little Brother. That ain't entirely possible no more, now you know that."

"Why not?" he returned. "Tell that Devil he owes me words. Never mind," he said, turning attention back on himself and doing up his shirt, "I'll tell him myself afore long. I don't appreciate being left to die. And I ain't the kind that forgets a thing." He stole a wide-eyed look at Saul and his leather gloved hands.

"All right," said Saul, putting a hand on Little Brother's shoulder. "We can all talk about that later." He turned to Gonz and said, "Ain't that right, Gonzy?"

Gonz only stood there, entertaining as a plank of wood.

"Oh, looky here," said Saul, feeling the inside of his smooth black jacket for something. "I got your Colt right on me." And he passed Little Brother a fine looking pistol.

Little Brother checked it over and aimed it at the wall above Raccoon's and my heads.

We moved further back into the shadow to be unseen.

He stuffed the gun in his waistband, saying, "Where's my knife?"

"Here," said Saul getting ready to pass it to hm. Only he dropped it on the floor. It clink, clink, clinked and spun around like a silver eagle, over to our bed board. I could see Raccoon was going to make a grab for it. I pushed him back and got to it first.

It was Violet's blade. An expensive looking thing. Ivory hilt with a wolf carved into it. I rubbed my fingers across it. Dug my nails into the nooks and crannies that made the wild dog howl. Then I felt a cold wind.

I looked up.

A tall man stood in front of me with skin pale as a corpse, and strange blue eyes, angry as a mad dog.

A gust blew the curtain off its hitch. The noon sun broke through the open hole. I blinked, and for just a moment, I thought I saw true Violet. A moment more and that white-faced villain had returned. And there I was, holding onto his precious knife like a thief.

He grabbed my wrist and clawed at my fingers, peeling them away, one by one from the blade. He bared his teeth at me, as he tore it back for himself. Once he got it, he let go of me.

I fell to the ground. I got up and ran back to Raccoon, holding on to all that was left of us now that Violet was surely gone.

Alley climbed up into the room.

Saul was looking at us.

"They're no trouble," Alley Mac said.

"Is that so," he said to her, unconvinced. His eyes were on me. I figured it was on account of him remembering me from the fight with Juan I won but never got rewarded for. But from the unfriendly look on his face, I could see that he did not. Or if he did, he didn't care a hoot about it no more. Or maybe he'd switched sides, and thought I was the enemy all along.

He asked Alley, "Where'd that one come from?" nodding to me.

I pulled my hat down over my face so he would not see me at all.

"Oh Boss, don't worry about him," she said. "He's no trouble. He's been helping the other one keep a look out the whole time."

"Is that so," said Saul.

"It is, Boss," said Alley, playing with her neck scarf. "I would never have let him up here if I thought he'd mean trouble. Nossir, not a chance."

Saul stood with his leather hands hanging on his hips, eyeing me up with one eyebrow hitched to the ceiling and the other hanging low on his brow.

"I'll see the pair look after the place, just in case the other comes back again and…"

Saul put his hand up to stop her from talking. "Let's not tempt the fates, shall we? I got enough curses hanging over my head as it is."

Little Brother went out the door with Gonz sparing not even a glance at Raccoon and me.

I looked at Raccoon. His eyes were wide, and wondering.

I turned to Saul. He'd had been watching me the whole time. When I caught him at it, he considered me with a sniff. Give Raccoon the quick once over, then goes back to me, only this time his face turned soft, with long lashes low and a smile shining through his eyes.

My heart went hopping over hills and ducking into rabbit holes.

Finally he tore his eyes away from mine. And with a snap of his tongue, like he was giddying up a horse, disappeared out the open door, and out of my sights.

For a time.

Chapter 13
Cherry pie

For weeks the mere sight of Violet-come-Little Brother made me shiver in my boots. Every time I heard him clanking his shiny spurs on the floorboards, I hid well out of his sight.

All the Shades were talking of the change. The story was, it seemed Saul had come and set Violet free, on condition that she start behaving like a man and not a female as she was wont to. Now, Violet only dressed in manly attire and went by his old name of Johnson, or Johnsie, or Little Brother as the Boss called him.

Raccoon and me took to spying on him on a regular basis. He was still pretty but wore a mean look with frowning eyes and a kind of hunch from being so tall, and having to bend under doorways all the while. He wore his hair tied up long as he had done when he was she, but now dressed in the same get up as Saul: a red silky waist coat with Chinese dragons beneath a tight black suit that fits a body fine. On top, a Spanish hat rode slanty on his head; black leather gloves peeled on his hands like a snake.

Together, smelling of leather and Chinese silk, they looked a fine handsome pair of brothers.

I tried doing the same. Tied my hair back like a horse's tail. Took to keeping my shirt too small for my body. Traded favors for a black waistcoat that I took to pieces then sewed up to fit my body tight like so. Come to wearing my preacher hat to one side, only mine was too slouchy and had a habit of falling off my head if I didn't keep on straight, and pulled down low over my eyes.

Saul's property was next door down from the Shades. Painted new with white wash and falling down less so. One time Raccoon and me were hiding outside the window peeking in. We could see the two of them together in a room with a large cabinet for keeping guns. Little Brother was having words with Saul.

"Where's the Jinx?" he said to him.

"Now will you just calm yourself, brother?" said Saul. "I told you before he ain't coming along. He has other business to attend."

There was snapping and clicking.

I felt the air around me go cold; I looked to the sky to see dark clouds were gathering together and making up a storm. My eyes caught Saul through the windowpane. His hair was cut like a knife-edge at the back. Only for a line of black that went to end of his neck. His ears were fine: set close and neat to his head. His eyes showed his youthful years, for I heard tell he was all but nineteen. Only found out later he was six years further on.

I watched him so. He was checking out a musket.

Little Brother had a gun also: the pretty Colt with the ivory handle, to match the knife. With one eye closed, he lifted it up, and aimed it at the window. With a steady straight hand he moved it, like he down before: in line where Raccoon and me were hiding out, only this time behind the sill.

I saw Raccoon was getting ready to say something to him. Like he was gone Violet again, but he weren't like hell. I put my hand across Raccoon's mouth and ducked him down low with me.

Then I heard Little Brother make a sound with his tongue. The kind you do when you're pretending to fire off a load.

With my hand still pressed against Raccoon's mouth, I flinched thinking it was for real. A moment later, I dared release his tongue so that's I could get a peek again. I lifted my head and saw Saul, with his black body looking fine.

Little Brother stuffed his Colt into his belt. "I see you're wearing my knife again, Brother," he said to Saul.

Saul stopped fussing with his musket. He lay it down against the gun cabinet. Started patting his pockets. He felt the inside of his jacket, which looked genuine tailor made. He took out something that looked like a switch. "Now, how did that get in there?" he said, holding it up like it was a stick of blowup.

"I guess you must have found it," Little Brother said, "like the last time. And the time before that."

Saul rounded on him quick. "Now hold on there brother," he said, pointing a finger at him, "I don't like your tone. I don't know what you been putting in your port, but I do not appreciate the way you are branding me with your fanciful crimes as of late. Now, if you don't find yourself a new occupation, you and me are going to have trouble, you hear? Now, this knife business is easily explained. We must have switched jackets again, that's all. Here, now you take it. And keep better hold of it this time."

I felt a cold shadow come over me. It made my skin chill and turn to gooseflesh. I looked up.

The tall, dark clad figure of him, who used to be Violet, stood by the open window in front of me. He bent his knees down to my line of sight and stared through the clear glass pane. And I saw him: skin, pale as a corpse. Hair, tied tight behind his head. His face had seen the sharp edge of a barber's blade only lately I could see.

Our eyes met. I caught sight of myself in his, only my hair had turned greasy, and my face was boney thin.

Thunder banged and shook the temples at the side of my head. A flash of lightning followed. It was somebody outside firing off a gun back of me.

Bullet fire rattled the window pain. I heard hollering. I looked all around and could only see the fleeting glimpse of bodies running: their feet stomping as they rode. I felt Raccoon grab me to go with him beneath the building, through a hole, underground where the rats live. I turned behind and saw more shadows a-coming back of me: running past waving pistols in their hands.

"Come on you bunch of cocksuckers," a gunner said, running down the street. "Goddam whores are going to get it this time," said another.

I swallowed down a holler and clung on tight to the window ledge.

"Come on Johnsie," I heard Saul say above me, which I took to be "Jonesy." I looked up to the light of where he was. But I soon saw he weren't talking to me, he was talking to Little Brother.

"C'mon," he said smiling at him, and hugging his neck, and kissing his cheek, "we're going to miss the whole goddam everything."

I stole a look at Little Brother. He was loading himself up with bullets and arms. He took time to lock up the cabinet and turned fast to follow Saul, both of them yahooing and banging out their home front door.

"C'mon," said Raccoon, dragging me down with him to the bottom of the house. "We need to get out of here quick. There's a war coming."

I followed him, crawling in the stinking dirt like a stray critter fleeing the rifle. I murdered countless worms and other crawly things that made my hands filthy. When we got to the other side of freedom, there was a rain barrel full of nothing but dusty moths and dead birds.

We were thirsty. Raccoon held on to the white wolf paw hanging from his neck and prayed with it, to the dark stormy clouds for rain. No sooner had he done begging with the Devil than the whole sky opened up and showered upon us. The noise made my ears deaf to all but the voice of heavy rain. I closed my eyes, lifted my chin, and opened my mouth to the sky. Cool water fell on my parched tongue. I swallowed sweet drops of heaven. When my thirst was quenched I turned to Raccoon. He face was raised to the sky and he was smiling high. His belly was jiggling and he was laughing, getting drowned by heaven's waterfall.

I pinched his belly when he was unawares. He flinched and hollered, then laughed when I did it again, covering himself up with his arms to stop me doing it, while daring me to do again,.

I chased him down the street, but he was too fast for me. He slowed down on purpose and I got him good outside the bakery store. Pinching his belly until he could hardly breathe with laughter. He tried doing the same to me but I squealed like a cut pig and we both agreed to stop as we was getting unwanted attention, and I was in no mind for making money on Dead Eye dogs today. In the end, Raccoon begged a cherry pie, too set with flies, from the baker. He rid the thing of all contagion, picking out the slimy wing critters and cleaning his finger on his shirt. Then when we sat under the boardwalk, and like a pair of ghosts, seeming free of nosy people, set down to feasting on our prize cherry pie.

Chapter 14
What's mine is mine

Every day the Suarez brothers saddled up: a gang of black crows, flying off together. Horses thundering. Guns slinging. Seeking retribution on the world for robbing a pretty piece of Mexico, and calling it California.

Meanwhile our world turned to gloom. We tried humming familiar tunes to cheer us up, but argued over how the song went.

We took to dancing, and it soon turned to fighting.

I said, "Watch your goddam feet. We ain't at a barn dance. Where's your deportment?"

"*My* deportment?" said Raccoon.

"Yeah, deportment. It means being orderly. As in, try being orderly with your feet and stop stomping over mine like a cow at the county fair."

We argued over how to make tea.

"Jones, that ain't how you do it."

"It is, exactly how you do it."

"No, it ain't."

"It is."

"Jones, it ain't."

"Oh well, fine then. Do what you want. It ain't real tea

from China anyhow. Only them crazy mountain mushrooms we been drinking the whole time. No wonder I've been seeing flying mice and Star Spangled Banners coming out the walls every night since I got here."

We both had our envy eyes on Violet's comfy bed, and soon all ideas of sharing it went completely off the table.

"Jones, I'm telling you to get off. I was her own first afore you come along. Now get your thieving hands off my belongings. You Confed traitor."

"Confed traitor?" I said, pulling on his fingers to get them off my neck. "What are you, blind? Besides, I ain't never been south of the Wichita. And if I recall, I didn't just *come along*. You asked me to live up here. And you ain't *her own*. I don't know what they been teaching you back there on your reservation but you ain't no *own* of Violet's, that's for damn sure. Now get your redskin hands off of me. I ain't moving from this bed one inch." I freed myself up and hitched my hands to the bedposts using my feet as a kicking weapon against Raccoon's chest.

"It ain't a reservation dumbass, it's a Rancheria. And I ain't a redskin, I'm Muwekma. The truth of it is, I only asked you up here because I took pity on you. Wouldn't have bothered if I'd reckoned you were gonna turn traitor on me and steal my claim first chance you got. Now get off my goddam bed before I kill you." He went around the other side and held my head prisoner again with his arm.

"Claim? What claim?" I said, trying to break his fingers with my own. "Oh, I see how the land lies. Violet's got a stash of gold some place around here and you want it all to yourself. Now get your greedy paws off my neck before you break it."

"Get off my bed or I will."

"Never!" I said. Then I broke free of him.

He went and found a piece of wood from the stove. Held it up like a sword.

I stood up on the bed. I reached for the empty water bucket outside the window. When I got it I put it on my head. And wore it like a helmet. "I know your plan, you lying Devil," I said to him. "Gonna leave me rolling in the shit with gutter-hogs while you go living the high life adventuring around the world with Violet's treasure."

"Jones, take the bucket off your head," he said. "You look like a dumbass."

"Fine then, dumbass me it is. Like I ain't had my hide tanned enough since I got here."

Raccoon threw the stick down. He sat on the end of the bed and sighed. I took the bucket off my head, and sat down next to him. For a time we said nothing.

Then I pointed to my neck and said, "Thanks to you, I'm gonna have bruises under my chin, for at least a week. Now how's that for business?"

He said there weren't nothing there to see, and was sorry if there was. He took the bucket out my hands and hung it on the hook outside. "Look," he said. "Violet ain't got nothing. No treasure, no nothing. And I don't know what, but something broke her down. Something changed her, and it looks like, for good."

I said, "Raccoon, when are you gonna stop playing blind mice? The truth of it is, she ain't got broken down. Violet's just a fella, gone crazy headed awhile, thinking he ain't. Now he's come to his senses and gone back to being himself again. Seen the same thing happen afore. Only being liquored up's usually to blame. Joe got crazy-headed all the time. But Angel Gabriel always comes. Talks him out of being melancholy. Though where was he on that day he drowned, I really don't know. Maybe he comes to take him with him. Back to heaven. Unless that devil dragged him down to hell. Oh Lord. Oh, Lord! At least Violet's still alive. At least they didn't comes to get her."

"Well, as far as I'm concerned Jones, she's gone. Just like my ma. And now I got nothing. Nothing at all. I ain't even got a grave to mourn by. Only this bed."

So I let him have it. At least I had the whole board in the corner to myself now. It was too drafty by the window anyway.

Chapter 15
The death of Violet

One day Saul and his two brothers, Gonz and the Jinx, rode in, wearing heavy frowns and smelling of blood. The door that led to their part of the building slammed. Voices hollered, furniture screeched across the floor, and the walls shook with things or bodies getting thrown at them.

The door opened, and a pretty girl called Reddie Mae comes rushing out, limping, holding her mouth and trying not to smile. She had hair as red as fire and wore a rust colored dress that shimmered like a new copper coin. One of her eyes was strange. Wally-eyed, they called it. One of her legs was shorter than the other to boot.

"What's going on darling," said Alley Mac to her, holding onto to the girl's tiny waist like a doll.

Reddie Mae made a gesture to be quiet, and Alley led her, and everybody who'd been listening at the door, into the Billy stove room.

It was stinking of old liquor and horseshit. Alley helped Reddie Mae onto the table where she sat, patting out her gown and all the petticoats underneath. Boys huddled around her like she was a fired up Billy on a cold night.

I was somewhere in the middle, but as more kids pushed in

closer to get to her, I found myself beside her. On the other side was Alley, and Juan, who taken the liberty of holding her hand.

"Oh, you boys ain't never gonna believe what happened," she said.

"Tell us Reddie Mae. Tell us," said Juan. Smiling, and taking further liberties with her fingertips.

"Little Brother's gone mad dog crazy," she said. "He's robbed the brothers blind and run off with all their treasure. They chased him from here to Sacramento."

"Lord Jesus," said Alley, "so what happened?"

"Jinxy caught up with him," she said, looking at Alley and me at the same time, even thought I was over there, "and he done the business on him."

"What kind of business?" Said Alley. "What are you saying? Is he dead?"

"No, no, he ain't dead. But I reckon he wishes he were. Brother Jinx gone and done something evil."

"What he do, what he do?" everyone called out, shuffling close, and nearly squeezing me to death.

"Took all his beauty from him as punishment," she said. "Scarred his face up for life. Now he's so ugly you can hardly look at him without wanting to run."

Everyone gasped and whistled. I looked about for Raccoon. I saw him standing in amongst the bodies, his mouth hanging open like a broken trap. I called to him. He came up close, and I pulled him in, by my side.

"Saul's went mad dog crazy for cutting his pretty face up and, oh, he gives Jinxy a real beating in revenge. The Jinx gets even more mad. Vows anyone mentions that white wolf's name again, he's gonna come in the night and cut that kid's tongue out, so he can't never speak the words again."

Hands and arms everywhere went up against lips.

Raccoon did nothing. Only stared at Reddie Mae without twitching.

"It ain't true about the cutting," I whispered to him, "I mean how that girl know what happened. They wouldn't tell her nothing.

She can't even see straight. And what's wrong with her leg?"

Raccoon looked at me. "Yeah," he said, "how would she know? I heard her talk all kinds of shit before. I don't believe nothing she says."

"Damn right," I said, crossing my fingers behind my back, and drawing the shape of a horseshoe in the dirty floor with my toe.

When she'd done telling, and giggling at the little whispers Juan was putting to her ear, a kid called out, "Tell us about Joaquin's head, Reddie Mae."

"No," said another boy, "Saul's hands."

"Yeah, Saul's hands," everyone agreed.

"Tell them both Reddie Mae," said Alley, winking at her. Reddie Mae relaxed her dainty hand from Juan so she could keep hold of it herself. I tried giving him snake eyes, but his were glued fast to her curly red head. I looked around for Belly Girl and the Blue-eyed devil: her face was grey as a tombstone. He was skulking at the back with his arms strapped to his chest like a belt.

"Yeah, tell them both," everyone said. And all got ready for listening.

"The Story of Saul's hands," she said, shimmering shiny copper, and making circles with her hands.

"You all know it," she said, he eyes black and wide. "He used to be Saul's best friend ever since they were kiddies. But them two boys became more than best friends. More than brothers. One day Saul's daddy caught him red handed doing the dirty on the other."

"Did I hear you say," said Alley, sounding as they do in the theatre, "that Saul did the dirty on him?"

"Uh huh," she said to us all, "and him got clean away, but Saul was in for it. As a punishment, his daddy made him put his hands out in from of him like this, then got a bucket of hot coals from the Billy stove like that, and filled his hands with them. And made him hold them until the clock rang exactly nine times. And that's why he never takes his gloves off."

Everybody including myself gasped and put their hands someplace safe, like in their pockets.

"Is that why Saul wears the black gloves all the time?" said Ally, talking to her, but looking at us.

"Uh huh," she said. "Then, Saul's daddy disappeared. Next time anybody saw him: he had just his head, and his two bare hands left."

Everyone took a long breath again. Except for Raccoon, who said, "Bull shit," in my ear.

"Some say it was the devil that done it," she said, answering a boy's question. "Some say it was one of them hooligans from the South side. Others say it was that white wolf himself, to pay old Joaquim back for destroying Saul's comely hands and killing off his mama."

"Killing his mama?" said Juan, holding onto his heart.

"Hell Reddie-Mae," said Alley Mac, "you never told that one before."

"No," she said, "I was saving it for the right time. Saul's Papa cut her up with a carving knife for saying Saul was most handsome of all men. And any woman who cast eyes on him would be blinded forever with passions coursing through her veins. And babies would come popping out like chicken eggs on a sunny morning in May."

"Oh, I can't listen to any more of this shit," said Raccoon, turning away. But it was too crowded. So all he could do was stay close by my side.

"I remember when you could pay two bits to go see old Joaquim's head," said Alley Mac.

"Oh and his hands," said Reddie Mae, "they were all on show at King's Curiosities on Kerney Street for a whole week before Sheriff made the brothers move him on down."

"Move him down where?" said Juan.

Reddie Mae said nothing, just looked at him with lashy eyes, then turned her head slow toward the door.

"In Saul's private bed chamber," she said, pointing in the direction of their house, "is a secret cupboard. A dark and terrible place," she said. "And that's where he keeps him. What's left of him, that is. And if you do wrong. Any of you, take my heed: Saul will put you in there, to do time."

"Are you trying to say," I said out loud to myself, "that the Boss puts you in the cupboard with his own pa's head?"

"And his hands," she said, hearing me.

"Is that so," said Raccoon, looking fishy.

"Well, I can't say I know it to be true for sure," she said sounding sweet and smiling. "I ain't never been in there, see? And I ain't never gonna be in their neither. But them that do: they never says a word about it when they come out. Only they're scared to death of going in. They say his headless ghost walks the streets of Sydney Town every full moon."

Silence stole through the air. Everyone's mouths were sewn up tight.

I swallowed courage and made myself speak. "What about his hands?" I said.

"What about them?" said Reddie Mae.

"Look," said Juan to me, getting edgy, "he ain't got none. When he comes to get you, he ain't got a head, and him ain't got no hands neither. Just his body and his legs come running after you. Get it?"

"Oh heaven help me," a kid said, holding onto his cheeks like a coward and looking at me.

"Is what you'd be praying," said his friend back of him to me, "once you done pissing yourself." It was redhead Freckles.

Everyone laughed at my falsely accused expense.

I turned to Raccoon, with my cheeks on fire. He was too busy squinting his eyebrows and thinking on Reddie Mae's words.

"Oh be kind, be kind to that boy," said Reddie Mae, talking of me, and scorning them with her brow. "Or I won't tell you all the rest of the story."

They apologized to her fast. She patted on her shiny copper dress, and beckoned me to come sit by her. I felt the hot knife of a boot toe to the back of my heel. Words of me getting my head dunked down the shithole for punishment as soon as the show was over burned my ears from behind. I clung onto Raccoon's arm for balance, while hopping on one foot and shaking my head, saying, "No thank you," to Reddie Mae, until it nearly fell off.

"After their pappy went," continued she, "the brothers were left to fend for themselves. And Saul brought that devil into the fold. And made him his brother. But now he's gone and turned mad-dog crazy. Got in with a real baddie. Bad as a rotten egg he is. Cockroach they call him. Robbing brother Saul of his every treasure. Now brother Jinx says he's a dead man walking."

"What?" said Raccoon, "what do you mean by a dead man walking?"

"Oh kiddie," she said looking pained, "he's as good as gone. I heard the Jinx say he can't wait to make him dance. He bought a rope, just for doing the job. And you know brother Jinx. He always gets his chores done. Ain't that a fact."

As soon as we left and headed back up to the attic Raccoon said, "We got to do something to get Violet back afore the brothers get her first."

"Raccoon," I said, "I seen this kind of thing before. It's the Devil's work. I don't think nothing can be done."

"Well, we got to try at least," he said, holding on to his forehead.

I went over to the comfy bed where he was sitting, sobbing. He moved over meaning I was allowed to sit there too, but only this once.

"Raccoon," I said, laying my arm on his shoulder. "I think it's time we put Violet to rest. Even if she did come back, if what Reddie Mae said is true about her being all cut up…"

"But it ain't true," he said, wiping his tears.

"But if it is," I said, "Violet wouldn't want to come back. I sure as hell wouldn't."

"Yeah," he said, drying his eyes with his sleeve, "well you ain't her."

Raccoon dug through some of her belongings and we took

the least valuable things he could find: a strip of cloth from an old gown, hair from one of her brushes, soap from her shaving things, and some China tea that wasn't. Together we took them and a kettle to a little spot by the bay, where no one was around to bother us.

Raccoon caught a fish, got it ready for cooking, and lit a fire. Meanwhile, I minded our little treasure.

While we waited for the fish to bake, we dug a little grave for Violet's things and buried them. We figured we ought to say a prayer but couldn't think of any other than the one she used to say, thanking God for our feast. We agreed it was how she would have wanted it. Besides, it meant we didn't need saying it again for when it come to eating our meal. And Violet once told us that a wise man is one who shows an economy with words, but still gets a thing done.

After the burial, we made tea without fighting, and had it with our fish. Then we laid back, humming our likeable tune, and watched the sun fall down behind the hills across the bay: making pretty fireworks in the sky.

Chapter 16
Difference between whores and Dead Man boys

I was leaving for work one day. Before I walked out the door Alley stopped me.

"Boss says for you to stay away from navies resembling this fella," she said.

She showed me a page in a penny weekly, of a comely looking man with short dark locks, a clean-shaven face, and lips like a cupid.

"Me? Why? Who is he?" I said.

"Why, he's the most famous poet that ever lived. Goes by the name of Byron."

"And he's Union Navy?"

"Union Navy? No, I'm talking about a navy that looks just like him. The real deal drowned in the bay 30 years ago. Boss says this one's a lone wolf. The worst kind."

I took a hold of the weekly. She went on explaining and I carried on looking. And mine eyes had never seen such a thing of "beauty", as the word was made to call.

"So, if you see a face that looks like this one, you come and tell me right away, all right?"

I said, "What?"

She snatched the weekly out my hands and chased a couple of boys off a bench by the Billy stove. I stood there as she poured us both a measure of grog, and lit a match on her boot to get her cigar going again. "Jones, sit down," she said.

So I did.

"Jones," she said downing a shot. "Do you know the difference between a brothel girl and a Dead Man boy?"

"I sure do," I said supping my cup. For brothel girls got made whole dollars for doing nothing and I got next to nothing for frigging my arm off and spitting spunk all day long. And ain't none of them looked like dear departed Mister Byron neither. Not even almost.

"Forget about him for the minute," she said, moving the weekly out of my reach. "Look, Jones. Have you been asked to offer any, shall we say, special kinds of services. The lying on your belly kind."

"What do you mean?"

"Anybody try buying your hole?" she said.

My face turned red as hot crab out the pan.

"It's just I thought we ought to have a talk about that, just in case something of the kind comes up. Which it sure as Hell will. If it ain't already."

I could only think of one thing. And one thing only: Juan and his blue-eyed devil going wild horses in the barn. I turned desert cactus and horny toad all at the same time, which only made me start going Jessie on my own self. Stabbing my thigh with my thumbnail until I bleed.

"It ain't already happened, has it?" she said.

I looked up fast, shook my head and said, "No, no."

"Good, good," she said, surveying me with her eyes.

"So, say you lost your senses, and risked your life getting strung up on the ceiling by one of Saul's Brothers, and you decide to try your luck and some high stakes. Dead Eye offers you gold to belly-down and you agree to the terms. Now, if Dead Eye turns out to be a son-of-a-bitch mad-dog and he starts beating on you, what you going to do?"

"Gut him," I said.

"And, where you been hiding the blade the whole time?"

"In my pocket," I said.

"What if you ain't wearing any pockets?"

"Why wouldn't I be wearing any pockets?"

"Because chances are, you ain't going to be wearing nothing at all."

"Oh," I said, digging at a nail in the table, with my finger.

"The thing is," she said, tapping her ashes on the floor, "that brothel girl lying on her back with a thigh over here and another over there, even if she's in the raw, she can start kicking that bastard on the back, pull that knife out from her hair, stab him in the belly. All the while she's punching him in the head. She can bite that son of a bitch's ear off while cutting off his prick at the same time. So, I ask you again Jones, what are you going to do?"

"Bite him," I said. "When my hands are by my head like this." I got on all fours like a critter, and put my hands by where my shoulders would be.

"Bite him?" she said. "Oh you'd be biting all right. Biting the board when you're getting laid into with punches to your back, after some old fat bastard's just finished fucking your ass for the third time in a row, hollering down your ear hole like this: 'You ain't going nowhere until I get my goddam money's worth you cheating little cunt!' Get it?"

I put my hand over my ears to stop her from yelling so loud. I sat up straight and moved over two spaces to get away from her.

Alley lifted the top hat off her head, ran her fingers through her hair, and put it back on again. Poured herself a measure and downed it in one. "So," she says, wiping her mouth, "that's why boss told me to tell you this warning: 'no getting fucked by nobody, and stay away from sailor-boy,' all right?"

I nodded, and felt my heart go banging against my ribs. "He said, 'me'?" I said. "I mean, he said 'me' in particular? Not nobody else, but me?"

She gave me a hard look. "It's a warning come from on high, Jones. And I believe it was meant for you. In particular."

"I heard you," I said, nodding. My heart going wild horses, crazy rabbits. The rest of Noah's ark thundering around my body making my whole self move. "Tell Boss, I ain't going to do nothing like that with nobody," I said, reaching over the table and grabbing hold of her hand. "Only what he says, is what I'll do," I said, praying. "Tell him that's the word from me, will you? Tell him it's God's honest truth," and I made the sign of the cross like they all done, and told her to tell him I done that too.

She gave me a long look then patted me on the shoulder and said, "I will do," then got up to leave.

Running after her, I held onto her sleeve saying, "Tell him I never thought of such a thing with nobody else. Tell him, the truth of it is I never saw such a thing to know how to think it and hope I never will neither unless I hear from himself otherwise. And I ain't going no place tell him, or doing nothing, tell him; I'm staying right here. Don't forget to tell him all that, will you? Will you please?"

And after that, and the long days that followed, of lying on my board waiting for Saul's almighty call; staring at the rafters, stinking of bear grease, my eyes stinging, my teeth grinding, my body bursting to spew. Counting nights watching mosquitos whizzing and whirling and killing themselves in the lamp light above my sweating head. By and by, after that, as the time passed,

Slowly,

Slowly,

I never heard another goddam thing.

Part 2
Months go by

Chapter 17
Sweet Virginia

I saw by his get up he was navy. He was young, which wasn't strange, but good-looking which was. He waited for a couple of wagons to pass, then crossed Washington Street, not looking at nothing, or no one else, but me.

"How much the dirty cost around here, sweetheart?" he said to me, smiling and jingling coin in his pocket.

I opened my mouth but nothing would come out. A gust of wind comes by, spewing sea and sand and dirt everywhere. My hair had been getting blown crazy, so I'd stuffed it under my hat to stop my eyes from getting whipped sore. When that gust blew, it nearly stole my hat off my head, and gave it to the Bay for nothing. Navy-boy was quick to rescue it. He stood there, turning it in his hands, while looking at my hair, blowing crazy in the wind.

"Oh, now I do like that," he said. "I do indeed. I mean, you're like a regular girly-girl ain't you?"

Then I remembered what Alley Mac said, about good-looking navies being overly eager for business. How Boss said they were not to be trusted. How they were all a no-good lying bunch of cocksuckers only out for what they can steal. And the first sign of a thieving liar is shifty eyes. But when I looked into navy's eyes, they were fixed as the stars in the heavens. So I figured Boss must have been talking about some other navy. Not this one, with his fine smile and jingle-jingle pockets. Finally my mouth started working.

"Well sir," I said. "It's two bits for 10 minutes, that's the going rate around these parts."

"Ten minutes of what exactly?"

"Well, that'd be for some dirty rubbing."

"Dirty rubbing," he said. "My, my. What a little sweet talker you are. Now what about a cock suck, darling? How much for that?"

"Same. And if you go up Jefferson way it'll cost you more and they only do 5 minutes, most of them that is. Although they'll tell you it's 10."

"Well I ain't seen nothing on Jefferson worth a penny. And then I come here and, well, look at you."

I bent my face down, to hide smiling so loud.

Navy turned from the wind and started making a small cigar from some fine smelling tobacco he'd pulled out from his coat pocket. "Well now I do like the sound of the words dirty rubbing," he said, thinking. "But, what I really want to know is, are you any good?"

"Well sir," I said, staring in his comely blue eyes. "You may have noticed how white my teeth are. I am the only body around town who doesn't have black teeth already."

"Well, that ain't even answering my question at all."

"It's just I do get complimented on my teeth, also."

"Well ain't that nice."

"As well as my hair."

"Uh huh."

"And the answer to your question is, hell sir, yes I am."

"Well," he said. "I'll bet you this cigar, you ain't half as good as me."

And I did not know what to say to that.

We hooked up down Dead Man's alley. Along the way, navy told me to call him "Mister Hakes". Told me how the God almighty Union had gone and seized all the tobacco from the wicked slave fields of Virginia. Told me he knew where it was hid and was going to take some for his self. To square things up with some bastard Spaniard who had it coming. Said he was going to make a fortune selling it. Buy himself some lowland up Sacramento. Start rearing horses for selling.

At one point, he stopped, and lit his fine smelling cigar against the wind. When it was all fired up and ready to smoke, he told me to open my mouth and taste some. Which I did. And I reckoned that puff of sweet smelling Virginia was probably worth a quarter ounce of gold dust. In fact, with the price of pure tobacco these days, the whole cigar might be worth a gold nugget. And that made me think of a more fitting name for Mr. Hakes. I decided to call him "Sweet Virginia". But only ever to myself.

I took him to the Dead Man and he gave me a kiss.

"Know why they call this the Dead Man?" he said.

"Well," I said, undoing his waistband, "they probably found a dead body down here one time or another. That kind of thing does happened a lot around these parts.""No, I reckon that ain't it," he said, stopping my hand.

I was about to ask him, "What?" when he put his hand down my waistband, and got hold of my thing. Began tugging me. And there was no hurting at all. Soon everything down there went crazy. My thing was beating fast, and made my body sweating hot. I held onto Sweet Virginia, while I was shook and panted loud like a Dead Eye dog.

In no time he was tugging faster. "You know that feeling," he said. "When the ship climbs the wave and you rise over top? When the wave comes down over, hard and fast like that? Are you getting it?"

"Yessir," I said, breathing hard. "I think I'm getting it."

"Feels like you're dying. Don't it?"

"I don't know," I said, "I never gone and died before."

"You know, when your soul's about to depart from your body and enter the gates of heaven?"

My eyes were squeezed shut and my heart was beating in my mouth.

"Well it's just like this," he said.

And that's when I died for the very first time. Not like some Dead Eye dog, but in the Frenchie way of meaning it. "Petit mort," Virginia called it. And I nearly died every time I thought about those words for weeks to come.

Afterward, he cleaned his hand. Lit his cigar and said, "Christ I'm starving. How about some hot eats at Mammy Jackson's?"

We were nearly at the door, when he stopped. A black cab was waiting on the other side of the road. Someone opened the door and Virginia said he had to go. Told me to meet him by the clock tower on Jefferson Street next Sunday. Then he passed me the rest of his cigar, jumped the cab, and off he went, on his fine-looking way.

Chapter 18
Heartaches for the living

For a whole week I could not stop thinking of him, and the precious dying thing he done, as navy gentlemen called it. I didn't think a second time about selling that cigar butt neither. Kept that piece of gold close to my heart. Lit it up once a day, put it to my lips and smoked it, just enough to smell Sweet Virginia once again.

Everyday I took to walking the long way home after working. I even took my chances walking Jefferson where Sweet Virginia said his gunner was docked, just to see if I could catch him with my eyes.

I lost all need for eating. Only stopped to fill my belly when I was hurting with hunger. I'd head on back to the Shades. Pull my boots off. Climb the three flights of rickety old stairs to the attic. Light the lantern. Lie on the board, and make myself die, die, die, all over again. Pretending it was Sweet Virginia doing the killing every time.

When Sunday finally arrived, I got down dockside early, not wanting to miss him for the world. I wandered around Jefferson in the rain, with my hands in my pockets and my hat pulled down low over my eyes, doing my best to try and hide from the world and the steely rain. Eventually I took refuge beneath the customs clock tower.

At three on the hour, it nearly rang my ears off telling me what I already knew, that I was dead on time. Sweet Virginia, however, was nowhere to be seen. Then a dark thought crossed my mind. Maybe I'd been a dumbass, and got the meeting place wrong. Maybe I was supposed to be at the clock tower down Washington Street. I was about to scarper when I heard a voice behind me say, "Well hello Mr. Jones."

I spun around on my heels, and saw it was him. And he looked good. He'd tied a white ribbon around his cap. It looked a little crazy.

"They let you do that?" I said.

"Find out soon enough I guess. When it gets confiscated off me. Navy's full of fellas who got nothing better to do than tell a fella what he can and cannot do every goddam moment of his born life. No peace at all from some I tell you. Anyhow. What about you? Been waiting long?"

"No sir, only just got here myself."

"Now that's a barefaced lie. Been watching you from over there at Irish Pete's."

I looked behind me, toward that old beat-up grog tavern, where I first landed, with three gunshot holes in the door, now five and counting.

A one-legged banjo player set himself down on a crate beneath the roof of the customs building, and started playing a sorrowful tune about that graveyard of tall ships, stranded out there, rotting to death, in the cold black harbor of St Frankie's Bay.

"Oh them sailors from the days back in '49.

All headed up the Sacramento River

With gold fortune on their mind.

Now them's all a ghosts who come a calling

Calling for my old soul.

To take me back to '49 and take away my gold."

Virginia leaned over to me. "Fella looks like he's gonna be a-joining them a ghosts any day now. C'mon let's get out of here before we catch a contagion."

I tipped my hat to the banjo player, threw a penny in his tin and hurried off to hitch up with Virginia who'd walked off ahead.

When I caught up with him, he told me what a waste of time that was. How most of sailors never found one single crumb of gold.

"Know how many of them idiots actually come back down from them hills millionaires?" he said.

I lifted my collar to keep the wind off and stop the rain dripping down my neck and listened.

"Hardly any at all, I heard is the answer to that. And the ones that did took it all. Greedy bastards. Left nothing for the likes of you and me. Well I guess you got a town out of it, but look at the place. One huge stinking pigsty full of piss-eyed lowbrows and crazy-headed villains who'll rob you blind first chance they get. I mean look at this place. Half-starved corpses are all I see around here anyhow. Nothing worth a bent cent. I mean, when was the last time you had a meal? Actually sat down all civilized and had something hot to eat?"

"I can't rightly recall," I said.

"No? Well there you have it." He stopped to light up a cigar and shake the match out. Then he passed it over, and watched me smoke it. "I bet you want some and a half don't you," he said, smiling.

And I was not sure if he meant the hot sit down meal or the dirty down the Dead Man where I could die, die, die all over again.

We passed all the sit down eating-places and then passed the Dead Man, and began heading up Madison Hill away from town, away from everything.

"Mr. Hakes," I said. "Where the hell we going?"

"Well, I'll tell you where we ain't going. We ain't going down some stinking lousy alley full of other fellas spewing spunk everywhere. Makes me feel unclean just thinking about it. No Mr. Jones, today I'm taking you to El Dorado."

Chapter 19
El Dorado

El Dorado, it turned out, was a pretty part of the Sacramento River. A little spot Virginia liked to call his own.

The sun had come out, and was shining on the water. Virginia took no time kicking off his boots, and stripping off into his cotton Johnnies. I followed him, watching him: his dark locks, polished in the sun.

We splashed around for a while, kicking feet and skimming stones. Then Virginia sat on a big rock, with a flat top like Abraham's altar.

"Come here darling," he said to me.

I climbed up and sat next to him. He took hold of my waist and put a kiss on my lips. Then another, a long hard one that made my belly fire up like a Billy stove. I was so dizzy with the kissing, that when he let go, I had to steady myself with my hands like a drunkard on his stool.

He told me to help him take his Johnnies off for him. I started by undoing the buttons on the front. The whole garment was nothing but quality. No holes or stains on it at all. I got off the altar rock. With my feet smarting in the mountain water, I pulled the clothes from his body by the legs. And there he was. All of him. And seeing a naked anybody was a rare thing.

I could not stop looking and regarding him so. Wondering if I'd ever become of such beauty myself. Or if I'd stay as I was. Scrawny, boney, and not much manliness to look at, at all. And I reckoned it must have been because of all the hard work he did on the ships that his muscles on his arms, and legs and everywhere were hard and strong looking. Like Goliath, if he'd looked like Angel Gabriel.

"Mr. Jones," he said, calling me to attention. "I order you, to stop gawking and get raw."

I was so thin my rib showed and my belly was round like a sick pup's. Besides all that, my feet had gone numb. I was shivering so my skin looked like a plucked goose.

I took my Johnnies off. Covered up what manliness I had with them and said, "I still got some growing to do."

"Well I don't know what you're hiding yourself for," he said, "I only saw your little pecker last week."

"Well, I know you did," I said, "But not all bare naked like this."

He stole my raggedy Johnnies out of my hands, and laid his eyes on my waist. "Well I can tell you for a start, you need to get your man standing to attention. Ain't making nobody feel good it lying there like a dead critter."

"It ain't like a dead nothing," I said, getting sore. "It's only on account of me being cold that he's lying low."

"Stop making poor excuses," he said. "I'm telling you, you need to get that thing fired up and ready to go. Right now."

I climbed back up onto the rock. Got close to Virginia's ear and said, "Mr. Hakes. Do you remember last week, when you did the dying thing on me?"

"What dying thing?" he said.

"The Frenchie dying thing. The dirty tugging thing you did, is what I'm talking about. I wouldn't say no to you doing it again. I mean I'll square up with you. Don't worry about that. I'll square up with you right now if you want me to. It'd be my pleasure, that's the God's honest truth of it."

He looked at my belly. My cock had come to crow, and to my joy, was standing higher than I figured it ever could.

"I guess you're right," he said. "You still need some growing to do. Eat much beef?" he said.

"No."

"Well, that's your problem. Take a look at mine. Now I always have beef at least twice a week. See what a difference that makes. You know I think I'm about ready for going to the gates of Heaven. C'mon, lets get out the river. I'm burning like a nigger out here."

We crossed barefoot over sharp splinters and slimy rocks to a patch under a tree covered with a smelly rug of pine. Virginia found a flat place where the tree roots weren't poking through, and made a blanket with his big navy coat.

He lay down on it. The way the sun was shining through the branches above, his whole body sparkled like a river. I sat next to him and watched him, studying the sky. One side of his face was the exact everything of the other. And everything on it: eyes, nose, mouth, jaw seemed the right size and shape for a face. Even the nasty scar on his left cheek, which should have ruined everything, somehow did not.

I was about to ask him where he got it, when he sat up, got hold of me, kissed me hard a number of times, and pulled me over, so that I was sat on top of his knees. I felt his cock hard between my thighs. I looked down to see it sticking up, all red and swollen. I was going to get hold and give him a tug, when he pulled it from between my legs, pushed me over so that I had to hold myself against the ground. Then he started digging at my hole with it.

"No," I said, "Jesus Christ, I didn't say nothing about you poking me."

He said nothing. Only kept tight hold and tried going in again.

I start fighting my way free, crawling away on the ground like a critter. "No," I said, "Get off me, goddam it. Get off of me I say."

Virginia let go, swearing and pushing me as he did. I fell on the pine needles, got up, and grabbed my clothes. Then I scarpered over to a tree. Leaned against its strong body. Folded my knees up to my chest, and dug my toes into the forest floor. From there I watched him, sitting on his coat. Rubbing his head in his hands. Cursing all alone to himself.

He threw a rock at a crow. It cawed and flew off. Another one came to tease him and he did the same to it.

"Mr. Hakes," I said. "I didn't mean to yell. It's just; they got rules where I live."

Virginia left the crows alone and turned his head to me. "What?" he said.

"I said the Boss's got rules. And one of them is no punks getting poked. Saul says that's what the whores on Union are for. Dead Eyes want that they go there."

Virginia looked at me. "Is that right," he said. "Well you ain't no punk and I ain't no Dead Eye. But now that were on the topic of cock-suckers, I'll bet Saul doesn't mind fucking his favorite boy every morning now, does he?"

"I wouldn't know about that," I said, "I don't think he gets up before noon. The truth of it Mr. Hakes, I owe him one. I got a home because of Saul."

"You know something Mr. Jones? I'm getting tired of hearing the name 'Saul' everywhere I go in this town. And it's starting to sound to more and more to me that you're sweet on him."

"Mr. Hakes, I only just live there. I hardly ever met Saul. Truth be told, I doubt he even cares I'm alive."

"Sounds like you'd prefer it if he did."

"Well, I wouldn't mind to be honest."

"Because you're sweet on him."

"No, I hardly know what he looks like. I only ever saw him in the dark."

"Oh?"

"What I mean to say, I ain't hardly seen him at all."

"Then if you ain't never seen him, and you ain't sweet on him, how come you never shut the hell up about him for?"

"Because I don't. I never talked about him once, until just now." I picked up a stick and started peeling its skin off.

Virginia went back to killing crows.

After a while he looked up and said, "Where's your Mama?"

"Gone. When I was two," I said.

"Papa?"

I shrugged. "Long gone." I made a kind of bird with the bark and threw it him. He picked it up and looked it over.

"Well," he said, fixing its wing. "I think you're lucky. I wish mine had died the minute he'd finished sowing his corn in my mother's belly. I reckon I've put every damn curse on him that there is in Hell. And I'll tell you why. That bastard sold me off to the navy when I was 10 years living. And do you know what that bitch did?"

"No," I said, twisting up a bark snake.

"Nothing," he said. "Not a goddam thing. Her fourth son is what I am. Three above me, two below. She was happy to pack my roll and wave me off to die with a bunch a salty, fish smelling, whore lovers. I was like apple pie for them bunch of motherfuckers. I hope the Iroquois come and do the worst to both of mine. Skin them alive for all I care. Hang the rest of them up for the wolves like they done me."

For a time we were silent. Then Virginia patted the empty place beside him and said, "Come here."

I went to him.

A patch of dark cloud moved over the sun. He lifted up his coat and made a kind of tent around our shoulders. I laid my head on his chest and started playing with the curls of his chest hair.

"Now listen," he said, putting a kiss on my ear, "I don't want you minding what Saul says. You ain't with him. You're with me. And you know me pretty good. I mean you like me don't you?"

"I find you pleasing." I said, "I mean it pleases me to look at you."

"You know why I brought you up to El Dorado, don't you?"

"But, you never said nothing about poking. I figured you were gonna be doing the dying thing on me again."

"I know but the thing is, I don't much like dirty work. Makes me feel just that: dirty. And you know how I took care of you last week?"

"Yessir, I do and I don't know why you're changing your mind, saying you don't like it no more."

"Well, I was just showing you how good a thing can be that's all. So you know for yourself. The truth is, you never felt nothing better in your whole life than when you're getting it the way I can give it to you from behind. I mean, last week: that was nothing to how good this is gonna be. I swear to you. I promise you. It's the most beautiful thing. There just ain't nothing better. Nothing better than giving you my seed which is all I got to give you, truth be told."

So I let him. And Alley Mac was right. Navies were liars. Because it was not the best thing I'd ever felt in my whole life at all. Not at first. Then it started getting a little all right.

Every Sunday for a month that day forward, I followed Virginia up to El Dorado.

And he was happy. Which made me happy. And I liked feeling him strong on me like so. His face buried in my hair, sweet kisses on my neck and precious words in my ear. Sweating pigs, howling coyotes, and shuddering wild horses. Rolling over next to me. Lying on his back, his arms spread wide, and his pretty everything smiling up at the sky.

Chapter 20
David's return

It was the third Sunday in June and the day was hot. Virginia and me were hanging around Union Square. We'd found a shady spot underneath the general goods store. Two stray dogs were fighting over a puddle to drink from. Virginia kicked at one and swore at the other. They went off, panting, looking for another hole to fight over.

He had his cap pulled low over his eyes, his thumbs handing from his pockets, with his boot heel set back against the general store.

I did my best to look likewise.

He lifted his cap and wiped his head and neck with a handkerchief. I looked for mine, and finding nothing, took my hat off and used it as a fan instead. I looked to see where he was looking. The building across the road: the US Mint.

A gold digger had come down from the hills. His face was scorched, his raggedy clothes layered with dust. He was going in to get his gold weighed and traded in for union dollars.

He went in.

He came out.

Next, he staggered over to the National Bank of California, to lock it all up in the safe keep.

Virginia relit an old cigar he had in his pocket.

"Wonder how long it'll be afore your precious Saul blows the walls off and scarpers off with all the winnings. Ever hear anybody talk about it?"

"I don't hear nothing," I said. "I never heard tell of Saul ever blowing nothing up."

"Oh, you ain't huh. Well, I heard he done such a job in San Marco and stashed all the winnings where nobody can find it. Not even his precious brother. A two-faced thieving liar is what he his."

The gold digger came out the bank smiling. Started walking across the square. Right away he got accosted by a bunch of hotel whores, dressed in silk and smelling of perfume. They were hustling hard saying, "Can I take you to the gates of heaven my lover? Any pleasure you want mister. Any pleasure at all. No exceptions."

"Any pleasure you want my ass," said Virginia. "They are one lying pair of clap-faced bitches. Truth of it is, you go in. They take all your goddam money. You stick your cock in. And if you ain't done in two minutes some buffalo in a dress stinking of whiskey grabs you by the arm and throws you out the door saying, 'Be off with you now. Next fella. Next fella's turn now. Be off with you.'"

I looked at him, then at the girls, and wondered which one he'd had for his pleasure and when, and how often. And how much it had cost him, to get robbed blind. In no time I turned to cactus. "Well," I said. "I guess the way the business is, if a fella's rich and comely enough, he can get what the hell he pleases."

"Yeah," he said. "Well look how rich I am. All I get is you." He threw the cigar on the ground and walked off.

I bent down to pick it up, and ran after him. "What did you mean by that?" I said.

He looked behind and saw me.

"Jesus Christ," he said, "Ain't there nothing worth looking at around here at all?"

I hurried to match his pace. "Why," I said, "what's wrong with the way I look?"

"Everything's wrong." he said.

"Didn't seem to mind me afore."

"Yeah, well, that was before. It ain't now."

"Changed your mind on me?" I said. "Changed your mind on me, is that it?"

"I ain't changed my mind. My mind ain't changed one bit. I got a good imagination when it comes getting my own needs, a man's needs by the way. And if there were a law, they'd be charging you for sale of false goods."

"Why you saying that to me for?"

"Because the plain truth is you are two-bits and the real deal's five eagles. Five goddam eagles that I ain't got."

"That ain't the truth of it, Mister Hakes."

"It's the God almighty, honest truth of it."

"It ain't the truth. I'm gonna be worth a fortune in gold one day. I heard it be told."

"A fortune in gold?" he laughed. Then he turned on me. "Let me tell you a fact of life. Soon as you start growing a beard, no Dead Eye's gonna come a mile of you. First sign of whiskers, you ain't gonna be worth a half bent cent to nobody. Soon as you stop bringing in the coin, your precious Saul's gonna kick you out on your ass. You're gonna be a gutter hog. Horse shit's gonna be worth more than you."

"It's a lie," I said, "A goddam liar is what you are Mister!" And I kicked him hard in the back of the shin saying, "I hope you rot in Hell. I mean I hope you die badly first, and then rot in Hell."

I ran out of Union Square and down Columbia. I got half way down the hill when I changed my mind, and ran back after him. I dodged wild riders, and four-horse carriages. I jumped back of the omnibus, and got off at the US Mint. I looked everywhere for him: the general store, the tavern, the hotel lobby, everywhere. I got chased, I got hollered at, I got met over the head by a broom for just for standing on the look out. And it was all for nothing. For I had lost him. And he did not come back looking for me. Not next Sunday. Nor the Sunday after that.

Chapter21

Dying ain't easy for sinners

I got sick. For a whole week I stayed wrapped up in bed. The sun was hot, and my body was sticky and shivering in sweat.

Raccoon got Alley Mac. She said I might be dying. Raccoon said I wasn't. He said he'd seen dying before and this was not it. Alley begged to disagree. She sent a medicine man from Chinese Town to call on me. Doc Chinaman said I was not dying. It was too much cheese in my belly causing all the trouble. He gave me a broth to sup and soon I stopped shitting, but still I was hurting deep inside where my heart was, which is what I'd been saying was the problem all along.

Next Sunday I was better and went out with Raccoon to get air. We sat on the pier fishing. Raccoon had a line out right by the place where Joe had been found beached up on the sand. There was nothing but waves rolling in and out now. Nothing to say he'd ever been there at all.

I hung my head over the side. The logs holding the whole thing together were thick with barnacles and seaweed. Purple starfish clung on. And I learned something watching those critters that day. No matter how hard the waves hit them, no matter how hungry the sea come, they stuck fast and hung on strong, and made little fuss about the trouble they was in.

Raccoon caught a fish. He pulled up the line, unhooked the critter and banged its head on the wood a few times to kill it fast. "Well there's three suppers now," he said. "I reckon we ought to get as many as we can and hang them up to dry out. We can store them up for the winter."

"I ain't living in a place stinking of fish all day long," I said.

"Jones, it's practically free food. The license ain't hardly costing nothing."

Which meant he hadn't paid for one.

"And the cost of store food in the winter's just getting too crazy. I ain't working just to pay some crook four times a thing is worth in the summer time."

Which was never, as he never paid for a goddam thing in his whole life. Unlike me, who was constantly getting stung raw in every pocket. The thing was, Raccoon had secret stashes everywhere, and wouldn't tell me nothing or give me a thing, and I was broke.

"I think I'm done with fishing," I said. "Think I'm gonna take a walk."

"Done?" he said. "Jones, you ain't done nothing yet."

"Well I just done nearly dying now, didn't I?"

"You ain't nearly died. Look, it'll do your bones good to get some real work done."

"Real work?" I said. "What do you mean by *real work*? Jesus Christ. You ain't got no idea of what *real work* is unless you done a day down the Dead Man, you bastard son of a bitch."

A fisherman yelled at us. Then told on us. An official come by telling us to stop cursing or we'd have to pay a fine. He asked us if we'd got our license.

Of course, we had not.

He threatened to reel us in if we didn't pay up right now. I was saying how the fishing weren't nothing to do with me, so hell if I was going do time for cheating, when a fella in a long navy coat coughed up and said, "Here, tell me what's owed. I'll pay it."

It was him. All smelling of sweet tobacco and soap. I looked up but the sun was in my eyes and made me blind. He moved in front making shadow. Then I saw his face. He was like an angel. The kind you see on those cards preachers pass outside the doss house door for nothing. If he'd worn a long white gown, folks all around would have been falling on their knees, clinging to his skirts thinking he was Angel Gabriel.

I waited for the official to leave then I went by his side. I smiled and tried thinking how I could say "thank you" to him without actually using the words.

"Hungry?" he said to me, looking happy.

"Starved," I said, smiling wide.

He nodded to Raccoon. "Whose the Injun?"

I looked behind. Raccoon was watching. I shrugged and said, "Just some kid from the Shades."

Chapter 22
The white wolf's return

Virginia and me walked uphill to Mammy Jackson's on First Street. It was sweating hot. My hair stuck fast to my cheeks. Virginia paid the halfpenny rent for the plate as well as the full cost of the supper. Cook stacked a pile of steaming ribs onto it, a big spoon of boiled Irish. Topped it off with a cob of corn and some fresh smelling pig dripping. The biscuit had just left the oven. It was another cent. In the end, Virginia insisted on paying for that too.

We squeezed onto a bench full of loud-talking fellas guzzling down ladles of water being passed around by Mammy's boys. Virginia grabbed some for us. It'd gone warm but it didn't matter, we were thirsty. He took out a fork from his pocket and stabbed at the potatoes.

"Ah damn," I said, "I ain't brought nothing to eat with."

"Use your knife."

"I ain't got mine. I think some devil robbed it off me when I was sleeping."

"Not a red devil I hope," he said.

I shrugged.

He put his fork down and pulled a switchblade from his back pocket. He wiped it on his trousers, slid it under the table and said, "Here, you can keep that."

And it was high quality. The hilt was made of ivory. I turned it over. It had letters etched on to it. And the figure of a wolf. A white wolf.

I spoke low, so those sitting by us were deaf to my words. "Mister Hakes," I said. "Where'd you get this knife?"

"Why?" he said. "What's wrong, don't you want it?"

"No I do, I do want it, it's just, Mr. Hakes, you ought to know, this here knife belongs to a certain body. And that body, and his brother, would not be too pleased if they found it in another man's pocket. And there's more. There's talk about a navy fella going around: a scoundrel kind. Looks like a fella called Byron. They call him a 'lone wolf' and I heard tell…"

"You heard tell huh? Let me guess: Saul again?"

"No," I said, keeping my voice low, "it's just, there's some bad talk about this navy fella been going around late, and I don't like the idea of seeing you in trouble for it. And I figure this here knife spells trouble, to those who can read the situation. So I need you to tell me who gave it you."

"Well, Mr. Jones, here's some news for you. I don't need to tell you nothing about nothing at all. But if you must know my private business, I won it playing cards. Now give it back to me if you don't want it."

"Do you know the fella then?"

"No, I don't know the fella."

"But you saw him? Was he the tall, skinny, pale-face type? Keeps long hair tied back like a horse's tail? Or was he navy like your self? A fella who might be your lookalike? The kind you might get mistaken for being brothers for?"

"Look I don't remember what he looked like, now give me back my knife if you don't want it."

"No Mister, please," I said, clinging to it while he tried stealing it out my hand. "I do want it, honest I do."

He let go.

I wiped our sweat off the hilt with my sleeve. I tucked it in my back pocket. Touching the toe of my boot to his I said, "Mister Hakes, I thank you for the knife. Most kindly, I do."

Chapter 23

The tobacco selling business

It was a Tuesday. I was down dockside when he showed up all smiles and smelling of soap. I was sticky and stinking of spunk.

We went to the grog house with the bullets on the door. We sat down at a table in a quiet corner. Virginia paid for the tins and we got busy drinking. Then he got down to talking about our tobacco selling business.

"With the war blockade on, supply is low. But demand is high. That means the price is also. Now, here's the deal. I give you two pounds of Virginia leaf. You roll them up like I showed you how. It's already shredded so it'll be easy. Then, go around every tavern in town and sell them off. I figure you'll get say, two bits a cigar. You keep one for trying out. Give the fella a blow but make sure he don't smoke the whole damn thing. You get it?"

"Yeah I get it," I said.

"All right. So you meet Sunday as usual, next week. I'll set you up with the stash."

"But, hold on," I said, "What's the deal exactly? I mean how much coin do I get to keep?"

"I don't know. Ten I figure's fair."

"Ten? Dollars?"

"Jesus Christ, no. Percent. You keep ten percent of the price of the cigar.

"Well how much is that?"

"I don't know. About twenty cents."

"How many cigars?"

"Jesus Christ I don't know. About a hundred. There, so you'll get about twenty dollars in all, which is the easiest money you'll ever make. I mean how many cocks you got to suck on to make that kind of coin, huh? And remember I'm the one risking everything. I get caught selling, I'll be shot. Or hanged. You're just a kid selling. Ain't nothing gonna happen to you. But I'm a grown man now. I'll be swinging for sure. But think, if we pull this off, by the time we're done doing business, we'll be rich as kings."

"Yeah," I said, "Imagine that. We could move into one of them rooms at that new hotel on California Street. I heard tell they got copper bathtubs, with water that comes boiling hot out the taps."

"Yeah well, one of them room's about $1500 a week. Gonna have to sell a whole boat load of tobacco for that, but, you're getting the idea."

We talked a while more about our future. After I done selling, we were getting shot of this shit-hole town. Going to catch the 9:15 to San Marco. Buy a forty-acre patch out in the hills. Raise fine-bred horses for selling. Be gentlemen of business. Go to the Mayor's Ball, the Governor's Ball, and even the President's when we getting to being millionaires. Get us a wife each. Breed some children, so they can run the ranch when we get being old-timers.

Up at El Dorado, as I lay there in the raw, my head on his lap looking up at his sleepy eyes, I figured my life was finally settled. And I thought, "Now, if only I don't go and blow my chances all to pieces."

Next week I was there, down Jefferson, right on time. Virginia was also. We found a back alley off the Dock Road, where he passed me a sack of pure Virginia gold. I stuffed it in the back of my pants and headed off back to the Shades.

I told Raccoon about my venture, and he was all for being a part-time associate in the business of selling. It took us a while to get the rolling right but once we got a hang of it, we had a heap a Mexican cigars worth a goddam fortune sitting like a pyramid in front of our eyes.

And we did just like Virginia said. Washed our bodies with soap, slicked back our hair with combs. Used a horse brush to get any mud off our best clothes. As we were about to leave I told Raccoon to wait downstairs, for remembering that time Violet dressed me up in lemon silk and petticoats, I had a marvelous idea for bringing in some extra coin. When I was done getting ready, we headed off. And stole into every tavern from Union to Columbia to get sell, sell, selling.

Raccoon was getting the best of business and I was getting nothing.

"Stop hogging all the customers," I said to him, pulling on his arm.

"Well I told you it was a bad idea wearing that get up," he said. "Ain't no fella in his right mind gonna buy a smoke off a girl."

"Well he ain't if you're gonna be muscling in on my business afore I even got a shot at the tin can."

"Alright, alright," he said, "take the next table, I need a piss anyhow."

So I made my way to a busy round of cards.

I caught several eyes.

I went up to the best looking pair and said, "Smoke, Mister?"

"Nope," he said looking back at his cards. He had a near run of nothing likely in spades.

My cigars were tucked inside a frilly garter tied around my calf. I lifted my skirts up to show him.

Fella looked down.

I waited.

Fella looked up. I met him with a wink and said, "Five dollars."

"Five dollars?"

"Five dollars."

"For?"

"A couple of fingers of pure sweet Virginia. Just for you, mind. Your friends stay here."

We shook on the deal. And headed outside, out back of the tavern.

Raccoon had finished doing his business. He come up to me and pulled me aside. "Jonesy, what are you doing? We're only supposed to be selling cigars."

"Look," I said, "you do business your way, and leave me to do mine." I shook him off and went to go back my lucky near straight.

Raccoon hung on to my arm. "You ain't punking on this job."

"First of all, it ain't called 'punking' when you're a girl, it's called 'whoring'. Second of all, take your unwashed hands off of me, you're damaging the silk."

"You're gonna get us both killed," he said, clinging on. "And you don't look nothing like a girl. No matter how hard you try."

"Oh, why don't you just go on home," I said. "Hang up some more fish from the rafters. I mean, the place ain't stinking enough for me already."

"You won't be saying that come February. When we're starved."

"Come February I'm gonna be living on my very own ranch. Up there in the hills, as rich as King Midas."

"Oh, what with your so-called navy friend 'Mr. Hakes'?"

"He ain't so-called, he's got the tattoo on his arm to prove the fact."

"Anybody can get the tattoo on his arm."

"Well, he ain't anybody. Him and me are business partners now. He's getting a piece of paper done, with the words stamped on it saying 'Jones & Hakes: breeders of fine-bred horses.'"

"'Breeders of fine-bred horseshit' you mean."

I could see my almost straight flush was starting to tire of waiting. "Oh to Hell!" I said to Raccoon, "All this talk is costing me business." And I made him stand over on the corner, playing lookout for punishment.

The Dead Eye turned out to be a fine fellow who played fair and square. For five dollars he got two cigars, a fumble up the top of my thighs and he was as happy as the day was long.

Raccoon wasted no time saying we were lucky and to head on home before it ran out.

News had come in by boat saying the Union had won another battle over the devils in the South. The whole of town was shooting off their guns and singing their heads off to "*Nothing but victory by fire will do*" and "*Mamma, take me to bed, I think I'm dying*".

We turned to go down an alley we didn't know so well. It looked like it might be a shortcut across town. We nearly reached the end of the road, when out of the shadows came a gang of boys. Four of the ugliest black-toothed bunch of dogs you ever saw in your life. All shabby and spitting chew all over the place.

"Shit," said Raccoon, "It's the Sydney Ducks." From Demon's Land.

We stopped.

They strode up to us and formed a line. From behind came another. The Boss of them all. I knew him right away. The same one who showed me his metal knuckles the first day I arrived in the city.

He broke through the chain, rolling a cigar around on his tongue and looking mean. He ran his eyes over me then spat on the ground.

He snapped his fingers. Next thing, two of his boys made a grab for Raccoon. They held him while another punched him in the belly.

Raccoon went down, gasping for air.

I looked either way for an exit.

"Come here," the Boss said to me.

I stood my ground.

"I said, come here cunt. Do as you're told."

I stepped up. When I got close, he blew smoke in my face and said to his boy, "Empty his pockets."

They left me alone and started stripping Raccoon of all the treasure.

Raccoon fought back, kicking and biting and cursing them all to hell. In the end they kicked him out cold and took everything he had.

The Ducks' Boss put his hand out. He held it flat in front of my eyes. "Give it up," he said, "and I'll tell the boys to be nice to you when the time comes."

I felt tears coming. I swallowed hard and handed over my dollars.

"Where the rest?" he said.

"That's all I got," I said, choking on my words.

"You're lying. Where you keep your savings. Up your pussy?" Him and his gang of black-toothed uglies started laughing.

I looked him dead in the eye. "I don't got no savings," I said.

"Why not?"

"It's spent."

"Spent on what?"

"On what folks regular spend money on. Food. Lodgings…"

"Where you sleep?"

"I rent a room over there," and I pointed to nowhere in particular.

"How much does your boss take off you?"

"My what?"

"Boss," he said, inclining his head to Raccoon, who was coming around.

One of his gang said to him, "Boss, know what we ought to do? Buy us one of them souvenirs they're selling down Columbia. Them nigger-collars. One of them would do nicely for lynching up Injuns."

The Boss said it was a fine idea, and that he should go and get one. He then turned back to me and, catching me unawares, punched me for being a "bitch-boy."

I held my belly and wiped the spit off my face. I looked up at him with angry eyes.

"Get a potato sack," he told one of his gang. "No rocks, I want to see if this one floats a while before it sinks this time."

I started shaking on the ground. I tried calling out for Raccoon, but no words come out my mouth. Piss was running, and stinging, down my thighs.

The black-toothed Boss got down to my level and sat on his heels. He blew smoke in my eyes and said, "You made a mistake coming on my side of the city, Bitch-boy. Ain't you heard of me? Don't you know who I am?"

Then I heard a body saying, "We know your name all right: 'Thieving cocksucker.' Soon to be known as 'no balls' by daybreak I reckon." I looked up and saw a gang of grown men, in white gowns and scarves wrapped about their heads. It was the Hooligans from Southside. A whole bunch of them sitting on horses and wielding scimitars. Shoulders heavy with firing arms too. It seemed the Ducks had been warring with them and now they'd come seeking vengeance. One lone rider on a horse lined a musket dead on with the Duck Boss's face. He, as it turned out, was nothing but a simple coward. He took one look at that lone rider and dropped his cigar. The lone rider lifted his hand to signal his friends. They spurred their horses toward the gang. The Ducks' Boss and his ugly boys wasted no time flying off in every direction of the compass to get away. All the while getting chased down by a couple of swordsmen screaming likes banshees in the wind.

I crawled over to Raccoon and tried helping him up. He shook me off, saying he was all right.

The lone rider moved toward us. I looked at the sword shining on his back. I put my hand in Raccoon's and we held on to each other tight.

The rider told me to take my bonnet off.

I did.

My hair had grown so long on its own I had no need for curls.

"Where is your father?" he said.

I told him he was dead.

"Brother?"

I pointed to Raccoon.

"You a half-breed boy?" he said.

Raccoon and me shared a glance. "No," said Raccoon. "My granddaddy was an Oholone chief."

The rider nodded. Then he pulled out a small bag. Fingered around in it. Took out a hunk of gold the size of Kansas. Held it up in front of our eyes. "I'll take your sister off your hands for this," he said to Raccoon.

I could only do like Raccoon did and stare at the riches in front of our eyes.

"She'll be safe with me," said the rider.

Raccoon and me shared looks again. I tried smiling with my eyes.

"Sir," Raccoon coughed up. "She ain't for selling."

"What?" I said to him.

"Be quiet," he said. "I know how to handle this."

"She's gonna die out here on these streets hanging out with you," said the rider.

"We made it this long," said Raccoon, "and she ain't died yet."

The rider turned to me.

"What do you want to do, daughter? Stay with your half-breed brother, and be turned into a harlot; walking the streets, side by side with the Devil? Or come with me. God willing."

I could not take my eyes of that lump of shiny yellow treasure in his gold-ringed hand. Not only was it beautiful, but also it was compensation for our getting robbed by the boys from Demon's Land.

"I got to talk to my brother first," I said. I pulled Raccoon up with me and said, "Raccoon, I got a plan for recovering our losses. You take the gold, I go with the Hooligan, and then I'll scarper first chance I get. It'll be easy. I'll make my getaway when they're sleeping. I tell you, I can't believe our luck. That gold makes up for the loss on the backie, ten fold over. Goddam it Raccoon, we're rich as kings!"

"Jones," he said, real calm. "We nearly just got killed. But, luck come our way and we're still living. Now, let me tell you something. I've lived around here all my life. These fellas here: they don't take kindly to being cheated. They got a mean way of getting vengeance. As soon as they find out you ain't a real girl your head's gonna be spiking on the courthouse gate. You rob them and who knows what's gonna happen. Probably kill everybody so much as looks like one of us." Then he left me and said to the to the rider, "Sir, I'm sorry but I can't be doing business with you."

"Why not?" he said.

"That hunk of gold just ain't worth my sister."

"Now hold on there," I said. "I'll have you know I just scored five whole Yankee dollars for just showing off my toes bare naked so don't tell me I ain't worth that goddam fortune when I'm worth a whole river of goddam gold. A whole mountain of gold. Jesus Christ. I'm worth every grain of gold in that hunk of beauty and the rest!"

Raccoon said nothing. Only stepped on my foot to say, "Shut the hell up."

Rider looked at his friends. They began having a conversation, and shaking their heads to the words. The rider nodded. And they all seemed to agree.

I watched, with my mouth hanging wide, as the rider tucked his shiny gold rock back under his skirts. Before I could speak, he clicked and turned his horse around. Then him, his Hooligans, and my gold worth went disappearing into the darkness of town.

Raccoon and me were left standing alone. I took one long hard look at him. He was brushing himself off and checking his wounds.

"I ain't never gonna forgive you for what you just done," I said, looking at him, staring at me with startled eyes. "You just gone and robbed me of my gold worth. My gold worth as was foretold by Alley Mac, and was right there in front of my eyes. *My* gold worth, you hear. *Mine!*"

We limped on back to the Shades in silence. Me with my arms folded tight. Him with his hands stuffed in his pockets. And he would not meet my attempts at staring him out. Not once.

Chapter 24
Fool's gold

I met with Virginia in the Grog House with the gunshots in the door. He sat forward on his chair and said, "Where's the money?"

I said, "I ain't got it."

"Why not?"

"I was robbed."

"You were robbed?"

"I was robbed."

"So, who's got it?"

"The Ducks got it."

"Why have the Ducks got it?"

"Goddam it Mister. Ain't you been listening to me once? I been robbed I tell you. I been robbed."

I put my head to my tin cup of whiskey and cried.

He pulled me off the chair and shook me like a bag of corn. "Well you just gone and cost me my whole fortune then, ain't you? Now thanks to you I got nothing you hear? Nothing." He carried on being angry. Told me I was fired from the tobacco selling business for being a goddam dumbass with cheese wheels for thinking cogs and macaroni for brains.

People were taking notice.

He shoved me back in the chair and ran out the tavern.

I followed.

"I owe people," he said, digging his hands in his pockets. "Goddam it I owe people. Who don't like being owed, get it?"

I stepped up my pace to keep up with him. "Mr. Hakes, I'm sorry," I said. "I'm real sorry. I swear I'm gonna get that money back for you, somehow I will, I swear upon my life."

We turned a corner into Union Square.

"How the hell you gonna make it up to me, huh?" he said. "They short on two-penny cocksuckers around this town or something?" He pushed through a crowd of fellas waiting for a dogfight to start. "The truth of it is, as soon as you start sprouting whiskers, you ain't gonna be worth half a bent cent anyhow. And you're hardly worth nothing now."

"Oh, what you keep saying that for?" I said dodging a horse cart. "Why you got to go and say things only to make me feel bad all the time?" We got out of the square and headed up a side road.

"There's fellas I know makes whore dollars fucking real proper," he said.

"Whore dollars?" I said, stepping over a drunken gutter hog. "Where? I ain't heard of that. I would have heard of that."

"Only you ain't man enough for making that kind of money."

"What are you talking about? Of course I'm man enough. What you think I've been doing up at El Dorado the whole time with you, if it ain't being man enough?"

We come out the side lane and into a busy road. He dodged a wagon that nearly went and hit me.

I ran after him. And dug my finger in his back like a gun. "Well," I said. "What do you say to that, huh? I'm man enough for anything. You don't know me by half, that's the problem."

He stopped dead and looked for an alley. He dragged me through a dark cramped lane with buildings nearly falling on top of one another. He pushed me up against the wall like a devil. Pressed his body hard into mine so that I went and started crying again.

"You think what goes on up there's fucking? That ain't fucking. I go easy on you, on account of me liking you. I go all gentle. I treat you like you're a little virgin on her wedding night every time. And do you appreciate that? No. You don't. Because first chance you get you go and lose my life fortune. So here's what I'm gonna do about it."

Then he kissed me hard on the lips. Digging his tongue in deep and caring less that I could hardly breathe. I held on tight and hung on to my tears, while I let him do the killing on me. And him talking gentle, sending precious words into my ear, numbing my brain with sweet gold promises and calling me his pretty young "beau".

When we got to El Dorado, Virginia wasted no time in getting down to the business of going easy. When he'd finished, he did as he'd always done, and lay down on his back, with his eyes closed, smiling in the sun.

This time though, he didn't stay on his back. He rolled over on his belly. The sun sparkling on him through the trees, like a river full of gold.

I run my hand down over him. His back was tight and strong. I kissed the freckles on his shoulders. I ran my tongue down the bones of his spine. I bent my head to look at him. And smiled to see him smiling back at me, his pretty young beau.

I kissed his ass. I sucked hard on his cheeks. It sounded like a fart and that made him laugh. I saw him open his eyes and look back at me, before closing them again, looking friendly, and happy.

I got on him, so my belly was on his back and my hardness was pushing on his ass. I buried my head deep into his neck and kissed him. I leaned over and put my tongue into his mouth. I grabbed a hold of his chin and turned it, so I could get to kiss it better. I pressed down hard as I could onto his lips, bruising them with kisses. I pulled away and looked. I saw they were red as forest berries.

He was breathing heavy. I put my tongue on his throat, and could feel his heart beating fast. And I figured it must be, that he wanted this. Or else he'd have kicked me off him by now.

I put my hand between his thighs. He did not protest.

I stroked the back of his balls, and still, he said nothing. Only seemed to breathe harder.

I poked my finger in his hole, and I wondered if he'd done "fucking real proper" more than a few times for him to know the difference. And right then I could not help myself. My thing was hot and hard, and I wanted to go easy on him the way he done with me. Only the thought of fucking real proper was making my body shake and my Billy stove burn. So I took my horny thing and poked it in his hole, and that's when all hell broke loose.

"What the hell do you think you're doing?" he said, beating me in the ribs with his elbow. He turned around fast, and flipped me down hard on my back.

I gasped for air. I looked up to see a clenched fist staring back at me.

I put my hand over my face to stop the blow. When it did not come I said, "Why you going all Jessie on me for? I thought you were liking it?"

"Liking it?" he said, drawing his arm back further to get a harder shot. "Think I'm some two-bit bitch-boy? A goddam whore only good for getting it?"

"I never meant it like that."

"You meant it exactly that."

"I never. The truth of it is, I'd rather die than say nasty words to you. Or do things that mean the same as nasty words."

He stared at me with angry eyes. I could hear his lungs breathing hot and heavy. When cooled down he undid his fists, and ran his fingers through his curls. He turned away from me and wrapped his coat around his nakedness.

I gathered some of my things together and started getting dressed. I watched him as I pulled my Johnnies on. I thought he might be crying. So I went to take a look. He gave me a punch in the arm and told me to go away.

I sat on the forest floor and played with the pines. "I only wanted to give you pure pleasure," I said. "Be all gentle the way you are with me."

When he said nothing, I could not help myself. I started sobbing, saying, "I thought you and me were partners, I thought that's what you said."

"We ain't partners no more," he said. "You're fired from being partners since you lost my precious fortune."

I cried.

He went quiet. Then he went shaking and shuddering under his coat. And I knew he was tugging his own self off, just so he could die without me.

I picked up a stick and threw it at him. "That's a bare face lie if I ever heard one," I said.

He ignored me.

"You got a whole stash of that backie someplace. You told me so yourself. Only you were too drunk to remember saying it, that's all."

He carried on with his killing.

"You're just a drunkard anyhow. Soap don't hide the smell neither."

I heard him getting close to paradise.

"You're full of lies. Probably ain't real navy neither. Anybody can buy a get up. Anybody can get a tattoo."

Then he went and died. *Le petit mort*, he used to call it, when he was glowing with the charm.

After making all kinds of racket, singing "Glory Halleluiah," he blew his nose with his handkerchief, let out some stinking wind, and wiped his belly clean with my own shirt. "I don't like fucking with my own kind no more," he said.

"What?" I said. "What 'kind'?"

"The "kind" wearing a cock and a pair of balls instead of a red juicy pussy and pair of nipples to suck on kind." And he started getting dressed. "The truth is, I'm a bull-blooded man," he said, buttoning up his braces, "which means I need a woman bad. Of course you wouldn't understand that. You ain't the same as me."

"I'm the same as you," I said, "I'll want that too, when I get older. Every man's got to get a wife sometime is what you said. Said you'd buy us each a one from Carolina when the war's over."

"That ain't never gonna happen to you," he said, laughing.

"Why not?" I said, turning my damp shirt the right way round.

He put on his big navy coat, lay down on his side and watched me dressing. "Because," he said, "you won't be able to stand the smell of pussy."

I said nothing. I was trying to get myself together, but some of my buttons had been robbed; probably by the thieving crows hiding out in the trees above my head.

He leaned on his elbow and looked at me. "Here's the thing, Mr. Jones," he said. "Do you like the smell of the bay at low tide?"

I thought of Joe.

"Nobody likes the smell of the bay at low tide," I said, looking for my neck scarf.

"Well, that's where you're wrong. Us navy fellas like nothing but that. Why do you think we spend so much time out at sea?"

I heard laughing. I said nothing. Only stared at him, with his pretty smiling face, and that ugly scar.

I got busy trying to find my shoes.

He lay down on his back. Pulled his hat over his grinning eyes, and pretended to be asleep.

I walked barefoot back to the river. I climbed onto the rock. Stared into the water and watched it spinning a leaf to death. At times I buried my head deep in my hands. At other times I looked up, between the branches of the ever-growing redwoods, and saw eagles taking turns soaring above my head, then nest down, disguised by the trees again. Thoughts circled in my head. Of the bay at low tide, and peculiarity; of sucking piss-stinking cocks of Dead Eyes at dawn; of poking and promises and dying while still living, and I wondered if I'd ever be riding wild horses on that goddam ranch with Virginia, or whether it was all plain fool's gold.

Chapter 25

Raccoon gets sick

I got back to the Shades. Climbed up to the attic room and opened up the hatch. As soon as I did, the smell hit me. Dried out fish, body sweat and puke. Raccoon was in bed. Shaking. Sweating. Mumbling to his self.

I stepped over the sick on the floor and asked him what was wrong. He talked a lot of words that made no sense at all. When his eyes rolled white I went and got Alley. She ran to Chinatown to fetch got the Doc. He came and said, "This here child here is dying. And only time will tell, if he's to walk with the living." Then he threw me out the room. Told me to take the blankets with me and burn them all to hell.

I moved back to my first home behind the beaten up chair. I had no blanket now mine had turned to ash so I slept in my coat.

I did not eat. I could not eat. I called for Joe to come a-rising from the grave but he would not. I begged Virginia to come and get me instead. Take me from this forsaken place. Forgive me for being a dumbass and costing him a goddam fortune. I had a waking dream that it happened so. I saw him come and get me on a white horse with a long black mane. And we rode fast. Over the river. When we got to the tracks I apologized for all I had said and done, and he kissed all my troubles away. We said goodbye to the horse and jumped the 9:15 to San Marco. I saw us smiling in the sun, taking turns trying to shoot crows from atop a boxcar. Then we lay down on our backs. Arms stretched wide, staring up at the wild moving sky. While that train puffed and chugged, running fast, fast, fast against the wind flying free. But he never would come to fetch me for that train. So I covered my head with my coat, and cried hard for my dear departed Joe instead.

Some Muwekma people came.

Saul met them. They were talking about Raccoon.

A crowd of boys gathered around Alley who was listening with her ear to the door. Soon heads turned to me as the word travelled down that Raccoon was dead.

Juan comes pushing through to me. He took my arm and said, "I'm sorry."

I pulled my arm back, told him to die in hell and pushed him out of my way. And I kept on pushing till I met Alley. I looked into her eyes to find the truth.

"Jones," she said, putting a hand on my shoulder. "You need to hitch yourself to the post, and get praying to Jesus for there's bad news on the horizon."

"I ain't gonna get praying to nobody," I said. "Jesus Christ ain't no friend of mine. All He's done is nothing, while his Pa gone and took vengeance on me, killing everyone I know. Oh, why was I ever born?"

I was wailing and banging my fists on the wall to make them bleed.

Alley told me to stop, and slapped me hard against the face when I didn't. She gave me a handkerchief to blow on and said, "Wait here."

She knocked on the door. Took her top hat off and held it to her breast while the key turned and she got let in.

She was in that room for what seemed like forever. I had my ear to the door but could make nothing out. Others did the same. Hands smelling of horseshit smoke and moldy clothes fell on my shoulder. Words come to my ear saying, "Don't worry Jonesy. I'll be your new friend when he's gone."

"Forget about him," said another in my other ear. "I'm your *true* friend Jonesy. I gave you my cheese that one time, recall?"

"What," said the other, "no you never did, you cheating prick, that was me, I gave it him."

"Don't call me words, you lying cock-sucker."

Then pushing and punching started, with me in the middle.

"Shut your traps," said Juan breaking it up, and holding me so. He took me away from the door and talked to me in private. "Just remember Jonesy," he said. "I found you. I rescued you. And it was me who was your first."

"You weren't my first nothing," I said, giving him the elbow. "And I don't know how you dare talk to me after my beating you that time." I tried pushing past him again but he got in my way.

"You didn't beat me," he said taking prisoner of my arm. "I let you win so I didn't have to kill you in front of the others."

"That's a lie!"

"It ain't a lie," he said. "It's the truth. And why you tried harming my boy anyhow?"

"What goddam boy?" I said tying to shake free. "I never done nothing to that ugly blue-eyed nancy of yours, now get off of me."

But he was strong, and held on to me tight. "My boy, my boy," he said shaking me. "That's my boy she got growing inside her belly is what I'm talking about, you dumbass little bastard."

"Oh well, bully for you," I said, and I went to bite him one.

The key turned, and Alley comes out.

I took my teeth out of Juan's arm, and he set me free.

We waited for her to speak.

"Well?" said Juan. "What's the situation? Is Raccoon dead?"

"No," she said. "He ain't dead."

I fell to my knees and cried like he was.

Juan put his hand on my shoulder and said to Alley, "So, how long before he gets to the other side?"

"I don't know," she said, "but he ain't got far to go. News is, the Muwekma folks are going take the critter back home with them. To the Rancheria, south of Frankie's bay."

I looked up and said, "What?"

"Jones, it's the only chance he's got. Evidently they got their own doc up there who deal with spirits, the kind Raccoon's people understand, and Chinese don't know shit about. Saul said you can go on up and say your good byes to him."

I got back on my feet, and dusted myself off.

Juan said, "I'll go with him," meaning me.

I could feel him on my back again. I pulled my arms close to my chest so I could get away.

"No," said Alley to him. "He said just Jones."

I ran upstairs to Raccoon, jumping over steps so I could get there faster.

I climbed the ladder to the hatch door. I lifted it up.

The sun burned my eyes. When my sight returned I saw him. Sitting up on the comfy bed. New blankets tucked around the mattress and everything. Two Muwekma women wearing white gowns were by him, feeding him from a bowl and petting his head like he was a pup. I took a long look at him. He wasn't even close to being dead.

I stood there waiting for him to pay me attention.

He was sat there smiling up at two pretty lady faces, while supping on soup, from a silver looking spoon.

I kicked at a piece of loose wood on the floorboards. It made a noise. But he heard nothing.

I stomped over to my bare board and jumped on it. It banged as I landed and made the kettle shake and fall. It ring ting tingled as rolled along the ground.

I lay down, on the board. Folded my arms, stared at the roof and waited.

"Hey Jonesy," he said, sounded fit as the devil. "Did you hear I nearly died?"

"I heard," I said. "And I nearly died after sleeping under that chair for three nights," and I raised my arm, and pointed to red mark where a long-tailed critter had got me. "We need to have words," I said to him, "in private."

He let a woman wipe his mouth with the handkerchief, then come over to my board.

I lit up a smoke.

One of his women told me to put it out.

I told her to go to hell and mind her own business.

"Be kind. They're nice," he said, sitting down next to me.

I spat on the floor and gave him snake eyes to look at. "What's going on?" I said.

"Nothing's going on," he said.

"Then what's all this talk of you playing turncoat and leaving?"

"I ain't playing turncoat," he said. "Looky here Jones, you'll never guess what but, It turns out they knowed my Ma. What's more is they said I could go back and live with them all. At the Rancheria, south of the city. I figure you can probably come too."

"What do you mean, 'probably'? Ain't you even asked them?"

"I ain't had a chance yet, but as soon as I do, I'm sure they'll say yes. I'll tell them we're brothers."

"Brothers?" I said. "Why, are they all blind?"

Raccoon laughed until he cried. I took another good long look at him, wiping happy tears from his eyes. His voice had fallen down low. His baby cheeks had gone and he had a manly jaw coming. Only it weren't all gawky and gangly and pimply like most around here. It was pleasing to look at. In fact he was getting comely. Which was the strangest thing I ever thought to see with sober eyes.

"Hey Jonesy," he said. "Let's do something. Just you an me."

I said, "What?"

"Give me your knife," he said.

"Why? What for?"

"Just, trust me."

I looked into his eyes for proof. When I saw he was for real, I got my White Wolf from my inside my jacket pocket.

As soon as he clapped eyes on it he said, "Hell Jones, that's Violet's knife."

"Well, it ain't no more," I said, polishing it up with my breath. "And I did not steal it if that's what you're thinking. But, I suppose if you must know my private business, I won it playing cards."

"Playing cards?" he said. "With Violet? I mean, Little Brother?"

"No," I said, testing the sharp edge on fingernail.

"Jesus Christ, Jonesy," he said, "it weren't that son-of-a-bitch Hakes was it?"

I kept my eye on the blade.

"Look Jones," he said, "there's something I been wanting to tell you. I wanted to tell you the other day and then I got sick and so I couldn't say nothing but, Jones. It's about Hakes, and you ain't going like hearing it."

I told him to never mind saying nothing about Mr. Navy-boy Hakes. I knew everything there was to know about him. "The truth is," I said, "I done being friends with him. Lying cock-sucker is what he really is, if the truth be told."

"He's more than that, Jonesy. He's the Devil in disguise." Then he tried telling me what he heard. I told him to say no more, for I already knew it, and I was done listening.

So, satisfied, he nodded and said, "All right." Then he lay his palm down on his lap, flat and wide and said, "Hold out your hand like this."

I said, "Why? What for?"

"Just do it," he said.

So, I did. Before I could protest, he flicked my knife open and tore the blade through my skin until a line of blood filled the cut. It ran like a slow red stream down my wrist. He then took the blade and did the same to his own hand. When his blood come a rising, he gripped my hand tight and together we pressed hard on each other's.

"Now we're Blood Brothers," he said to me. "That means our spirits are joined up forever."

"Forever?" I said. "But, what happens now?"

Before he could answer, two Muwekma men climbed into the room with Saul on their tail. I was told to get lost so I did. I waited down the hatch. Hanging on the ladder, looking up at the way back in.

The door lifted. A rush of light come and blinded me from above.

I skedaddled out the way of the Muwekma men climbing down: two tall dark bodies smelling of cedar smoke and meat.

Saul followed.

They all waited at the top of the stairs for the two women in white to come. They wrapped their skirts around their legs as the lowered themselves until their toes touched the ground.

I looked up at the brightness in the hatch above my head and waited. Then he comes. Climbing down from Jacobs ladder. Smelling clean and looking tall. One of the women brushed his hair with her hand and he smiled at her with glowing eyes. Raccoon put his fingers in with hers. The other woman wrapped a shawl around his shoulders and pressed him close to her bosom.

I waited for him to see me. He did not. I was over-shadowed by Saul and the other two men, standing in my way. I looked at my hand, wrapped up with a piece of dirty red cloth. It'd done a bad job, keeping our brothers' blood from running. I held it up at Raccoon to say hello.

He saw me. And did the same. As soon as those women caught sight of his bloody wrapped up hand, they started fussing and moaning. And gave me hard looks like it was all my doing.

When they all started heading down stairs, I realized Raccoon was leaving.

I stood alone at the top, looking at them going down. "Raccoon," I said, with my heart beating hard.

He was walking with his head leaning on a woman's shoulder. He turned to me and said, "Don't worry, I'll be back. Just make sure the fog and rain don't blow on the fish and make it moldy."

"Don't worry," I said, "I'll hang them over to the Billy stove."

"Yeah, but don't let them get smoked black. It'll turn them sour."

"I won't, I won't," I said. "I'll hang them to the back."

"Hang them to the back, all right."

"I know, I know, I just said I would. Hey Raccoon, I reckon they'll do fine in a potato pie come Christmastime. Did I tell you I make a fine potato pie? Boil up some Irish and onions. Let them cool down some. Mash it all up with your fingers. And it's just right for eating then. I reckon if we put the fish in, it'll be tasty. Tastier than beef pie any day."

And then, he was gone.

Part 3

Some weeks pass by

Chapter 26
Beat the Devil

It'd been slow as mules down Washington dock. Two jobs won, only four-bits earned. A potential customer passed me by. He was clean and looked spendy. I ran after him, hustling hard; starting high and beating down the price of the other kids chasing after him doing the same.

I pushed my way to him, hanging onto his coat tails. "Take ten minutes of your time at the most, mister," I said.

Some kid back of me gave me the boot from behind.

I got my elbow in his gut and he backed off. "Entertain you better than the rest," I said to the fella now I had his ear. "Faster service guaranteed with me."

He took one look at my face and snorted like a hog. His eyes wandered beyond my gaze, to another kid. A younger kid. With blue eyes and angel-face looks. Canny as a crow, he was. Saying he was seven when he was all of ten. Scoring more coin than all of us boys put together with that cunning device. Only yesterday he was on his bragging chair saying how a lawyer paid him two five gold dollars to dress up like the Blue Boy, hanging in the courthouse. Said all he had to do was stand on the dinner table singing "Oh, if I were but a boy again" and pretend to cry. Foul little shit he was. Words come out of his mouth that would have made the devil shy. And he was a gold digger. Offered free cock sucks to anyone who'd hand over his regular to him. So he was getting all kinds of valuable trinkets while dumbass punk boys like Juan went starving. He tried it on me and told him to go and fuck his own self.

"Never mind him," I said, to the Dead Eye now. "He don't know nothing about giving pleasure, whereas I know it all. Mister, you can pick any card up from my table. Any card. A no-hold game of Chase is what I'm offering you here, get me? Get what I'm saying there, mister? What do you say? Deal with me? You wont be disappointed. I guarantee it with my life."

But Dead Eye turned out to be a waste of my precious time. He shook me off his arm and went to that cunning son of a bitch standing over by himself looking pretty and lonesome like a young blue-eyed dog.

I spat on the ground close to where he stood, and ran off back to my crate and my tin of boot black calling out, "Shoe shine. Shoe shine. Two bits for the regular, seventy-five cents for the special service. Cost of a slug of whiskey sir, gets you the best shine you ever had, guaranteed. What do you say?"

A fishing boat docked up. Seagulls circled above, making noise over its open belly. Every now and they'd take a chance on the fisherman's pikes. Taking turns, diving down. Stealing themselves a silver body: shimmering and squirming in the overcrowded net.

At three o'clock the customs clock rang. Told my belly it was time for food. An army of black rain clouds was moving fast across the bay. Which meant no more business for a while. So it seemed like a good time to head up to Mackenzie's for some hot eats going cheap.

When I got to the corner of the road where I was heading, two of Saul's riders were there, wearing long black coats and mean looking guns. They had some fella cornered with their horses.

It was a fella called Strange Sticks.

"So where is he now?" a rider said. It was one of the Brothers. Jinx.

Sticks stood there stammering like a fool. "Last I saw him was yesterday at the tavern down Jefferson. I swear on my mother's grave I ain't seen or talked to him since."

"So why are you pissing yourself, if you ain't seen him?"

I did not wait around to find out who it was they were looking for. I pulled my hat down low over my eyes, and snuck in behind a gang of dockworkers heading for the tavern on Monroe.

The black cloud comes a-calling.

It burst, and rain poured down heavy on my head. Like everyone else I ran looking for cover when I heard someone call out, "Kid."

I turned and saw a fella standing in an alleyway. His face was unshaven. His eyes were hiding. His top hat was coming apart at the brim. He wore a dirty dustcoat, and was holding onto himself like he was dying.

I got ready to keep walking by. Then I heard my name.

"Jones. Kid, it's me."

I took a second look.

He lifted his hat up.

It was *him*. Sweet Virginia.

He had a black eye. His cheek was swollen and blue.

I went running to him. "Mr. Hakes!" I said. I went to put my arm around his shoulder. He winced and drew me back with him into the shadow. I looked at him close, all damp and dripping in rain. One of his eyes was closed up tight and puffed up like a fish's belly, the other was blood red and streaming tears.

"Jesus Christ, Mr. Hakes," I said. "What the hell happened to you? What, were you robbed?"

"Quiet," he said, moving out of the rain and under a dry roof. "Where you goddam been? Been looking for you for goddam hours."

"I was down Washington like I always am."

"I thought you worked Jefferson."

"No," I said. "You know I work Washington. Why you saying you think I work Jefferson for?"

"Jesus, shut up, shut up!" he said, looking up and down the road. "Saul around?"

"How would I know?" I snapped at him. But I could see he was fretting over something. "I saw his brother," I said.

"Which one?"

"The Jinx."

"Oh just my luck," he said. "Just my goddam luck. Someone must have cursed me for sure. Where's that devil now?"

I told him where, and said, "Are you in some kind of trouble with them? Are they after you?"

"Be quiet," he said, squeezing my shoulder tight. He looked out again for anybody coming, then turned to me. "Do I look bad?" he said.

"You look like you had a beating."

"Do I look real ugly?"

"Well, you don't look pretty."

"Jesus, is it so bad?"

"Don't fret none," I said, brushing the hair from his forehead. "The bruising will wear off. Then you'll be back to being handsome again."

"The thing is I had business with somebody important, somebody high up, with money, and I needed to be my best looking."

"Well, just explain you got robbed. Anyone would be forgiving."

"There ain't no such a thing as forgiveness in this shit hole town."

"It wouldn't be so bad if you had your navy things on. They got robbed too?"

"My whole life's been robbed."

"Looky here," I said, fixing his hat brim. "I saw a navy get up just like yours in the second hand on Columbia. I figured the fella must have died but…"

"Shut up," he said. "You trying to tempt fate on me? Devil's on my back enough as it is without you inviting the reaper along to keep him company."

"Sorry," I said. "What I meant was…"

"Thing is I owe people," he said wiping his good eye. "I damn owe people, who don't like being owed. I borrowed off of folks that don't like handing out something for nothing. I'm a dead man walking is what I am."

"No you ain't," I said. "You and me, we can get that train and get the hell out of here. Start over in San Marco."

"They know me in San Marco."

"Doesn't have to be San Marco. Can be any place. Can be up north. I heard tell Columbia's going be the new place. They found rocks of pure gold up on a river up there, and soon everyone's going to clear out of Frankie's Bay and head up to where they got snow for grass and whales the size of Kansas swimming in the sea. We can hitch a ride on board a whaler. You and me. Nobody else. Just us."

"You must have found a tree sprouting money instead of leaves," he said.

"I'll get some," I said. I reached in my pockets and handed him what I had, which wasn't much.

"Oh stop talking shit, will you," he said taking the coin from my hand. "Besides, I ain't never getting on another boat as long as I live. I hate the goddam sea."

I was about to remind him how he said he didn't when I heard, "Boy. You there, boy."

I jumped.

Standing at the end of the dark dripping alley was a well-fed man in a white hat and a long brown leather coat. He was holding an umbrella against the rain.

"There you are," he said, not looking at me.

I said nothing. I waited for Virginia. He said nothing neither. Only slid further back into the shadow and let the rain do the talking.

I saw Virginia was hiding, so I walked up to the fella.

He smelled of beef pie.

He gave me the once over about ten times running. "This is what you had in mind?" he said, looking to the shadow.

I followed his eyes back to Virginia hiding in the dark.

The rain was getting angry and calling on the thunderclouds to come and make hell-fire across the piss-yellow sky.

"Do you know the Pacific Hotel?" the fella said to me.

I caught sight of the fine white suit beneath his coat. He had thick gold rings squeezed on every knuckle of his fingers.

"Yessir. I think I know it," I said.

"Good. I'm looking for a boy to help me with my bags. Interested?"

I looked for his bags. He didn't have none. I looked to Sweet Virginia, to see what his eyes said. Even if I had seen them they would have told me nothing. They were so closed up they could not say a thing. His hands were busy digging in his pockets, fingering our small fortune: rustling my two-bits' worth of everything between his fingers. I wanted to go to him and say, "C'mon Mr. Hakes, let's cut and run from this city and all this Dead Eye shit!" But that Daddy was dripping in gold. Gold rings, gold buckle, gold watch chain peeking through his clean white jacket. Everything about him said white picket fence and high living. His beard was cut smart. Which meant he saw a barber every day. His eyes were all lined, as you would expect from a gold digger who'd been out in the desert sun too long and who was pretty close to being an old-timer. His cheeks showed he'd had the smallpox at some time in his life. But being ugly didn't mean nothing. Being rich did.

I looked behind me, to Sweet Virginia. I ran to him. I put my hand to his arm.

He forged a smile.

I shot a fast look at the Gold Daddy. Then moved closer into the shadow with Virginia.

"Mr. Hakes," I said, "I'm going to get us a ticket out of here. Tomorrow, we'll be on that train going anyplace. Any place away from here, I promise you." And I kissed his ear, and his cheek, and I could not find a word big enough to say what I felt for him right then, so I said, "I love you, Mr. Hakes," instead.

And he said a whole lot of nothing. When I went to kiss his

lips he turned his head and said, "Ain't you got a job to do?"

So I let him go.

When I neared the end of the alley, I turned to give him a last look and held up my hand to say goodbye. He gave me a little nod.

I turned back to the Gold Daddy. Took the umbrella from his hand. Held it over his head to save him from the rain, and headed up to Pacific Hotel.

Chapter 27
The Golden Daddy

When we got to the hotel, I could see it was all class. No drunks or panhandlers anywhere. The outside was painted white and there were fancy posts holding up the roof. A union flag was laying low up top, dripping in the rain. There were velvet blue curtains on the windows, and polished brass railings along steps. A fella dressed in a red jacket, with white gloves and a top hat, was there to greet him. He held the door open bowing and nodding at the Golden Daddy like he was the president of everything.

We went inside. The carpet was like a Chinese vase. It stretched from every corner of the entrance hall: a red sea set with yellow roses and thorny leaves. High polished shoes shuffled across it. And big words about the benefits of war and the rising price of everything hummed over it. Somewhere, stringed up instruments played. Not barn dance music. Or the kind you hear fiddling down dockside. But dreamy, colorful music, as my ears had never heard before.

I looked up.

I saw a chandelier. There was enough candlepower to brand

a poor boy's eye. A high-class dame dressed in shiny silk and smelling of perfume caught Daddy's eye. She had a boy helping her too. He was dressed like a music box monkey and holding onto a bunch of hatboxes staked too high for small hands.

The old Daddy tipped his hat and said, "Mam."

She nodded and said, "Mr P," and they asked how fine each other was. And would he be coming to the Governor's Ball?

He would.

And wouldn't that be a delight for her and her husband, Sir "so and so", from "such and such". For any occasion without the presence of his honorable big daddy self was just a terrible bore. Oh! And did he know that "so-and-so", with that wife of his, and that child of unknown paternity was coming?

No, he did not.

And fie fie fie, for shame! What a scandal that story was. For she had all the intel.

He looked forward to hearing all about it.

And she looked forward to telling it.

I looked at the boy. A hatbox squishing up against his nose. His eyes slid to mine.

I smiled.

He slid them back to the box.

She said her goodbyes waving a lacy fan in front of her cheeks and rustled off up the long windy stairs, with a high polished railing, to her boudoir, as she called it.

Daddy slid his coat off and handed it to me. He peeled his gloves off one finger at a time and held them and his cane out for me to take. I juggled his things in my arms, like an entertainer in the square, until everything was steady, then I followed him up the windy stairs.

My hat was wet. It was dripping down my face. I looked all around me. The walls were covered in silver grey stripes. There were paintings of people, in gold laurel frames. They were following me with their beady eagle eyes.

"Damn," I said to the old Daddy, "you could probably buy a horse for what they charge a whole night to stay this place.

Most folks down dockside think sleeping's what saloons are for. Cheaper to buy six shots of whiskey and get your head down on the table for the night."

"You always talk so much?" he said to me.

"No sir. I hardly ever speak at all."

"Good," he said.

We got to his room. Daddy unlocked the door and went in. I followed.

Once over the threshold, he locked the door behind me. He took the key. He put it in his pants pocket. Then changed his mind and hid it someplace else.

I stood there waiting: a dripping coat stand with feet.

My hat was wet and loose, and falling over my eyes. I watched him from underneath. He was polishing up a fancy wood box with his handkerchief. "Hang them over there," he said, pointing to a brass pole with hooks over by a dresser that looked newly made.

I went and done what he said. Smoothing out his long leather jacket as I did so. And wiping the moisture off his hat with my sleeve. Which was wet, and left a mark. I tried spitting on it and rubbing it with my shirt-tail to get the dirt out. That failed, so I checked around my pockets for my handkerchief.

"Leave that and get your things off," he said to me.

So I did. I left my hat on, but took my coat and went to hang on the hook next to his.

"Not there," he said.

There was a velvet chair sitting in the corner. I went to lay my jacket on it.

"Not there either," he said.

So I held it in my hands while I looked for someplace else.

I saw the bed. A big one: enough for at least three people and one at the bottom. The railings had been polished high. I caught sight of my face in the bed knob: as comely as a wet stray dog.

I went to hang my coat up on it, when I caught his eye. It was a hard look. So I kept hold.

I went to lay it on the carpet.

"No," he said.

I moved to where there were only nail boards, and put my coat down there. And he said nothing. Which meant it was all right.

I stood there saying nothing, counting on the clock's ticking. I watched him tinkering with the brass latch on the fancy box of his. It was one of them that had another kind of wood laid in it to make it look expensive. He paused to scratch his chin. His whiskers were nearly all white. He put on a pair of eyeglasses. I figured they were made of diamonds and pure gold.

"Mister," I said, "Do you want me to talk business now?"

He said nothing. He was busy thinking. And staring at the fancy box in front of his eyes.

He put his hands in his fine white tailored pockets and soon I heard the familiar jingle of coin.

I waited to see what he had to offer.

When he took out two five-dollar coins and dropped them both onto the bed table, my knees nearly give way.

Ten dollars of gold. Ten whole dollars of gold in minted coin. I watched them shiny tickets to happy fortune flicker and dance and sing "glory halleluiah" to my ears when they fell down on the table. I could smell the forge still on them. I looked up to heaven. "Oh Lord," I said to Jesus, "Grant me just one of them beauties, and from now on I promise you, I'm taking to church on a Sunday. I'll tell Virginia there ain't no more fucking on a Sunday, only churching from now on. God be praised."

Daddy had been watching me praying. When he caught my eye, he snapped his eyes shut and said to me, "How old are you?"

"Pa said fifteen years living come Christmastime."

"That's a disappointment," he said, "I was led to believe you were younger."

"I can be, Mister, "I said. "Hell, I'll be however old you want for the right price. Twelve. Nine. Just roll the dice, I'll be any number you call."

"Is that so," he said, his spectacles hanging low on his nose. He'd turned to his pocket watch. Had it opened up and was winding up the spring to make it living. He wore a heavy frown as he did so, breathing loud through his open mouth. "Out of curiosity," he said, "what deal were you planning to offer. What's my generosity worth to you?"

I was no dumbass; I knew he weren't thinking of parting with that whole ten dollars. It was only there to show he meant business. And he was willing to pay. So, I figured it was time I raised my usual price. I reckoned on how much two tickets to San Marco would fetch started higher. "Five dollars gets you ten minutes of pure pleasure," I said, "the kind of pleasure, you ain't never had the like of. Guaranteed. Five dollars. A solid five."

"I know plenty of low life degenerates who'll do the same for no cost at all," he said, snapping his watch shut. He put it in his top pocket. The gold chain hung down like a King Midas lasso.

"Mister," I said, "if you don't mind. I ain't no degenerate. I ain't nothing like that. I know I look the poor sort, but, the truth is, my things is getting done at the wash house, so I'm only wearing these rags on account of waiting on time."

He paid me no heed at all. Then lifted up the lid of the box and kept it open. It was a small version of a music box. I could see the brass pin with all the studs on it for making music. I reckoned it must have been worth at least two fine-bred horses, and the rest.

"Now," he said, to me while looking at his little piano. "What I would like is for you to remove your clothes, place them neatly on the floor, and lie down on the bed facing the wall."

"Now hold on, mister," I said. "We got to talk business first."

He left his singing box and looked at me hard. Took the glasses off his head and put them in his jacket pocket next to his gold watch.

"You have trouble understanding words?" he said to me.

"Nossir," I said.

"Then follow my instructions carefully. I want you to remove your clothes, place them neatly on the floor, lie down on the bed facing the wall and stay quiet. One thing I do not like is unnecessary noise. Now get your things off, and do as I ask." Then he turned from me again. And opened up the top drawer of the dresser the music box was sitting on.

"Mister," I said. "I understand you want to do a deal. But, I can't do something for nothing. I can only accept coin or something of similar value. Something I can turn over in a jiffy. Like one of them five dollar coins you got lying there. The truth is my Pa ain't well. And I got to take him on the 9:15 to San Marco tomorrow morning for his life's sake. Now I figure two tickets is about five dollars. And for five gold dollars I'm talking the best pleasure a fella ever had in his entire life. Because I treat a fella like he's the president. So I do more than just the regular. I do other while I'm doing too. All kinds of other. To give a fella pure pleasure guaranteed. That's how good I give it, and that's how good I'd give it to you. I swear to Jesus: this is going to be the best pleasure you ever had in your whole life."

I watched him. He wore snake eyes and rode them all over me, up and down, and up and down again. A drop of spit fell from his lip and landed on silky rug. He wiped it off his mouth with his tongue. He lifted his chin at me and scratched his silver beard. "I hear you're an orphan," he said. "Lodge with those Mexican bandits: The Suarez brothers. Is that correct?"

I could tell by his words he did not approve of their company, so I said, "Mister, that is a lie. I don't know nothing about no Mexicans, no brothers, no nothing. Now, about this deal?"

"Tell me of yourself, son," he said.

And they were strange words to my ears. So much so that I stopped and looked at him with new eyes.

"Well sir, the truth of it is, Me and Pa come to California looking for honest work. We were meant to get off at San Marco but hitched the wrong boat…"

"Your father white?"

"Sir?" I said.

"Your father. The man who sired you. Is he a white man?"

I thought about it and said, "I ain't never got to asking. Thing is sir, we landed here at Frankie's Bay instead of where we were supposed to be going. Now he's got sick and I'm only trying to get solid coin together so as we can get back to San Marco."

"What about your mother?"

"I don't know nothing about her," I said.

"Not a squaw, is she?" he said. "I thought I made it quite clear that I detest the red skin. And the Mexican. Cuban is tolerable. The Puerto Rican also. A certain complexion of Negro has the most charm and delights of the races." Then he walked up to me, pinched my chin as he lifted it, and rolled his eyes over my face. He said, "Perhaps you're a mulatto's bastard. Either way, you're not of pure blood. No white boy would talk as you do. Unless his brain had been injured. At birth or some unfortunate fever or accident. Do any of those apply to you?"

"I had the fever not long back."

"Degeneracy is an unnatural trait of the white blooded man animal. However, it is found in its abundance in the colored races. You are not white if your blood is mixed with a colored. So you have no business posing as a white if that is so. Do you understand?"

I nodded at the daddy's words, apologized, and slid my eyes to those two shiny gold coins of fortune.

"I have no love for the Mexican, "he carried on saying, turning away from me and jingling more coin in his pockets.

"I ain't from Mexico," I said. "The truth of it is, mister, I ain't never been south of the Wichita. They're Kansas folk. Pa and me hung with them awhile although I ain't one of them. They called me White Bones on account of me being of the white-blooded sort, and said I carried dead spirits with me. So Pa and me had to sleep outside the whole time. Except for when it was winter. Then they'd showed kindness and let us set in a corner by the fire."

"I cannot tolerate the Mexican," he said, polishing his glasses, "I have no respect for men who cannot decide matters of business for himself, especially when a fair deal is lying on the table staring him in the face. It's the sign of a yellow belly." And he looked at me.

"I ain't no yellow belly, sir," I said.

"No?"

"No," I said, shaking my head to make it come true. "So now, mister, was that a rub or a suck you'd be wanting today? Five-dollar coin. Fifteen minutes of pure pleasure. Best you ever had. I guarantee it."

Daddy put on a frown that weighed heavy on his face and made his cheeks fall down. "You would charge me five dollars," he said, "For you, a mongrel, to pleasure yourself in such a way with my person."

I saw I was losing fast. "Okay, fine," I said, "A fuck. Fifteen minutes. Five dollars. Best you ever had. Just the other day a fella offered me a hunk a gold the size of that music box right there for to have me so. That's how sought I am in town. And I'm a man about it too. I guarantee you ain't never had a boy as good as me. I ain't hardly ever done it neither, understand what I'm saying? But I did enough times for a fella not to be uncomfortable when he's doing it, if you get my drift. Five dollars. How's that?"

His bottom lip bulged out like a frog. His face went red and shook like a steaming kettle ready to blow.

Then, to my surprise, he shook his head and said, "This is not how I wanted it." Then he went to the door. Took out his key, unlocked it. Stood holding it open saying, "Get out."

My heart sunk to my shoes.

"Why?" I said. "What I say?"

"That's the thing with your kind," he said, "it's all filth with you. Now, leave. Go on, get out."

"Sir," I ran to him. "Mister, wait, we can do another deal. A better deal." I grabbed his sleeve. I held my fingers up. "Four dollars. Fifteen minutes. I won't say no more coarse words I promise you."

"You are not at all what I asked for," he said. "I was told you were a clean white boy. What you are is a degenerate and a mongrel."

"I'm a clean white boy," I said. "I swear I am. Pure as snow is me. I swear to Jesus on my knees I am." And I got on my knees to prove it so. "A clean white boy. Twelve years living. Ten years living. It's just I can't do numbers well and Pa told me to say I was older, that's all. Here's a new deal," I said. "Three dollars." I held my fingers up again. "Fifteen minutes. Nobody can beat that."

He only stared down at me, looking angry.

"Oh, fool me!" I said. "Mister, you ain't seen my hair yet." I put my hand to my hat, lifted it off my head, and all my hair fell down to my shoulders. "Some say I look just like the Blue Boy hanging up at the law house, only not quite so fair. Fella paid me five dollars, " I says smiling, "just to dress up as such, and stand there singing God Bless the Flag."

Then he comes around. His dead eyes comes a-looking for me. His mouth dripping down likes a rabid dog. His chest going: chug a lug, chug a lug. He laid his gold ringed hand on my head. Began brushing my hair behind my ear, and rubbing it messy all over my scalp. When he pressed my body tight against his hips, I could tell he was hard up for the sport. He took hold of my chin, and pulled my lip down so my teeth showed.

I looked up at him with my eyes wide open like a lone, lost pup. "Three dollars." I said. "Ten minutes of pure pleasure sir, and three dollars is all."

He let go of my chin.

I took hold of his hand. "I won't disappoint you, I never disappoint a body, no sir."

"I will be the decider on that," he said, looking me down.

"Shake with me sir," I said, clinging to his fat fingers. Rolling in gold. "Three dollars for ten minutes of pure pleasure."

And so I won.

With the deal sealed, he shut the door, and hid the key again someplace on his person. He pointed to the bed and said, "Go do as I said. Right way now boy."

I went to the bed, stripped off my clothes and, with my back to him, got my thing fired up hard so as to look like I was keen. All the time I was frigging, I kept checking with my head to make sure he didn't see me cheating.

He was at his music box again. I heard him wind it up. It played a familiar tune. A union song, about glory and virtue, courage and swords. Men fighting and dying for the fatherland. The Gold Daddy was humming along to it, going, "Dum, dum dum, bom, bom, bom." Tapping on the dresser like it was a piano board. Undoing his tie. Hanging up his white jacket, while stepping on mine and kicking it someplace else on the floor.

I was lying down like he said, "right way", which I took to mean right side up, with my back to the mattress: soft with feathers. "I did not say to lie like that," he hollered. "Not a good sign if a boy can't follow simple instructions now, is it?"

I apologized for being a dumbass and turned around, belly down. Hung my head over the brass and looked to the floorboards.

The music box played and him went, "Dum diddy dum."

I tapped my fingers on the rail to the beat. Heard him undoing his belt.

"Done this before, you say?" he said.

I did not know what answer he wanted to hear so I played dumb. Then before I knew nothing, I felt a sharp poke go up and I flinched so. Next thing Daddy starts fishing around up there, inside of me, with what has to be his fingers, or so I figures at the time.

"Sodomite," he says. "As I thought."

My ears burned fiery red at hearing those words, which did not belong to me. Only some worshipping Devils living in Hell.

Next thing fat old Daddy's on top of me and for a moment I could not breathe. I pulled myself up a little further, so part of my chest was hanging over the bed. But old Daddy yanked me back down hard, and got me how he wanted me. Then starts going in. And I weren't a dumbass no more. I fucked enough times with Sweet Virginia to know a thing or two about a thing, so I thinks right then, I had a pretty solid idea of what was coming next. But I was wrong. For if I'd have known what was coming, I would have bolted out the window, jumped two stories down to the road below. When it did come, it was like an angry bull on a cattle ranch fucking a body hard. I thought I would scream. Put my hands to my mouth to stop me doing so. All the while, old Daddy sweating hogs on top of me. Sliding in his own juice. Taking long pauses to catch his breath—for he's too fat for the business—then starts hammering at me again. Not like Virginia's going easy. Not like him at all. More like a mad-dog crazy would do a whore after paying her minder to put cotton in her ears, and look the other way. He calls me a degenerate and filthy little sodomite, which becomes his favorite words for me. After he stops for breath a third time, I knows for certain what's coming next. My eyes fill up with tears thinking of it. And, every time I tries prying myself away, clawing my way to the edge of the bed, that son of a Satan's bitch pulls me back down. Swearing at me. Starts thumping me in the arms. Lays a heavy blow into the low of my back just above my hipbone.

I couldn't help it, I cried out.

Daddy punches me in the shoulder to shut me up.

My chin was trembling like a broken branch in the westerly wind. Sweet Virginia's name fell from my lips. I begged him to come and break the door down. I watched that door and made myself see him coming through it, with a Colt .49 raised high in his hand.

"Goddam son of Satan's bitch," he says to old fat Daddy. He puts that gun to the old Daddy's head and blows the back of his skull clean off and all his brains go spewing everywhere, turning his clean white jacket into bloody red rags.

I come back from my waking dream. I looked over to where my pants were. Made myself stop crying so I could see them well. They were lying on the floor, with my Sweet Virginia's pocket knife tucked inside the back pocket for safety. Which was no use to me at all, right now. So I lay there quiet, like a critter playing dead. Praying inside my head to Jesus, Mary, and all the angels in heaven to come make that fella hurry up and spew. And after what seemed a hell of a lot longer than any ten goddam minutes—my prayers were answered. And he was done.

Chapter 28
Hoodwinked

Daddy rolled over and I could breathe again. I lay there, my face still staring at the nail-boards. I played chance and turned my head. I saw him. Lying on his back. Puffing and blowing like a steam engine. His pockmarked face all purple and red and covered in sweat. I watched him with his pants undone, one hand over lying on his cock. The other on his forehead. Breathing heavy, like he'd climbed the mountain and stole a river of gold.

I slid off the bed. Everything felt sore. I picked up my clothes from all over the floor, and got ready to put my property back on. First thing I did was pull out my handkerchief. I wiped my ass clean and saw there was both blood as well as shit. I put my hand to my mouth to stop myself from screaming.

I took my hankie, and plugged up my hole. Sobbed without tears, not knowing what the hell was happening. Thinking how women bleed. Thinking how I done wrong. Fucking my head off like a whore with the Golden Daddy full of shit.

I turned to the door. I wanted just to run right through it. Get back to Sweet Virginia, with them ten dollar coins held tight in my hand. Tell him what the old mad dog daddy done. And we'd wait for him later. Get when he was unawares. Hogtie him up. Drop him in a sack full of stones and horse-draw him down to the bay. Push him in the water. Watch him sink down to hell.

I looked at them two gold five dollars. I looked at the Golden Daddy full of shit. And I knew the Lord loved me. For the Sons of Jesus, down the doss house on Columbia, told me so just the other day. "He loves poor folks," preacher told me. "It's the richies he ain't proud of. They got a better chance of poking a needle's hole than getting into heaven." Which meant they had no chance at all. So if I was to get caught, saving Sweet Virginia's life, with those two gold coins, then I was going straight to heaven when I die. For Jesus ain't approve of no law but the one his daddy put down to Moses. And Virginia and me were going straight to heaven no matter what the man's law says.

I stepped up to the gold dollars. I brushed my fingers over the face on them. I looked up at the Gold Daddy.

He was still asleep. Snoring like a broken horn on a hog's head.

I saw his watch hanging on the bed knob. I flicked it open to see the ticking of my time. I closed it up and held it tight.

Daddy stopped snoring. He was just laying there, his arm still stuck to his forehead. He had his eyes open. He was staring at me. And his gold watch held prisoner in my hand.

"I was just looking on the time," I said, letting go.

Daddy took his arm away from his eyes, and started doing up his waistband. Lifted his hog head to see what he was doing. Pulled a new face that made him look like a toad.

He was trying to pull the two ends together, but they would not cooperate. He grunted and sat up and sighed.

"Come here and do me up," he said.

I'd turned my thinking now to getting paid and getting the hell out. So, I got beside him. Got on my hands and knees, and pulled and tugged at the two ends of his unmentionables until they met, pressing hard with my fingers to get the buttons forced through the holes.

"Now my boots," he said.

I lined up boot with foot, slid on, pushed hard, and took the whole force against my chest, until nice and snug. Then I did the same with the other. Figuring I'd done a fair job, I sat back on my heels, swept my hair behind his ears. Laid my hand open, hoping I'd see at least three silver dollars fill the empty space. All the while I kept smiling at him. Smile, smile, smiling; with my shiny white teeth.

Gold Daddy took his time.

He lit his cigar.

Tick, tick, tick. Took

More time pulling on it.

Tock, tock, tock.

All the while, I was sweating to get out.

At long last, he put his hand in his pocket. Coins jingled and fell into my own.

I shot up, headed over to the corner, to the window, where the sound of rain and seabirds, and the crazy hustle bustle of Frankie's Bay made for warm comfort.

I stood counting my hard won earnings.

When I finished summing it all up, I stopped and stared into my hand. The count was wrong. It weren't no three dollars. I was tired, that was it. I must have added up incorrectly. So I did it again. Now there was less than the first count. That can't be, I said. How can that be?

I spun around on my heels. "Mister, you made a mistake," I said. "This is only a dollar and a half worth you give me here."

Daddy sat, hunched over, wearing his gold-rimmed spectacles and busy winding up his watch. "No," he said, "you have been paid correctly."

"No, mister," I said, "I ain't."

He stood up and faced himself in the mirror. "Son," he said, doing up his collar, "you stated your fee as being three dollars for twenty minutes, am I correct?"

I said yes.

"That's what I thought had been agreed. So, you have been paid correctly."

I said, "What? What are you talking about mister? How's that, when I'm only holding one dollar and a half in my hand?"

He turned to me doing up his tie. "Because son, it only took ten minutes, not twenty as I agreed to. That's why."

"It only took ten minutes?" I said. "What only took ten minutes? I don't get you?"

"Well, I can tell here by my timepiece, that it was exactly ten minutes to the hour when I began and it was exactly on the same hour when I was done. That is precisely ten minutes according to the laws of chronology. Not twenty. So the correct price is one dollar fifty."

I felt my face go red. My heart started flapping in my throat. My fists tightened, my mouth went dry. There was a clock-face on the building opposite to the hotel. I ran over to the window to see it. It read an hour's time past from when I first got there. "Now looky here mister," I said. "I been here till the next hour's come and gone. So it took longer than any ten minutes. The problem is your goddam watch is wrong."

"My watch is not wrong," he said. "I set the time before proceedings commenced. Twenty minutes you agreed. Ten minutes is what transpired."

"Now looky here mister, " I said, "it don't matter how long it took you. It's three dollars. That's how much this here cost." And I pointed to the bed.

"Well, it seems to me," he said, fixing his cuffs and shaking down his sleeves, "that you don't know how to do proper business. You're selling all wrong, son. You need to state that it's three dollars for the service you are offering. And explain that the maximum time is twenty minutes. Otherwise you can't then go blaming the customer if he calls you on it."

All I heard was *I been cheated, I been had!*

I felt for the knife in my back pocket.

"Now you listen here, mister," I said, creeping up to him. "You got what you paid for. Don't matter how long it took to get it over with, now give me the rest of my goddam money."

"You know," he said, facing me. "You have one hell of a foul mouth. And it is a shame. A real shame."

"What are you talking about," I said. "Why? Why is it a real shame?"

He ignored me and went to the window. Threw it open. Called down below: "Thompson."

"Yes, Mr. P," said a voice from below.

"Go and get Joeb for me. I got a problem up here."

I held the wolf knife behind me.

Daddy nodded to my hidden hand and held out his. "Give it to me son, or you'll be in more trouble than you already are."

I kept hold and backed up toward the door. "One thing I ain't, mister, and that's your goddam son." I put my back to the door and used my free hand to jostle the doorknob. As soon as I did I felt the lock go and the door blew open, knocking me down.

A couple of big fellas pushed through together and grabbed hold of me right away. First thing they did was steal my knife. Handed it to the Daddy. Stole my money and handed that to him too. Took my precious coin and stuffed it in his pocket. Took my knife and began looking it over like he was going to buy it. Stared at me like I was a criminal. Tapped my knife in his hand like it was his. Passed it back to one of the fellas and said, "See this gets back to who it belongs to."

I said, "It belongs to me."

"Does it now?" said the Daddy, stepping up close to me, being held prisoner by his two thugs. "I suppose my timepiece belonged to you too?" he said.

I spat at his shoes.

A thug slapped me in the back of my head and I howled.

"Well, you are a poor thief," Daddy said, getting close.

"Thief?" I cried. "Where'd you get that from? I ain't no goddam thief."

"Son," he said. " I caught you eyeing my gold watch when we first met. I saw your eyes on my gold watch not two minutes ago. You've been coveting my belonging the whole time. I turned my back to pay him," he said to his boys, "and he had it in his hand."

"I was only looking on the time," I cried, "Looking ain't the same as stealing. I ain't no goddam thief."

"You use that language in front of me one more time, " he hollered, "and I'll get Joeb here to beat you for it. Take him out of my sight," he said to my guards.

I protested like I had never protested before. Kicking and yelling and getting beat all the while. They treat me like I was a prisoner for the Gaul. Tied my hands up with burny rope and smacked me all around, dragging me down the staircase. Dragging me through the hotel door, then the hotel hallway with everybody in the world staring at me and pointing at me, going, "Tut tut tut," to the Devil. Into a kitchen full of fine smelling food, and cooks shouting and banging pans. Threw me out the back door so I landed on my knees. Scraping them all to pieces. Pushed me out another door, and all the way back to Union Square, to the Sheriff's, and his Devil's house of bars.

Chapter 29
Jailhouse Floyd

They dragged me inside the jailhouse, and stood me outside one of two iron bar cages. I could smell the prisoners in one of them were drunks. Two of them appeared to be sleeping it off. The deputy on duty searched through a big ring of keys for the right one. In the other cage, a dark shadow of a man stood with his back to the wall.

"Judgment day's a coming," he said.

Sheriff freed my hands. They were biting sore, but I could do nothing about it.

"Get to the back, Floyd," said Sheriff.

"Lord's gonna burn this town to the ground, and everybody in it.", he replied.

Sheriff told Deputy to unlock the prison bars. He, in turn, wrestled with a jangle of keys until he found the right one. "Deputy unlocking the bars," he said.

Sheriff gripped my arm tight and stood me by the cage.

"Deputy done unlocking the bars."

I dug my feet into the floor.

"This town's a shameless whore," said Floyd. "Full of wanton desires and sinful hungers of the flesh. God's retribution gonna come, Clarence."

"So you keep saying, now to the back I said."

Floyd's feet made noise in the straw as he moved deeper into the cage.

"Deputy opening the doors."

The cage door creaked and groaned. "Deputy done opening the doors."

"Thy will be done oh Lord," sang Floyd from the darkness. "Thy will be done."

Sheriff pulled me closer toward the cage, but I stayed stuck to the ground. He then lifted me up by the back of the arms and forced me to move. I tried pulling free. But he had tight hold of me. And tried forcing me inside the cage. I clung to the bar door, and put my foot against the iron so to stop me getting hauled in. I got booted in the back of the knee, and I came down. I was lifted again. Then thrown inside: banged up, locked up with crazy-headed Floyd singing songs of damnation.

I stood staring at two walls, a ceiling I could touch with my hand, a bucket for shit, and a floor full of hay that stunk of piss. I was like that bear they had locked up Southside for baiting Monday. My eyes locked on Floyd. His face was sweating. His head was shaved—looked like he'd done it himself. His eyes were carved deep into his skull, and were looking straight at me.

"I got the Devil out of her," he said to me. "She'll be breeding no more demons. I done cleansed her with my seed."

I backed up to the bars. I turned around and pushed my nose through the iron saying: "Sheriff, sir, I swear on Jesus' grave I ain't done nothing wrong."

"He ain't able to hear you," said Floyd.

I grabbed hold of the bars and spoke louder.

"Sheriff sir, if only you'd send a body over to Gunnybags. And get my brother. His name's Mattie Hakes. He's serving the Union Navy. He'll tell you I ain't never stole nothing in my life. Sir—"

"Devil gave them mule ears. So all they hear is noise. Except for the call to sin."

I watched Sheriff: sitting, with his legs up on the desk, playing cards with Deputy. Pouring out whiskey from a bottle. Talking about the bear bait, and what dog was going to win.

Floyd comes up close from behind. "What you in for, boy? Thieving is it?"

I said nothing.

"They'll string you up for it," he said. "Now the Hanging Judge is in town. When's the last time you done and prayed?"

I put my face to the bars. "Sheriff," I said, "sir. Please, be kind to a poor soul. Listen to me, will you? Please?"

Floyd took possession of my hand and said, "Come here boy. Pray with me, son. I'll learn you to ask the Lord forgiveness."

"Get off me," I said, "Jesus, get off me!" And I wrestled my hand free.

"Leave the boy alone Floyd," said Sheriff, "or I won't read from the Good Book when your time comes. And I mean that."

"Clarence, I"s only trying to save the boy from eternal damnation. Give me that at least, will you?"

"It's your soul that needs attention, Floyd. If I were you, I'd get praying. Come dawn, you'll know if you've been successful. Or not." Him and deputy chuckled.

"Now why'd you go and say that for?" said Floyd, his eyes going wide and his jaw shaking. "The Lord in Heaven ain't never gonna abandon me. He loves me like his own son. I am his soldier. His warrior. Prepared to fight for the side of heaven. Not like you all. Bunch of Satan's whores. Bunch of buck nigger lovers. It's all them niggers and chinks and red skin heathens that's made this place what it is: a shameful, naked place. Sinful. Full of sinful hungers. And demon breeders. You are all gonna burn. All of you. Every single one." Then he started wailing tears. When he'd done, he started hollering again. He ran up to the bars. Started banging his whole body against them, like a wounded bear, trying to escape the bait. When his coals ran out, he clung to the iron and cried sad like a child. He turned to the darkness and held his hand out to me. Begged me to take it.

I shrunk back into the shadow. Crept toward the far dark end of the cage, and held on tight to those cold iron bars.

It was nightfall, and I was aching tired. I waited for Floyd to go asleep. When he did it were all fits and starts, full of angry moaning and weeping. I stayed upright, watching out.

My stomach was cramped up, and I hadn't stopped feeling the need to shit since the hotel. When I saw Floyd was in a quiet moment of slumber, I took the opportunity to get rid of the rag I had stuffed up my ass. I pulled it out. It was messy. I buried it underneath the straw, and wiped my hands clean with the hay too. I tore a piece of cloth from my Johnnies, and stuffed my hole back up with it. As I did, I thought about a story I heard, about how when women bleed, they stuff rags up their woman's hole. And here I was, having let myself get fucked like a whore for nearly nothing. Leaking like a woman too.

Corked up a fresh, I took a last look at Floyd. Then making sure he was out for the count, I curled up by the bar door. Lay my head against my knees, and tried to sleep.

I must have nodded off. I hadn't been unconscious long when the sound of puking guts woke me up. It was coming from the cage next door. One of the drunkards. It stopped. I dozed off again. Then a second noise woke me. One of the drunkards started singing. About a man waiting to get hanged. It seemed he'd killed the wrong fella by mistake. And now he was sorry. Because he'd never ride his horse, taste Ma's biscuits, or hear Mary Lou singing hymns on a Sunday ever again. I wanted to cry. I held on to the bars to see the fella singing. He stopped, and started crying for me.

Next morning, the smell of hot food woke me up. I got to my feet. Day broke through the window and shined on my face. Deputy had a basket of hot vittals in his hands. He was giving to the drunkards. They were saying thank you. Floyd was behind me. I pulled my arms close to my body and told him to get the hell away from me. But he was only interested in the food that was being dished out. When Deputy comes our way he put his arms out to take his meal through the bars. When he got it, he moved to the back of the cage and started eating likes a dog. My mouth was dripping. My belly was growling and biting at my insides. Deputy shoved corn bread and a piece of bacon in my hand and I wanted to kiss his fingers for the kindness, but he was quick to get away. There was a tin of water outside the iron for me to drink. After stuffing the cake in my mouth I carefully lifted up the cup so as not to tip it over, and drank every drop to quench my thirst. I saved the bacon for last on purpose. Jesus Christ, the meat was tasty. The salt burned my tongue. My belly was happy now it had hot food sitting in iFloyd hadn't bothered with his tin of water, so I stole it for myself. As I drank, I heard the sounds of a cage door being opened. Then sheriff told the two drunkards to get lost.

I put the tin down, wiped the grease off my lips and licked my hands clean. I was dying for a piss but that meant heading over to the Floyd's part of the cage. So I held on. Wondered if they'd be moving me to the free cage any time soon. Away from crazy-headed Floyd. But they didn't come. Just went back to playing cards and smoking fine-smelling tobacco. And sipping whiskey alongside their tins of coffee.

I felt like sleeping again. But Floyd was wide awake and talking to somebody only he could see. Just like Pa used to. When the Angel come. At one point Floyd and his unseen friend got to fighting. Floyd gave him a blow with his fist and everything. Then they weren't on speaking terms no more.

And every thing was quiet again.

Then comes an almighty bang, like an explosion, as somebody boots the jailhouse door open.

I stood up to see what was going on. A bunch of long coats carrying guns burst into the room.

There, behind the bars, I saw in front of me, the tall, dark shape of Saul Suarez. Surrounded by sunlight: the angel Gabriel, come to deliver my body from Satan's paw. Two of his brothers: Boney, and the Jinx, was by his side.

"Well, well, well," he says to Sheriff. Hands on his hips, wearing a smile that made his teeth shine. "So it was not a lie.

You really are the new law around here after all. Old pie-eyed Clarence McGovern. How's your pretty wife doing these days, Clarence?"

Sheriff kept his mouth shut.

"And looky here," he said, turning on his heel to see Deputy. "If it ain't Longjaw DeJong. Hell, and I thought you were dead already. Jinxy, didn't you think Longjaw was dead already?"

The Jinx rustled up Deputy, looking for weapons that might be out of sight. "The day's only young," he said.

Saul clapped and laughed.

"Shit, Clarence," he said to Sheriff. "Your old pal Mr. P must be down to the dregs if you two are all he's got to keep this town safe."

"Now look here Saul," said Sheriff. "If it's your boy you come for, it's out of my hands."

"Boy?" said Saul. "What boy? What are you talking about, Clarence?"

I started waving to Saul from behind the bars. But he didn't notice me at all. He was busy sniffing the jug of liquor on Sheriff's desk. He downed a swig, and then held it up to the Jinx like it meant something to him.

"Now Saul," said Sheriff, "this is no fault of mine. Your boy here's been caught thieving. One of Mr. P's boys brought him in yesterday. Caught him in the act. And I'm sorry to say, the boy's already wanted. So that's three counts, two of them capital. He's determined to see justice done. So my hands are tied."

Saul picked up the jug of liquor and swigged it.

"Your hands are full of dirty money, Clarence," he said.

"No, Saul. That is not the case."

"I prefer Mister Suarez, if you don't mind, Clarence."

"Well I do mind, son," said Sheriff, getting up and taking the jug of liquor with him. "Now listen up to what I have to say," he said, pouring a shot. "Forgetting for a moment, the wanton destruction of federal property—and the loss of life that nearly was. Your boy offered to take Mr. P's bags to the hotel. Mr. P agreed, thinking he was doing the poor lad a favor," he gestured over to my cage. "Gave him well over the odds for it too. More than generous. Boy attempts robbery in return. So," he said, downing a cup, "Despite your attempts to turn him into a law abiding citizen, which I'm sure was always your intention, he's gone bad on you." He passed the other whiskey on to Saul.

He wouldn't take it.

"Always a rotten one in the crate," Sheriff said, slugging the other cup. "It can't be helped. It ain't your doing and it ain't mine." He went back to the jug and poured two more shots.

Saul opened up his long coat. He had a pretty pistol sitting on his hip. Next thing it was in his hand.

I heard the safety snap.

Clarence downed his shot and shook his head. "C'mon Suarez, I know you're a sensible man. Like your pa was before you."

"I know you're a turn coat liar, Clarence," said Saul, standing tall, with his leather fingers steady on the trigger.

"A traitor," said the Jinx from behind. I heard him cock a rifle.

"Son," said Sheriff to Saul, "you, of all people, know I am not, by any account, a traitor."

Saul was ready for shooting. He had one foot back and his good hand lined up dead straight with Sheriff's head. "I ain't your goddam son, Clarence," he said,

Sheriff had his hands in the air. "Saul, your pa would not have handled things this way."

"Mention my pa once again, Clarence, and you'll be wearing my bullet at your funeral."

I heard laughing behind my back. It was Floyd.

"Wearing my bullet at your funeral," he said. "Fella, you got a fine sense of humor."

Jinx comes hurrying over to the cage. I ran back into the dark.

The Jinx looked in. "Shut up," he said to Floyd.

Floyd pushed his face up to the bars. "Gonna break a fella loose?" he said to Jinx. "I'll see it's worth your while. Name your price. I'll see you get it."

"What's he in for?" Jinx said to Sheriff.

"One of your cousin's half breeds," he said. "He got at one."

"*Got at?*" said Saul. "What does that mean, got at? Is the girl still breathing or no?"

"No," said Sheriff, his hands still riding high above his head, staring down at Saul's steady aim.

"She had demons in her," said Floyd, "That's what they do. Get white man's seed and turn out the Devil's children."

"Shut up," said Jinx.

"Oh, poor boys," said Floyd. "Your mama's daddy made a hog hash of your pedigree, didn't he? Got him back for it though didn't you. Devil looks after his own, don't he?"

"He's for the rope at ten sharp," said Sheriff.

"No, I think he's for the rope now," said the Jinx. And he went banging out the jailhouse door.

When he came back, he had a length of rope. Wrapped it thirteen times to make a slipknot.

"Give Jinx the keys," Saul said to Sheriff. When he did not move, Saul, put his finger on the trigger.

"Deputy, unlock the door," Sheriff said. Deputy comes to our cage door.

Jinx stood by.

Keys jing, jing, jangling as Deputy opened up the lock. When it clicked open, Jinx shoved him out the way and went straight for Floyd. He was in the corner, with his hands over his head, singing, "Get away. Get away from me."

Jinx grabbed him by the neck with one hand. Punched him in the face with the other until Floyd dripped with blood and could barely stand. Boney came and held Floyd while Jinx strung the noose around his throat. They dragged him over to the bars by the neck.

I moved to back of the cage and cowered like a beat dog.

I watched Boney thread the long part of rope through to Jinx who'd gone around to the other side. Jinx pushed his boot to the bars, and pulled hard on the rope, pulling Floyd up against the cage with it. Floyd put his hands to the cord around his neck, and trying pulling on it to get it free from his throat. But Jinx pulled tighter. The slipknot was well strung, and there was no escaping it.

I stood watching as Floyd's eyes bulged out of their caves. His tongue stuck out, and swelled up, purple like a dead cow's. His legs danced on the straw.

I once seen a baby lying on the road. It was kicking its legs in the same manner as Floyd's were right now. Pa picked that child up and took it to a woman. Said she'd know what to do. Floyd was making sounds. Terrible sounds. Like when a pig's getting its throat cut. I put my hands to my ears to stop it from coming inside my head. I smelled he was shitting himself. I wondered where that baby was. And how much I liked that town. It had a pretty church and the mountains were blue like the Bay in sunshine. So, why'd we ever leave there for? Then Floyd stopped moving his legs, and I felt mine go falling to the ground.

When I woke up, Sheriff and Saul were engaged in conversation.

"Then why are you buying my southern bastard whiskey from my enemy?"

"What?"

"Southern bastard whiskey, I said. Gone deaf, old man?" Saul had his gun out and was pushing it deep into Sheriff's cheek. "Same as my Southern bastard tobacco. All belonging to me. Stolen from me and all of mine. And I know you're selling it on. Making profit for my enemy while living on my land. Taking advantage of my good nature. While I let you and your ugly brood live in peace while the rest of us got a goddam war going on."

"That just ain't so, Saul. You're getting it all wrong."

Jinx come at Sheriff from behind and roped the noose around his neck. Sheriff's eyes went white the way a horse's does when it's getting whipped.

"All right Clarence," said Saul, putting his gun away for to let Jinx do his job with the lynching, "I'll give you one last chance to show me exactly where your loyalty lies. Now tell me where's that cockroach son of bitch hiding?"

Boney had locked Deputy up in the empty cage. But my cage door was still open. At first I stood looking at dead man Floyd, and I was too scared to move. Then I made my feet start walking and edged my way to freedom.

I made it slowly to a corner then stayed down, hidden in shadow, beside a tall cupboard.

"I don't know," said Sheriff, squirming and hanging onto the rope around his neck. "I only know he's doing business with Mr. P because I heard his name mentioned in my company. That's all I know. Take the key to the safe. It's on the ring. Third one from left. There's enough in there to compensate you for any loss."

Saul went to Jinx and took the keys from his pocket. Rattled them in his hand while he come to the tall cabinet where I was hiding.

I made myself small.

He unlocked the doors and cleans out a strong box.

I leaned my head over to see inside. There were a couple of guns, paper dollars, coins, watches, and other things that must have belonged to past prisoners of the jailhouse. Then I caught sight of it. Virginia's knife. My knife.

Saul picked it up and flicked it open. The sun from the window hit the blade. It shone like a sharp diamond.

"Where did you get this, Clarence?"

"Your boy had it," he said, pointing his finger at me. "Your boy, not mine."

Saul's eyes caught me.

I shrunk further back to the wall.

"He was threatening Mr. P with it," said Sheriff. "If he hadn't called for help, who knows what would have happened? The old Daddy would be dead. Boy'd be swinging for murder as well as blowing up government property."

"What government property?" said Saul.

"Customs house," he said, choking. "It's all chaos down

there without it running." He made a squeaky laugh. Until Jinx started laughing. Tugging on that hanging rope, wrapped around Sheriff's neck.

Saul walked up to me, his spurs clicking on the floorboards as he did. He looked down at my head. "Get up," he said.

I staggered as I stood. I wiped the sweat from my brown and then I saw him. Short sides, and a moustache trimmed to perfection. Hair was oiled smooth and parted fashionably. Black leather gloves, covering his hands like skin.

He held Virginia's switch in front of my face and said, "Where'd you get this knife?"

I tried to swallow, but my mouth was dry. "I found it," I said, my voice cracking.

"Found it where?"

"Outside Mammy Jackson's."

"You were there, why?"

"I ain't sure. I think I got lost." I heard the shuffling of feet and sound of strangling.

"He's lying," said the Jinx from back of the jailhouse. He and Boney were dragging Sheriff along the floor ready to bang him up in the cage with Deputy. The jail door slammed, keys jangled and the lock got turned.

"Is my brother right?" said Saul.

I looked down.

"Look at me when I talk to you," he said.

I looked up at him. Tall, dark eyed, dark skinned and handsome. "Nossir," I said, clearing my throat. "It's just like I told you. I found it."

"When?"

I shook my head.

He made a sign for a brother to pass over the whiskey. He took it from the Jinx, passed the jug to me and I swigged. Coughing and wasting precious fine liquor down my chin.

"When did you find this knife," he said.

"I reckon, maybe, a fortnight ago?" I said. "I lost my way in the fog. That's how I ended up there."

"Too foggy to know where you where going, but eagle eyed enough to find a blade that happened to be lying on the ground?"

I felt my knees going soft again. I clung to the cabinet with one hand to keep myself standing tall.

"Know who this knife belongs to?" he said.

I shook my head.

"Know what these words say?"

I looked at the etching of the wolf, and the letters beside. "It's just I ain't too good at reading," I said.

"Are you blind?"

"Nossir."

"Are you fool headed?"

"Nossir."

"Then tell me, what kind of critter is this?" He held up the hilt of the blade.

I studied the wolf; like it was the first time I'd ever set eyes on it.

"A wolf," I said.

"*The* White Wolf," he said, rubbing his black gloved fingers along its body. "You ever had seen a cockroach?"

I looked up.

"A clean-shaven white boy?" he said. "Dresses up like a navy. Curly hair. Lips like woman. Big scar going down his face like this," he took the blade and slid it down his face without touching his skin to show me. "Hangs around Sydney Town looking for stray children to fuck for nothing. Seen him?"

"Nossir," I said shaking my head, "I never met such a fella in my life."

"No?" he said, staring me out.

"Nossir," I said, letting my eyes fall.

"Did you try and kill the old Daddy?"

I looked up.

"Well did you, or didn't you?"

"I weren't trying to kill nobody," I said. "Only he come at me like this," and I showed him, "I was only trying to defend myself like that," and I showed him that too. "That's the honest truth of it."

Saul's eyes were buried deep in mine.

I was sweating. My heart was beating in my mouth. I stopped breathing. Felt myself going dizzy.

He bent down, put his lips to my ear and in a whisper said, "You didn't burn down the customs house, did you?"

I looked into his eyes. "I was trapped," I whispered back. "They had me prisoner. I thought they were going to kill me first."

He drew his head away, and stood tall. A shiny white smile grew on his face. He lifted his chin, and tucked the blade in his pocket. Put his leather hand on my shoulder and rubbing my sore bones with his fingers said, "C'mon Little Brother, let's get you home."

Chapter 30

Two horses and a whip

Outside the city jailhouse, the brightness stung my eyes. I blinked until I could see again. The rest of Saul's black coat brothers were sitting on horses and smoking cigars, with loaded up rifles resting on their knees.

Some coatless gutter hogs were sleeping between the sides of buildings, all missing their boots and probably anything else they had of value by now. A blind beggar and his friend with no legs, but carrying a fine looking set of riders with clean soles, set up work outside the general store. Each had a tin can for money, and a scrawny looking dog to keep the rats away.

A couple of brothers threw them some coin. Made a game of getting pennies in the tin and watching the blind fella and the legless one scramble on the ground for the ones they missed. The blind one eventually sold the boots for one paper dollar and a half silver. A spoon went for two bits. So with the price set for today, nothing less than an eating tool in fine condition was worth bartering for down the Dead Man. You want a cock rub. That'll cost you a fork. Want me to kiss you while I'm doing it. That'll be a wooden spoon please. In fact for the whole eating set you can have my ass on a plate, and I'll take a pair boots into the bargain if you please.

More early risers were around, heading into town to fill in a day of paid work. They walked past me and Saul's gang. Heads down, going about their own business. Not minding anybody else's at all.

Three unmanned horses were still hitched up outside. I wandered over to them. My eye caught a real prize beauty: a tan filly with a white diamond and socks to match. I knew exactly who she was: my Darling from the barn.

Gonz come up behind.

"Get on," he said to me.

I turned to him, then back at her.

"Me? Get on the horse? You mean, this horse?"

"Don't ask dumb questions," he said. "The Boss says for you to get on the horse, you get on the horse."

So I got on the horse. Held on tight to her saddle. As soon as I did, she started stepping sideways. I put my boot in the stirrup. Began following her sway, dancing with her until I hauled myself up. High up. So high, I could see the bare hills behind me, and a hotchpotch of ramshackle houses, all different sizes, and all with their own crazy-headed means of construction.

She pricked her ears, sniffed and tried getting a good look at me. I bent to give her a show. Stroked her mane and whispered gentle words in her ear. Let her know I was the kind sort after all.

There was another horse hitched next to me: a chestnut with a white diamond, and white spots on her belly. She began stamping her hooves, digging at the mud, and shaking her head. I wondered what her fussing was all about. Then I looked up and saw Jinx coming out the jailhouse door.

He had his rope coiled around his arm like a snake, and was heading straight for her.

As soon as Jinx got close, she backed away, knocking into my horse; Saul's horse. She in turn twisted her head, and bit the other in the neck, making her scream. She reared up, spinning her front legs wild in the air. Meanwhile, Darling started fretting, shivering and shaking underneath me. I held on tight for I was sure she was getting ready to bolt.

Jinx grabbed his horse's rein and pulled her down, cursing her all to hell and calling her a worthless whore. He removed the whip from the saddle, and whacked her over the head with the end a couple of times saying:

"What's wrong with you? You cowardly bitch."

Darling stepped sideways and shuddered. She began to grunt like a bull and dig her hooves in. I figured she was getting ready to fight or run or do something that meant me getting thrown off and landing on my ass, in front of the whole of the world, when Saul came out the jailhouse door. Then she quickly calmed.

Saul strode up to her in that manner of walking he had, like he was about to start dancing. He got by her side, ran his hand along her belly, and kissed her. With hardly any effort at all, he got on her back, behind me, and took quick charge of the reins.

Jinx, meanwhile, had pulled his horse down. He was now on her back, whipping her hind.

Finally the horse screamed.

"Jinxy," said Saul, "hold your goddam fire, goddam it. You've already wasted two good horses in two years running. A third, and you'll be riding bareback on a mule."

Some fool on a horse started laughing when he heard those words. Another followed suit. Then another.

Jinx shot the last one a look.

Then the second.

And they both shut the hell up.

When he turned his attention to the first, the fella was still laughing. And Jinx starts laughing with him.

Quietly at first. Then louder.

Throwing his head back and shaking his shoulders. Until his rope started sliding down off his arm. And the slipknot hung low, swaying loose beneath his hand.

Everybody watched it swing and swing.

The fella stopped laughing. Spent the rest of the time making his apologies to Jinx. Offering him all kinds of tokens of sincerity. His watch. His new ivory dice. His sister. His belt buckle, which he got off a fella he shot for fucking his sister. And his gun. Jinx settled for that. And they moved on.

Saul shook Darling's reins and we flew, with Saul and his brothers blasting shot in the air, yelling, and going like hell-fire out of Union Square.

Some of Saul's black riders went off on their own, so it was only Jinx and Gonz riding with us now. Saul, and me saddled up behind him, leading the way.

We rode into a part of town where families tended to reside. An old man stopped painting a post and looked up. Some children playing with a broken cartwheel let it fall to the ground and started running alongside us. Plain looking women with hard faces were hanging out laundry. They carried on, but slower, and called for the younguns to come out of our way. Saul nodded to all and touched his hat in a friendly manner, saying "Mister" and "children" and "Ma'am" to each and every one of them. And they looked up and smiled with wide-open faces. He pulled his horse up to a two-story building with all the white wash peeling off. The brothers hitched up the horses. Gave the children pennies to mind them, and walked to the back.

There were stairs leading to the door and Saul climbed up them. He stood, removed his hat, tidied his hair with his hand, fixed his neck scarf, smoothed his moustache and knocked.

A woman answered. She had her hair up. It was dark. She wore a white shirt that left everything to the imagination. And a full skirt, a nice shade called cornflower blue. She stood in the doorway with a baby on her hip. It was eating something soft and wasting most of it down her clean shirt.

"Mrs. Monroe," said Saul, holding his hat on his heart. "How are you this fine day?"

She did not reply.

"I must say ma'am, you are looking a true portrait of comeliness this morning."

"What do *you* want?" she said.

"Ma'am, if I might be allowed the privilege of a quiet word with thee?"

"I have nothing left to say to you." And she raised her hand like she was going to whack him one.

But Saul got to her arm first. He pulled it, her and the baby toward him until they were all hanging on his hip like a gun.

He smiled and said something only the two of them could hear.

She started smiling back and then, she let him in.

For a while everything was nice and quiet. Except for the sound of the baby, yelling out every now and then. And for the chickens in the yard, clucking amongst themselves.

I looked around. Lots of empty boxes stacked up against the other house beside. Figured there must be fresh warm eggs hiding around here someplace.

I was about to go hunting, when voices started coming from upstairs.

It was the woman. Hollering at Saul like no body's business. Raising Cain. Cursing him all to hell. Calling him a son of bitch bastard and heap of other hellfire names. Said she knew about another woman and hiding the fact would get him nowhere fast. Then, as if Satan himself had got in on the conversation, the baby started screaming. It was a wonder the glass on the windows hadn't broke. Come to think of it, it was a wonder the glass on the windows hadn't been robbed. Probably get a few eagles for clean pane like that.

Finally, Saul fired back. Said she didn't know what the hell she was talking about and that she'd got it all wrong as always and why was she always making out like he was the one committing sin when it was all her doing in the first place.

Then it went quiet.

But for the chickens.

And the baby. Cawing like an angry crow.

I turned to Gonz to see what he was doing. Smoking his pipe and watching bugs climb up the stair rail. He squashed one and rubbed his thumbs together. Wiped the mess off on his knees.

Jinx was pacing up and down the yard, running his hands through his hair so it was sticking up right like a Cheyenne warrior's. He stopped and looked up at the door.

"He's going easy again," he said to Gonz. "Got rot in his spine." He carried on pacing. Then he stopped.

"I told you it's all these good for nothing goddam books he's been reading. Thinks he's the professor of… of bull shit."

Gonz shrugged.

"And it ain't my doing about the damn horse. It ain't been damn broke. Those skiving Injuns up there robbed us. For a second time too many if you ask me." He stood waiting for Gonz to reply.

He'd gone back to his bugs.

Jinx swore, spat and grabbed the rail. He pulled himself up the steps, his spurs clacking on the boards as he did. A chicken followed. He kicked at it and missed. It got in his way again and he tried grabbing its neck to strangle it one, but it ducked between his legs and flew off the edge of the stairs to safety. Jinx pulled out his new gun and aimed at it with his shooting arm.

"Nope," said Gonz. "Brother, it ain't worth the price of a bullet. I ain't had time to get a fresh batch going and we got that purchase."

Jinx growled and put it away. Then he went for the door handle, but stopped short of turning the knob.

New noises had started coming out from behind.

Fucking noises.

In no time flat, Saul and her were going full gallop. Riding all the way to Kansas.

"What the hell…?" said Jinx. "Sounds like he's getting fucked instead of her."

The thought of that made my face burning red.

"I mean, that just ain't right at all. What the hell is wrong with him?"

"Don't know," shrugged Gonz. "Guess he must be really sweet on her."

"Guess he must be really sweet?"

Jinx tried looking through the window. "The problem is," he said, "is that pussies got him horsewhipped."

It was steaming up.

"And she's loosening up his tongue."

He tried wiping it but the moisture was coming from the other side.

"Gonna be telling her every goddam thing there is to know about you and me like nobody's business."

He tested to see if it would lift open. It didn't.

"I mean she's loyal to old pie-eye and his ugly mother-fucking kin not us. She's a goddam spy in my book—the only book worth looking at. And I cannot believe how neither of my brothers can not see what's right plain in front of you all."

He turned to Gonz. He was standing with his back facing the yard. And something was going on. Had his hands down his trousers. Doing the dirty on him self is what it was.

"Oh for Jesus Christ's sake," said Jinx. "Brother, you're too old for that now. You'll be wearing spectacles for the rest of your life. Every time I see a fella wearing spectacles, I remind him how he got to be wearing them. Be wearing that shame for the whole of your life."

Then he saw me.

"What are you looking at?" he said.

"Nothing," I said. "I was watching the hens. I was looking out for eggs." And I made myself look busy doing so.

I was bent down searching between crates when I heard Jinx's boots coming down the stairs. Before I knew it, I was looking down at his feet. He had fancy metal tips on his toes and wore one fine looking pair of spurs.

"I know who you are," he said to me.

I held on to my hat and looked up.

"You're one of them cocksuckers from down Washington, ain't you? One of those Dead Man bitch boys."

And he was not ugly, but nor was he a portrait of comeliness. He had scars on his skull, where hair wouldn't grow. His beard was short. Well trimmed. Had the same kind of patches as was on his head. He wasn't tall like his brothers. And he had a way of looking at you, like it didn't much matter if he killed you or not, because you were hardly worth living anyhow.

I straightened my back. "I only been working for you since April gone," I said.

"You don't work for me," he said.

"I mean your brother."

"You don't work for my brother."

"I mean all of you… brothers."

"Where the hell you get that idea from? You pay us a board. That's all you do. You don't work for us. Little bitch boy."

"That's what I meant."

"You have nothing to goddam do with us."

"No."

"You're just some ugly little street rag too shy of work except for when it's getting your hands dirty on another man's prick. So where do you get off saying you work for me or my brothers?"

"I guess I got it wrong."

"Got it wrong. What were you doing in that hotel in the first place anyhow?"

"Nothing," I said. And I started creeping backwards, moving further away from him with every step.

"Where you going?" he said.

"Nowhere," I said, while my eyes caught sight of a tall stack of crates with chickens perched on the top.

Behind them was the house next door. I'd seen a chicken come out from underneath the building not long before, meaning there was a gap running along the bottom, a crawl space underneath. A getaway.

Jinx was rounding on me fast.

"I said where you going, I ain't finished talking to you yet."

I got ready.

"I said get over here, little bitch boy. Now."

Then I dropped low and made a run for it. I could hear Jinx coming: his boots sucking up the mud as he did.

I dropped behind the high stack of boxes and then pushed the crates over, right into Jinx's path. The box tower came crashing down, with birds squawking and flapping everywhere.

Jinx booted all aside and kept coming at me like a steam train.

I slipped and skidded on his knees and tried to claw my way into the crawl space. As was my luck, it was too narrow. I couldn't even get my head through. And Jinx was right on my tail. So I pulled at a plank of wood hanging loose above my head, and tore it from its hitching, nails and all. Still crouched down, I spun round in the mud to face Jinx.

And there he was, standing over me.

I held the wood and got ready to whack his legs with the sharp rusty nail end.

Then a bang and a clank resounded as the door to the house slammed shut.

We turned and looked up. Saul came out. Smiling, singing and jingling a bunch of keys in his hand while dancing down the stairs.

Jinx snatched the nail board off me while I was caught unawares. I sat there squidging, blinking and reaching to protect my head from getting beat.

"What the hell was you thinking of doing with this?" he said, holding it up.

"Mister," I said, "I'm real sorry. I didn't mean nothing. I just thought with what you done with the crazy headed fella before—the thing you did."

"What thing I did?" he said, like he didn't know nothing. "What thing you see, bitch boy?"

"Nothing, nothing," I said. "I never saw nothing. It's just, I thought you had it in for me just then, that's all."

"You thought I had it in for you?"

"Yeah. Yeah I did," I said, trying to smile. "I reckoned you did."

He looked to the crooked rusty nails poking through the board in his hand, and then back to me.

"Well I didn't," he said. "But, I do now. Bitch boy."

Then he tossed the plank aside. Gave me a mean look, and walked on off, back to his brother.

I sat there, squashed up in the chicken shit, wondering what the hell I'd done to myself now.

Saul tossed the keys to Gonz and said, "Here, open that cellar up will you."

Gonz caught them with both hands. Bent down and undid the lock. Then, he and Saul got down into the cellar.

Jinx was looking up the stairs at the door where the woman was. She'd come out again, holding the baby.

She watched them take a barrel of her liquor.

Saul and Gonz lifted it up from the cellar. Saul wiped his brow and said, "Jinx, you and the kid roll this back and get the others to come and get the rest."

"Brother," he said, "I ain't rolling a goddam barrel any place. I just ain't doing it. And I sure as hell ain't doing it with that dimwit son of a bitch boy."

I piped up and told Saul I didn't mind doing it on my own.

Jinx spun around and told me to, "Shut up. No one's talking to you. You ain't got a goddam opinion about nothing." He walked up to Saul. Tried talking low so I wouldn't hear but I could hear it all. "Brother," he said, "that little prick's nothing but trouble. I say ditch him. In fact I'll ditch him for you."

"Jinxy," said Saul. "Can we get this thing on your horse?"

"What?" he said, "Why the hell's it got to be my horse for?"

"Because your one cost the least. And the kid stays all right."

"What the hell for?" he said, following his big brother to his horse. "Why's he so special all of a sudden?"

"Because I like him," said Saul, tightening up his saddle. "Any body who'd try and put a hole in the Golden Daddy is a goddam hero in my book. And did you know he burned down the customs house?" He stopped for a moment. "Now, I'd never of even thought of that." Then carried on strapping.

I looked over at Jinx.

He had his hands on his hips, watching Saul, wearing a face like a storm.

Gonz got his rope from the saddlebag and together with

Jinx's noose, they tied the barrel on top of the barrel. Jinx's horse was unhappy at being rustled, and the three of them fussed over the barrel until the whiskey was sitting tight still back.

It was taking too much room up on the saddle for Jinx to sit as well, so Saul ordered me to ride with the liquor on Jinx's horse, while Jinx, cursing his elder brother all to hell, had to leave his horse and ride behind Gonz.

I could feel Jinx's eyes digging into my skull. Hacking away into my brain. His slipknot still hanging from his rope: now tied to the barrel of Southern Bastard whiskey, sitting right in front of me. Reminding me how close a lynching was. How much closer it could get.

I tried not to meet his eyes.

As we were about to leave, I looked up at the woman in the doorway. The way she was holding that child in her arms, it made her look like an idol I'd seen, of Jesus' mother, Mary. Except angry.

Saul tipped his hat to her. I did the same. And for no reason at all, she stared back at me with eyes as sharp as knives.

Saul blew her a kiss and then we flew, horses blazing, back to the Shades.

Chapter 31
Hero returns

I sat on the stairs and got ready to pull my boots off. The Shades was quiet. All the Dead Man boys were still sleeping. The place honked of pig fat from the last night's lamplight. There were a few more ugly smells. The liquored-up kind. Someone had puked up on the steps again and not one body had bothered to clean it up. Nor would they ever. I thought of heading back out to get a bucket of water to wash it down, but I was more than tired. And I was badly in want of a scrub, never mind the stairs. I thought about doing just that. Getting cleaned up. But then I figured, "No. I'll sleep first." For I was dead tired. I figured after a good long rest I'd go down to the shallow part of the bay and take a dunk. Get all looking nice and smelling sweet again for when I see Virginia. I wondered where he was. Back at Gunnybags, I figured. Sleeping off his beating like I was about to. I needed to dispose of that ugly rag before I did anything more.

I looked at my knees. Covered in chicken shit. My shirt was coming apart at the sleeve. That meant a needle and thread. But Golden Daddy full of shit had all my money. And Saul had my precious knife. I played over in my head what I'd say to Virginia about all of what had occurred when I saw him. Say,

"Now Mr. Hakes, hear me out. This fella you won the White Wolf from, he's an outlaw amongst outlaws if you get what I'm saying. Now you don't know it, but you've met this fella face to face. Played cards with him and played him dry. Beat him. Beat him fast. It's a wonder he didn't shoot you for winning his knife off him like that. In fact, I'm not saying you're a dumbass or nothing like that, but Jesus Christ, Mr. Hakes, you don't know how close you come to being killed by the son of Satan's bitch-dog. Goddam lucky to be alive is what you are. Not like Floyd."

Then I started feeling melancholy again. More than melancholy. The silence started to make a sound all of its own in my ears, buzzing away s like a trapped wasp. I put my hands over my ears and turned to go on up to my room in the attic.

Just as I took my first step upstairs, the door to the back parlor opened up from behind.

A fella comes out saying, "Hey, are you the kid called Jones?"

I looked around and shrugged.

"Boss wants you," he said.

Before I knew it, I was being led to Saul's door.

I waited outside. The door was slightly open. I could see walls were painted red, and a cross was hanging up. It was the almighty Lord Jesus looking like he'd been got at with a six-shooter and hung out to dry. There was blood everywhere. Running down his face, running down his hip that was almost bare naked. And pouring out from his hands and feet where the nails were meant to be. Then there was an idol of Mary on a cabinet. She was looking pretty. Killing off a rattler with her bare feet. And I remembered how the Sons of Jesus told a story that time when they were handing out free cups of hog soup for listening. Of how Jesus come and rescued his mama from being stoned to death by a bunch of no-good ugly thugs, calling her a wicked whore and all, whose soul was damned to the Devil for sinning. When she was only trying to win a few coins to buy bread for the table. And I thought how Alley done the same to me that time. Telling me off for whoring even though I wasn't. For it's a Devil's game for certain. For how close I come to being drowned without stones. Until Lone Rider comes. And Raccoon ruined everything. But then Saul comes again for me. And saves me for a second time.

I was told to go on in the room so I did. I heard voices. Girls. Giggling.

I followed their noises. There was more carpet on the floor. The costly kind, like at the hotel. My feet were bare. The rug was smooth and soft on my soles, which were dirty from my boots. I tried scraping the muck off with my toes so as not to make marks on the good quality beneath my feet.

I got to a door. It was half open. I kept behind it and peeped in.

I saw Saul. Lying on a bed that could have provided slumber for four people, maybe six depending on the size and how you arranged the sleeping.

With him were two half-naked girls. One had dark ringlets and was almost pretty. The other was Reddie Mae: a flaming mane of red hair going out in all directions. She was straddling him like he was a horse, swinging her hips from side to side and singing like a cat.

The dark one began hugging his neck. Pulling on him. Telling the red one to get the hell off of him.

"Carlotta," Saul said her. "Get your nasty hands off my neck, you're strangling me to death."

"No, no, I won't," she said. "Not until you tell Reddie Mae to get off of you. It's my turn. And I don't know how you can like her anyhow. She's ugly. And she's got the clap."

"I ain't got the clap," said Reddie Mae.

"Then what's that all over your face?" said the other.

"It ain't nothing," said Reddie Mae. "I ain't got nothing all over my face. I ain't never gonna catch nothing, 'cause I use that thingy George give me." And they started arguing back and forth with Saul in the middle yelling at them to shut the hell up for Jesus Christ's sake.

But Carlotta had her mule ears on. She began pinching Reddie Mae. When Reddie Mae pinched her back, she slapped her one. Hard across the face.

Reddie Mae held her sore cheek and started to holler her head off.

Saul swore, threw Reddie Mae off of him, and grabbed hold of Carlotta's hands saying, "That's it. I had enough of you."

He got up. His shirt was undone. He had hair on his chest like Virginia. Only it was straight and parted nicely like a crow's feather. He dragged Carlotta off the bed by her hair. He beat her hard over the head a couple of times until she began to holler.

There was a door in the wall. It was in so tight that you could not tell it was there, until Saul opened it with a key. Then you could see the whole cupboard inside as clear as day.

He tried making Carlotta go inside. She stayed fastened to him tight.

"No, no," she said. "Please, baby boy; I don't want to go in there again. I swear, I swear. I didn't mean it. I'm just scared of her taking you away from me, that's all it is. I don't mean nothing, baby boy."

"Taking me away from you?" he said, shaking her by her hair. "I don't belong to you. Where did you get that idea from? Now do as you're told and get in there before I hide you with my horsewhip."

"Oh but baby boy. Please, please, don't lock me up in there again. I don't like the dark. Oh, please don't do it baby boy. I swear I'll be good. I swear. I swear."

"Shut up," he said, biting down on his teeth, "I couldn't give a bent cent. You deserve all of what comes to you. Beating on my precious Reddie Mae like that. When she ain't done nothing to you. You nasty little bitch. Now get in. You're doing time."

So he shut her up in the cupboard and locked the door with her screaming and banging on the door from behind.

He stood there rubbing his hands through his hair and cursing women all to hell. "Shut up," he hollered at the door, nearly tearing his hair out as he did so, "or I'll get the Jinx in here. Lock you up with him for a while. Then you'll you know what it's for.After that, she went quiet as a rat. If it were not for the fingers poking out from underneath every now and then, you'd never know someone was in that little closet at all.

Reddie Mae was twirling her hair with her finger. She'd been watching me.

Looking somewhat comely.

Here and there.

Something still wrong with one of her eyes.

"Who's this?" she said to Saul, tying her arms loose around his neck.

"This," he said, freeing himself from her, "is the one I was telling you about."

She looked me up and down. Twirling more hair.

I gave her snake eyes to look at.

She paid no heed. "Oh fie fie fie," she said, laughing and pretending to slap Saul's cheek, "It's a boy! Why, I thought you got another girl."

"Got another girl?" he said, grabbing her behind, "Why'd I want another girl for, when I got you, darling?"

"To take Carlotta's place," she said. "When she's gone, like you said. But she ain't gone. She's still here. And I don't like her much."

"Well now, Carlotta ain't all that bad," he said, putting his black-gloved hands up Reddie Mae's skirt. She started to squeal like a happy pig, laughing and doing up her hair with her hands so it went even more crazy.

I put my hands to my ears and looked at the closet. I saw Carlotta's fingers peeping out from underneath the door. I swear I could see her eyes shining under there too. Seeing everything that was going on.

"Now," said Saul to Reddie Mae, "this here is my kid. My new Little Brother. Who just nearly gut the old Gold Daddy."

"Why," said Reddie Mae, "this little boy couldn't do such a thing."

"Could and did," said Saul, "using this…"

And there it was. My precious knife. The White Wolf, held tight in Saul's black leather hand.

"Oh my Lord," she said. "How'd he get hold of that?"

"Never mind, it's not important. Now listen, he got the White Wolf and got ready to slice his neck open like this." He put his hand to neck to show her. "Then pulled his knife like that," and showed her that too.

"Oh baby boy," she said, smiling. "Be careful. Not your pretty face. You know how much I like looking on it so."

"Just as he was going to send that ugly bastard to hell," he said, "the law comes in. Robbed the kid of his destiny." Saul let go of the blade pressed flat against his throat. "Did you know it was him who burned down the customs house?"

Reddie Mae put her hand to her neck and swallowed hard. Her chest was berry red, and beating like a lizard's belly in the sun. Next, she come running over to me with her legs on show and draped her arms all around me, saying in a whisper, "Did you really do all those things? Is it the honest truth of it? You ain't telling lies now, are you?"

"But," said Saul, looking up to the ceiling and nodding. "All of this is part of His plan. For me and my brothers."

"Oh! The Lord's plan," said Reddie Mae, clasping her cheek as though she was on the stage. "Oh, now which one is it: The Final Retribution, or the Great Revenge that's coming?"

Saul did not reply. He was talking quietly to heaven. He put the White Wolf to his mouth and kissed it. Showed it off to the cross of Jesus, and kissed it again. Then set it next to some statues and a photograph, where it lay, burning in their holy glow.

Reddie Mae turned to me and said, "I think that means both of them."

I edged his way to the handsome cabinet and my knife, with Reddie Mae partially attached to me by the arm. There, I got a good look at the photograph.

It was Saul, looking dandy as hell. Reddie Mae explained who everybody was. The prize beauty of a woman sitting in front of Saul was his wife Ramona. On her lap was the real baby boy: Pedro. The two younguns, handsome like their daddy, were little Saul and little Gonzo. Little Juanita, his precious daughter: "Well now, she's the one to look out for. Any man so much as looks at her sideways will have his eyes put out and fed to Saul's dogs for supper."

I tore my eyes away, moved quickly away from the handsome cabinet and over to a chair. I found a book with pictures in it. I sat leafing through it while Reddie Mae got comfortable on my lap. I watched Saul humming to himself, tapping his toes and combing his hair in a long mirror. I saw him put his comb away, undo his tie. Unbutton his shiny red waistcoat, with the gold dragons running all over it. Then his shirt: crisp and clean as the first snow of winter.

"What's your name, baby boy?" said Reddie Mae to me.

I looked deep into the book. No pictures on this page, just lots of words that meant nothing at all.

"You're pretty," she said. "How old are you?"

I almost turned to the compliment, but stopped myself, and continued my work of trying to read words. She was wearing sweet perfume that was making my head dizzy. Her lips were painted, and her cheeks.

"I'm 16 years living anyhow," she said. "Lottie's 18 although she lies and says she's younger."

Her titties were sparkling. They were overly big and nearly coming out of her corset.

"That's real gold dust I got powdered on," she said. "Want me to put some on you?" I nearly said yes. Took stock of Saul who was almost naked by now, and

continued leafing through my book instead.

"You sure have comely hair for a boy," she said stroking my head, "I wish my hair was so."

Then Saul called out,"Reddie Mae, get me my pipe."

Reddie Mae jumped off my lap and got it. She opened up a small box and took out a long thin looking contraption like what they sell down Chinese town.

Saul took it, played with it in his gloves, and gave me a

narrow look out the corner of his eye. Then he sat on the side of the bed, pulled out a pouch and started filling it up. Not with tobacco, but little black crumbs, like what you find in a coal fire.

"Reddie Mae," he said, "go and get some body to tell George I want him. Tell him I need some tailoring done. Tell him I need some water. Hot this time. And some pure pleasure: but I don't want crumbs again, I want whole pieces. Make sure you tell him that. You got that right?"

"I got it all, baby boy," she said.

"Not like your stupid friend in there," said Saul, inclining his head toward the small door. "Last time I had a bath it was cold. Because you did not tell them what I told you to say. That the water has to be steaming when it leaves them. Or else it's cold by the time it gets here."

Carlotta started mumbling something from behind the cupboard door.

"Shut up," he said. "I hate hearing your voice. It ain't sweet like Reddie Mae's."

I looked to see what Reddie Mae thought of that, but she'd already gone. And now it was just the two of us. And the girl in the cupboard.

Saul lit his pipe.

It smelled of some strange smoke: heady and sweet.

"Come here, Little Brother," he said.

I slunk up to him.

"Sit," he said.

So I did. On the edge of the bed. Shaking. And hurting with all the beating I'd got done. My head spinning like a hurricane. Visions of Floyd and his choking eyes one moment, and Gold Daddy and his sweating hogs the next.

Saul handed me the pipe.

He took a drag. It was nothing like Sweet Virginia's. Or the dried up horse shit Raccoon and me were used to. It was like smoking perfume.

I pulled it from my mouth, spitting, and wiping my lips.

Saul started to laugh.

I saw him.

He held out his black gloved hand, and I passed it back too him, coughing. Then I looked down at my own hands. They were covered with something sticky, like pitch.

Saul lay down on the bed. Had his chest on show. Straight black hair going down to his belly. No scars. He took a long drag this time. Made a sound of heavenly comfort. For a moment it seemed he'd just died and gone to paradise.

I thought about him dying. I put my hand so it touched against the side of Saul's thigh. I looked up to see what he said. But it was hard to tell what Saul was thinking. At one time he was smiling, next he was giving me peculiar looks out the corner of his eye that didn't look entirely friendly. So I took my hand away. Besides my head felt strange. Dizzy. My mouth was drying out fast.

I licked my lips.

Couldn't feel nothing.

I pinched them with my fingers.

Couldn't feel a thing.

I felt sleep begging me to come. So I collapsed on the bed, with my legs dangling over the side, looking up at the ceiling. Watching the candlelight flickering and licking the walls with long dark tongues. Getting longer and darker each time I blinked my eyes.

Someone was playing with my hair.

It was Saul. Smiling this time.

I smiled back.

He started laughing. I started laughing. And everything seemed happy. I could not recall any time in my life when I'd felt this kind of happiness. Except for that first time with Virginia down the Dead Man.

Soon Saul and me were both laughing like crazy-headed loons. And I wanted to kiss a body bad. But to do so meant I'd have to move. And moving seemed an enormous effort. So I lay there hoping an invitation to his lips would be coming soon.

Then Saul stopped playing with my hair and I heard the

smack of kissing. Some body was getting it. And it wasn't me. It was Reddie Mae. When the hell had she come in? Saul was kissing her like a crazy man. Full on her lips and then her neck and then her face again, and chest and arms and everything. He couldn't get from one place to another fast enough. And he had his hand right up her petticoat. Inside her drawers. Together they pulled them off and tossed them away, nearly landing on my face, with me lying there like a dumbass. And I could see everything going on between her legs. All copper curls and black bound fingers, rubbing up and down inside where her crack was. And I felt myself going cactus. But could not look away. So, I was busy watching when an almighty noise made us all jump up and out of our skins.

Chapter 32
New clothes

At first I thought the ground was going to open up and swallow me whole. Instead, a boodle of people came charging through the door in the next room. They were dressed as they do in Chinese town: blue pants and loose fitting shirts hanging down to their knees, with shaved foreheads, and a single braid of black hair going all the way down to their backend. Some had poles on their necks, and buckets hanging from the ends shouting, "Hot! Hot! Hot!" Two carried a tin tub and set it down on the floor. It was soon filled to the brim with the steaming water.

I saw the door to Saul's place was open. I got ready to make my getaway. I used my forearms to crawl to the bottom end of the bed, and prepared to make a run for it. Out of Saul's boudoir, and back out to the hall and up to my old attic room. But getting out from underneath something, with a body that's been fourteen years living, is a clumsy business. I could not escape without being fully noticed by every eye in the place.

One fella pointed and called out, "A boy! A boy!" as though he were saying, "A rat. A rat!" It's a wonder he did not pick up a broom and start whacking me over the head with it.

Then came Saul.

"Oh, there you are," he said. "Where the hell you been hiding out?" He put his arm around me, and swung him around to face George.

"Now George, this is my new little brother. What do you think? Ain't he the likeness?"

George, by the look of him, was a her. She looked me up and down.

"Too young," she said.

"No. No. No," he said. "Well, of course he's too young. But, I'm talking ten years gone. Isn't he the plain image? Did you know he nearly killed a man yesterday? And not just any man. The Gold Daddy, Mr. P. Done time for it too. Busted him out this morning."

"Oh," she said, as if that explained nothing.

"I mean the clothes are all wrong," said Saul. "See if you can't fit him into something."

He drew me over to his wardrobe and went rummaging through his things. Whipping out shirts and pulling out trousers. He only stopped making mess to show George an item he said he thought had possibility. He'd hold up a shirt and she'd say, "No, I can't possibly do it." He'd hold up a pair of trousers and she'd screw her face up and say, "Maybe so, but not likely." Finally they settled on some things they could both agree on.

"I can fix this but it is difficult. And very expensive. A lot of work."

So they bartered on a price and before I knew what was happening, I was hauled in front of the mirror, to get measured up here and there and everywhere.

I looked at my likeness in the glass. I was raggedy as shit after being in that cell all night. And I could see Saul in the reflection, sitting on the bed with George. She was peeling off his gloves like she was skinning off a snake.

She held out his naked palms and studied them, as a fortune teller would.

I stared hard in the mirror to get a good look at them.

At first I saw they were wrinkled like an old-timer's. An old-timer who'd had his hands steeped in bucket of seawater for all eternity. But then it became clear that this was an illusion. George had been rubbing some white ointment over them. And it was only when she finished making it disappear into his skin, that I saw the truth of it. For his fingers were like those of a body that's died and been left to dry out in the desert. Only his still had red flesh holding on to them, so they were not wholly like a skeleton's.

George put the ointment back in her bag and took out another. Rubbed it into his shoulder. Then stroked his hair, helped to get him undressed, and snapped at her boys to get out the way and get to work while she led Saul to the hot tub full of water.

Saul covered up his manhood with his bare hands, and got in. Right away the whole place began to smell of something sweet and spicy. George ordered her boys to the tub. They got busy bathing and shaving him while he and her talked business.

I meanwhile was in front of the mirror, wearing Saul's dandy clothes over my own sorry rags. The boiled white shirtsleeves hung down over my scrawny looking wrists, while a soft pair of dark trousers hung from my hips. A fella, carrying a mouthful of pins, and wielding a sharp pair of scissors, was cutting at my shoulders, then cutting at my feet. When he'd done snapping and pinning, he made me take it all off. Then began stitching up the whole thing again.

Saul lay slouched back in the tub with his long legs hanging over the end. He said to me, "Get your things off kid, you're getting in."

I stood there wondering how the two of us were going to fit in the one tub, without me having to sit on top of him. And with the whole of the world looking on too. And with all of what just happened in the hotel and that rag and all. I weren't fit for such entertainment, and feared I never would be again. For, during the long night in that jailhouse, I'd had time to think. And talk to Jesus. It was then I made a bargain with the

Lord. I said that if He, the Lord Jesus Christ, let me survive this ordeal, that on my very soul, I, Goldsmith Jones, promised that I was done with getting fucked. I said I'd take better steps next time, to ensure it never happened again. Not even with Sweet Virginia. Who had a sweeter part of the deal anyhow, I was sure as a Union dollar about that. In fact, until a more, fair arrangement—like a fifty-fifty partnership of sorts—could be made, I was done playing bitch and hound for good.

But all that worry was for nothing. George held out a cotton sheet and Saul stood up and got out the tub. And Saul's cock sleeping was twice the size of mine when mine was wide-awake and crowing, so it was just as well.

I looked around the room for somewhere to change. I saw there was a screen with girls' clothes hanging over it and spilling out from behind it. One of George's boys were busy filling a wicker basket with them. I went behind the screen and prepared to get naked.

I hopped around like a dog with three legs getting the last of my Johnnies off. Then I pulled out the rag loaded up my ass and stuffed it inside my undergarments. I rolled the whole thing up into a large ball and tied it together at the arms and legs. When I saw basket boy wasn't looking, I crammed it deep inside amongst the other dirty laundry.

I came out from behind the screen, holding onto my manhood with both hands—one on top of the other, so there looked to be more of something than there actually was, then tiptoed over to the tub.

I got in the tin bath and sat down.

Quickly, my bones warmed. It felt like they were melting into water. I sighed like I'd come to the gates of heaven, only my prick had nothing to do with it.

I looked around to see who was going to be doing the bathing. But no one seemed to be coming my way. I looked at George and prayed to Jesus it would not be her. It had not gone unnoticed that she did not like the look of me one bit. And who knows what treachery she might get up to, with me lazing there, in all my nakedness.

I looked at Saul. He was getting dressed again and looking smart. Had his leather gloves peeled back on. He was saying to George, "I said to you I want whole pieces this time."

"No, it's too much," she said.

"You mean not enough. It's not enough I'm telling you." Then he lifted his lashes to me. And shone a white smile saying, "Am I right, Little Brother?"

I smiled back saying, "Right," to whatever it was he was talking about. Then I slid down into the warmth, laid my head back in the water and wondered if I'd just been adopted. And that would be like striking gold. But, what about Sweet Virginia? And wasn't Reddie Mae crazier than a loon? Saying all kinds a girly nonsense about heads in cupboards. Some of the things she said were just plain ridiculous. But his hands. I'd seen them with my own two eyes. All burnt up and mangled. Oh, but Virginia and his goddam southern bastard tobacco. I had to get to him. Before he wound up jigging on the end of Jinx's rope.

After a while it was clear no one was coming to rub me clean. The soap was somewhere in the water. I kept sliding on it. It seemed to prefer a home under my ass. It was a damn slippery devil too. A smart fish that wouldn't be caught. With each failed attempt at capturing the villain, my hands wore a coat of victory: clean smelling slime that bubbled and slid over my shoulders and chest. And then nearly blinded me in the eyes when I washed my face.

That made Saul roar with laugher.

George came over tut tut-tutting at me, and wiped my eyes dry with a clean cloth. Then sunk her nails deep into my skull, and nearly tore my skin off as she washed my hair. Done with that torture, she proceeded to begin another by scalping me with a fine-toothed comb. I hollered, splashed at her, and shooed her away in protest. Saul told me to keep my fists by my sides and mind my language or else. I took one look at what else: that tiny cupboard, and the prospect of being stuffed up in it with parts of Saul's daddy and apologized until I was told to shut up about it.

Then George, not done with her persecution, went and told Saul that I had critters living in my hair. Before I knew what was happening, I was doused with a potion smelling of rotten eggs and cat piss. She brought her fine-toothed weapon out again and combed the critters out. They dropped down dead onto my new clean shoulders. And littered the bath, now cold and uncomfortable, with their green-yellow bellies.

She pulled me out the bath, wrapped me up, ready for burial, and passed me over to the tailor who dressed me up for living again. When he was done, I looked at myself in the mirror. It was all a blur. My stinging eyes were puffed up red and streaming with tears that I did not cry. Then firm hands come to rest on my shoulder.

"Well, well, well," said Saul, standing tall beside me. He brought his comb to my hair, and made a gentle part down the middle like his own. He took his time patting down the sides and tucked the long lengths behind my ear.

The fog finally lifted from my eyes and I could see myself again. I was nearly good-looking. It was just that my nose was getting too long, and my cheeks were bony from not being fed on a regular basis. But I certainly looked manlier. No body with sight could mistake me for being a girl, no more than they could mistake Saul, who stood over me saying, "Yes, this is much better. It's like looking back in time. I mean, look at us. Exactly the same, don't you think?" George said, "No, it's not the same. And you don't want the past."

"But," said Saul tapping his chin, "what bothers me… no, I say what terrifies me, is how much do you think Ma Wong would pay for a boy like this down the House of Happiness?"

George kept her mouth shut.

"See I heard she'll pay $40. A straight exchange. Once he's inside—off with his balls and there you go: a girly boy for all those Frenchies and Englishmen who prefer a eunuch to anybody else."

I dug my hands deep inside my new pockets and took hold of all I had for safekeeping.

"So, say Little Brother was to venture off into the wrong side of town. Start hanging with the wrong kind of folks. Start talking about things they might overhear in passing. Foreign rouge could make an easy 40 dollars, am I right?"

"Forty is too much," said George. "Thirty-five, maybe."

"Well, 35 dollars is 35 dollars George. Hell, these days a man can do a week's lodging down the Sons of Jesus for that money. So now listen here, little brother. These are the rules: you don't go out unless you're with your older brothers. And you don't open your mouth about nothing to nobody. Absolutely nobody. Except me. Got that?"

"What about when I go work down the Dead Man," I said.

"The Dead Man?" said Saul, hoisting up an eyebrow. "You're in the terrifying trade, ain't you? The Gold Daddy's watch: you nearly got it off him, didn't you? The Customs House: blew it sky high, didn't you?"

I nodded.

"Get any coin from it?"

"Only what they stole from me."

"That's right," said Saul, fixing up my collar. "A man steals from you, you go after him. Get your gold worth back. And plenty more for all the trouble. You are not some poor, pitiful, two-bit tomcat from some stinking alleyway, now are you?"

"Nossir."

"I only let those boys stay at that shithole, because I know they ain't got no place else to go. I could collect board three times what I get paid for them but I do not. They call it benevolence. Ever hear of that word?"

"Nossir."

"Well, remind me to teach you how to read. I mean it's a man's own choice if he wants to dishonor himself by being another man's bitch. Just not if you're going to ride with me, you understand? I mean sucking off another man's prick. You're nearly a grown man now. You get a woman to do that for you. Teach her how. She'll learn. Just like when I teach you to become a literate. Now, you are not the kind who's going to let another fella dishonor you, are you?"

I shook my head until it nearly fell off. "Nossir," I said.

"Good. That's what I like to hear. Now what I do not want to hear, is you ever talk about the Dead Man ever again, alright?"

"Yessir."

"You stay away from them boys from now on, you hear."

"Yessir."

"You stay right here with me."

"Yessir."

"You can be my muse. Did I tell you that I'm a poet?"

"Nossir."

"Well I am. Had some rhyming verse published in the San Francisco Review only last month. You know, there are plenty who allow themselves to be dishonored and I'm not just talking about whoring themselves out. Some fellas will sell their own wives and daughters for the right price. They'll sell off their land—the same land that's belonged to them for centuries. They'll drink away every penny until their sons are left with nothing. Make their own sons the slaves of other men's sons. Sell their own hole for pennies and squeal like happy pigs while their own people die around them with only ditches for graves. But you ain't one of those ball-less pussies, are you?"

"Nossir," I said.

"Alright," said Saul, slapping me on the back. "Now. Where's my whole bits gone? Get me my pipe. Where's my Reddie Mae?"

Saul stopped. He looked at George. She was in conversation with basket boy. She had possession of my johnnies, all tied up safely in a knot. Then somehow, she undid the whole thing. I could only stand there watching with my mouth hanging open as it all unraveled before my eyes, and hung from her hands like the Star Spangled Banner. Only this flag was a blank canvas. Save for an ugly patch of brown where some sorry ass would normally be.

"What the hell is all that?" said Saul. "What'd you do? Shit yourself?"

Then some one pointed to the soiled bloody rag lying on the floor.

"Contagion," someone said.

"Jesus Christ," said another. "It's the contagion. The contagion's back." Everyone quickly covered their faces and backed away from me like I was the Red Fever.

Saul rushed over to the other side of the room wearing a handkerchief over his nose. He then replaced it with his neck scarf, wrapping around his mouth like a shroud. He stood with his back to the wall and yelled through the muslin, "Go and get the doctor. Tell my brothers they ain't to come anywhere near here. Now git."

George pulled out a pair of spectacles and began inspecting my rag. When she was done poring over that she began picking over me. Putting her hand on my forehead, and under my arms. Pulling on my eyes and trying to look into my mouth, which I kept tight shut.

"It's alright," she said to Saul. "It's not contagion."

"Can you be sure?" he said, an eyebrow hitched to the ceiling, his black leather hand clinging to his scarf for safety.

"Very sure," she said.

"Well, what's wrong with him then?"

"He's a Dead Man boy," she said. "That's what's wrong with him. He's been got at. Must have been yesterday."

I felt like I had a bird trapped in my chest. I held on tight to myself, hoping I could stop its wings from flapping. The more it beat, the faster I kept breathing. The faster my lungs went, the less air there was in the room to breathe.

Saul unraveled his scarf-mask and tossed it on the floor. He put his hands on his hips and moseyed up to me. He looked me up and down.

"Who did this?" he said.

My heart banged against my ribs.

"Don't tell me," said Saul. "It was that white devil Floyd, wasn't it?"

I shrugged.

"Where the hell was Clarence?"

I shrugged again.

"Somebody get me my brothers," said Saul. "Now, I said!"

Soon the scuttling of feet; the lifting of a tub; the shutting of a door, the opening of a door and the tall body of Gonz slid into the room.

"Goddam Clarence," said Saul to him. "I've had enough of that puny-dicked motherfucker. Goddam sits there drinking my whiskey. Smoking my tobacco. While little brothers getting violated in front of his very eyes. Where's the Jinx?"

"Out," said Gonz.

"Well, wake him up. And tell him to get his lasso ready. I'm going tie that ugly bastard to the back of my horse and ride him around the whole of Sydney town on his bare ass."

"No," he said. "Jinx is out cold. Carlotta got to his whiskey. He ain't gonna be coming round till way past high-noon."

"Goddam that scheming little bitch," he said, "Well, never mind. C'mon, let's go have some fun. We're going take old pie-eyed for a real ride. Give him a taste of his own poison."

"No," said I. "It weren't Sheriff's fault. It weren't Floyd."

"What? Well who was it then?"

I kept my mouth shut. The sound of clacking spurs told me bad company had arisen from its poisonous slumber and come into the room. And I dared not look to see its ugly face staring back at me.

"Well, it sure as hell wasn't old fat belly Mr. P," said Saul. "Know what I read in the El Dia last week? His wife used to be Napoleon III's consort. Do you know what a consort is? That's the highest class of whore money can buy. So I got a pretty damn good idea of what he likes and it sure as hell ain't you."

Then I heard the Jinx's voice. "Why don't you tell us the story of how you got that knife again, Little Brother?"

I looked over at him. His eyes were red. His face wore the angry welts of wrinkled up bed sheets.

Saul turned to me and ordered me to start talking or else. I didn't think twice. I told the story I made up back at the jailhouse. The problem was, I was not thinking straight. I kept forgetting my lies, and therefore had to make up new ones.

Only they were too forgettable to remember, so I was quickly caught out.

"You told me you found it outside the restaurant, by the hitching post," said Saul, "and now you're saying you found it in the alley way behind. Your fable ain't worth nothing even as a piece of fiction. Now what would you be doing down that back alley anyhow? You got a hole between your legs as well as your ass? That's the only kind of whoring going on around that part of town. Well? Answer me."

I stayed dumb. And felt my knees go loose.

Jinx walked over, beating up the floorboards with his heels. He grabbed me by the throat and pulled me up off the floor and shook me around saying, "Answer my brother little bitch, or you're gonna have more than shit coming out your ass. I'll pull your yellow-belly guts out with my bare hands."

I panicked as I felt my legs start to dance. I grabbed at Jinx's hand, and tried pulling it off my neck in vain.

"Hold your fire, Jinx," said Saul, "I just paid an eagle for that shirt. Now get your hands off my collar."

Jinx grunted and did as he was told. When he let go, I collapsed at Saul's feet. I lay there like a critter caught in a trap, gasping and hanging on to my neck for dear life.

Saul got down to my level, and put his hand on me and squeezed my shoulder overly hard.

"Now why don't you just tell me the whole story from the start: the truth this time."

I kept my mouth shut and my eyes on Jinx and his metal tipped boots. Saul sighed, and released his grip on me. "Look," he said, "Never mind Jinxy. He's just doing his job protecting his brothers. You just ain't won his heart yet, that's all."

I looked up at the Jinx: his eyes all ablaze; breathing through his nose like a bull.

"C'mon little brother," said Saul, holding me close, "the truth now."

I put my head to Saul's, kept my voice low, and told him all of what I knew about a navy called Mattie Hakes. How he'd won the knife in a game of cards and gives it me in exchange for eternal friendship. I even told him about the raising horses on the ranch. Only I left out the times at El Dorado, the southern bastard tobacco, and the jumping the 9:15 to San Marco as that information would only complicate matters. Finally I told him about the hotel and the Golden Daddy of Sacramento, and how I'd been wrongly accused, and ended up in the jail in the first place.

When I'd done confessing, Saul pats my shoulder and said, "Thank you, little brother. You've done the right thing telling me everything. Now I know for sure that you can be trusted." He kissed me softy on the head three times. Then he stood up, and stared down at me, saying nothing, for what seemed an uncomfortably long time: his black-gloved fists opening, closing and cracking by his hips.

Saul shifted his weight to his other foot, and I thought he was getting ready to boot me one. And if he started booting me one, then Jinx and Gonz were sure to join in and kick me all the way to kingdom come. So I curled up tight into a critter ball, covered my head with his hands, and prepared for it all to come.

But it did not come. Instead, Saul ordered his brothers out the room. One more hollering from Saul, and both brothers left. With Jinx cursing the world and slamming the door so hard it flew open again.

Curled up on the floor, I watched it beating the wall as it swayed back and forth.

Saul moved over to his bed. He took out the black incense George had left him and said, "Goddam bastard, he give me crumbs again," then filled his pipe and sat with it in his hand.

I got off the floor and stood up straight. Fixed my shirt collar, and tidied back my hair. I looked around for my hat and boots, and put them on. Stood for a moment and watched Saul smoking his pipe. Took one last look at the White Wolf, lying there on the handsome cabinet. Tipped my hat to bleeding Jesus. Then, saying nothing, turned and walked out the open door.

I walked down the hall. Then I walked out the front door.

I nodded to Alley and she nodded back. I carried on down the steps. Got to the stables and climbed on the first horse I laid eyes on. And, giving the reins a stir, I rode off.

Chapter 33
Horseflies

Clay Street was usually quiet at three o'clock in the afternoon, but today was the fourth of July. The day George Washington freed the world from a bunch a mad-dog Englishman. Only he forgot the world weren't all white folk. Now president Lincoln was going to free the world proper. Or so everyone kept saying.

This day, it was hot and it was crowded. White and ruby streamers ran from building to building. Either side of the sidewalk was a horde of men, women, and children waving little union flags. Cripples with only one leg and a crutch whistled and cheered. Invalids, not long for the grave, carried in carts and wheelbarrows, rolled their eyes to heaven and thanked the lord for still being alive to see this very day.

All the stores, the hotel, and the gold mint had their white washed faces marked with union flags. And down the center of the road filed a great procession. A whole bunch of well dressed drummer boys. Behind them marched armies of well-fed school children: singing "The Battle Cry of Freedom." Next came the benevolent society: the Christian women society, the Christian men society, the reformers, the do-gooders, and the unions: the bakers, the fishermen, the hat finishers, the pipe makers and what seemed to be hundreds more, all took their time, strolling down Clay Street in the sun.

Next came the San Francisco fire department. Some cattle herded down the street, followed by the Butchers Union—doing some kind of military salute with deadly looking cleavers. They had a real live buffalo caged up in a cart. That was something.

The glue factory—they were holding a banner up that evidently said: "We stick fast to the Union." Which I thought was real clever.

Finally came the military. Army first. Then, the one I was waiting for: the navy. Marching in rows of six. A sea of dark blue: with a gold stripe going down the leg and two going around the cap. I set my eagle eyes out looking for Virginia. Row by row, I inspected each one of their faces. When I drew a blank I rode my horse further down the road, ignoring all the yells and the waving arms telling me to get out the way. I did the same again twice more. Re-positioned myself looking out for Virginia. But, I found nothing. He simply was not there.

When the procession finally ended, everyone decided to leave at the same time. Omni buses, two man buggies, and horse riders jostled for position to get down the wide road. It was impossible to get moving anywhere.

As I approached Parliament Square on Kearny, I could tell there was something else going on. Horse traffic slowed up to a halt and the road, although wide as a river, was clogged up solid.

I sat high on my horse to get a look-see. There looked to be a crowd of top hats down the street causing the hold up. I asked a rider in front of me, "What's going on?"

"Rally," he said. Union on the left, secessionist on the right.

I lifted my head to see a story high podium on one side of the square and the same again on the other side. The one closest, to the left, was decorated with large star spangled flags, and banners full of black lettered words.

There was a man, talking to the high hats. Drum was the speaker's name. The richest man in San Francisco. I tried moving in closer with the horse, to get moving at least, when I heard what Drum was saying.

"So I say to you gentlemen, liberty and union are one and the same. They cannot be separated. It is the union, the whole union, and nothing but the union."

A rally of support followed. With men hat waving, and hand clapping. Drum then waved his hat to the crowd of cheering onlookers, nodded his head to say thank you, and disappeared from the podium. A band playing music quickly replaced him.

When that was over, everyone removed their hands from their ears and turned their attention to the other side of the crowded square.

I set my eyes at looking for a way out. Any square foot of space that opened up before, I filled it with my horse. My plan was to edge my way to the other side of the square in this manner: A slow but sure plan of escape.

As I moved closer to the secessionist's podium, a familiar sight caught my eye.

Standing up above was a portly man in a white hat and suit. Wearing a face like a pitted bullfrog.

It was him: The Gold Daddy. The man who robbed me blind. The man I could have killed but failed to.

He had his spectacles on. The afternoon sun glinting on the gold. He was shuffling papers in his hand. Talking to some other men by his side and chuckling. Shaking hands with them. All looking happy with themselves.

I hid amongst the sea of black cabs. From there, upon my horse, I looked up and watched him, adjusting his glasses, shuffling his papers. I noticed his fat hand was shaking as he did so. And the son of a bitch had dared call me a yellow belly. And so I was, if truth were told. I had my opportunity handed on a platter and I failed. Saul had called me a hero. Well, I was no fool. I knew exactly what I was to him. A music box monkey. Like the one down Jefferson dock. That critter wore tailor made clothes too. To attract more customers. Ten cents' worth of amusement, and the only thing that monkey did was wind up a machine, and jump up and down while it played a tune. Which is what monkeys did anyhow. A lousy dollar and half and a boy called Goldsmith Jones gets nearly ripped in two by that old fat frog up there in a white suit and gold rimmed eyeglasses. But, when it was all said and done, at least I got some nice clothes out of it. Probably get a dollar just for the shirt. Maybe more if I was canny.

"A free state," Mr. P said from above.

The onlookers kept on looking.

Mr. P pulled on his bowtie and cleared his throat.

"A free state," he repeated. "A whole free state, and nothing but a free state." There he stopped. And waited for the high hats to respond.

Down below cart wheels creaked. Horse hooves clopped. Men smoked. Men mumbled. Men folded their arms. Men tried slipping away.

Men close to the Gold Daddy, the ones on the podium, shouted, "Here, here!" and clapped, as if to instruct those below how to put their hands together and make noise.

Mr. P wiped his brow with a handkerchief. Tucked it back in his top pocket, and did something I had not seen him do before. Smile. And what a strange face it was. His eyes became two slits. His cheeks bulged like crab apples that'd been got at by worms. When he grinned, his mouth became a cave, his tongue a snake, an eel slithering and wagging from the dark within.

The blood in my veins ran for cover. Something burned in my belly and shot up to my throat.

"Are you not intelligent men?" Gold Daddy said. "Do you not work hard for your lot? Your wives, your children?" Men stopped in their stead, and top hats everywhere seemed to nod.

"Now gentlemen, you do not need a government on the other side of the continent telling you what to do. You are not children. You are not women. You are men. Free men. Your granddaddies fought to free yourselves from tyranny. And you have shown your gratitude, by living like free Christians."

Quiet clapping followed. Top hats bobbed. Flies buzzed.

"Now gentlemen, I can see in your faces that you know who the true tyrant is here. And I am not talking of our dear Mr. Drum. He is but a tadpole swimming with the sharks. The real tyrant is of course, a lawyer."

Top hats looked to one another and chuckled.

"Abraham Lincoln is not a man of law. He is a disrupter of law, a destroyer of the law. A cheap wordsmith, my fellows. A man not worthy to clean your granddaddy's shoes, let alone stand in his boots."

"Here, here," the top hats said.

"A man driven by greed, who, at this very moment, is making bedfellows with the very princes our forefathers fought to free us from.More cheering.

"Robbing from hard working men like you, Jeremiah Crump."

Crump nodded. Hands patted Crump on the back. More clapping. "And you, Mr. G."

Mr. G nodded. More clapping.

"Stealing from the honest living white man."

"Here, here," went a wave of claps and nods, while flies whizzed around horses' heads in a frenzy.

"Taxing you, gentlemen, for a war you did not agree to."

"Aye aye aye."

"Dictating laws for you to abide to, as though it was you who are a slave, who must show fear and respect to your master, Abraham Lincoln. I tell you gentlemen, California is free to make its own laws: a free state, a whole free state, and nothing but a free state."

Men threw their hats in the air, clapping and cheering. Mr. P was sweating like a water hog, wiping his sopping brow and yanking up his waistband, falling low down beneath his fat belly.

I turned my horse toward my freedom. And let the flies buzz on.

Chapter 34
Peg legs

I zigzagged back up several narrow side roads and moved onto Clay Street again. Further down this time, close to Pacific dock. I could see a paddle steamer blowing coal and an army of seagulls and fishermen fighting over an overflowing net. I rode along Pacific dock to where it met Jefferson. I stopped at the tavern with the five bullet holes in the door, now seven and counting. It was heaving with men getting pie-eyed. Some women in dresses: blue stripes, white stars, red corsets, were dancing with their legs flying up in the air, while a fella cranked out a bawdy tune on a piano.

I hitched my horse. I went in and asked around the card table for a navy called Mattie Hakes. As fortune would have it, the first fella I came to knew where he was: the gambling tent on Mackenzie.

I found the tent, ducked under somebody's arm to get in.

It was sweating hot. I asked at all the tables. But it was waste of precious time. I was laughed at, kicked at, ignored, told to beat it, or asked to go out back and shine John Thomas for a lousy two bits' pay.

Tired, my legs aching, my chest raw from running, my brain hurting from thirst, I left.

I dipped my head in the first rain barrel I came to, drank, washed my neck, and wondered what the hell to do next.

I shuffled back to my horse with my hands in my pockets and tried thinking what to do. It was about that time that I noticed the horse had muddy boots. I pulled a rag out from the saddlebag and dusted her off. That's when I saw her white socks. Goddam it, if I hadn't gone and stole Saul's prize beauty! I figured I ought to forget about Mattie Hakes and return the horse right away before they come after me for stealing.

I started to panic. I thought of what the hell I was going to say. Say it got loose and wandered off on its own accord? Or maybe say someone else rustled it and I went on the rescue. Chasing that rustler up and down town then hogtying him with a rope I didn't have. But Saul had more smarts than me. And would want to know who, where, what and everything besides.

I kept my hat pulled down low and looked out for people looking at me. Which seemed to be everybody.

I stole into the shadows every time a rider happened by, and ducked for cover every time I heard Spanish.

I passed Kong Sung's where you put anything they had on a plate for a $1, if it could fit, and remembered I was hungry. I had nothing in my pockets. So I went around back of the restaurant and stood in the free scraps line, hoping to get some pigswill before it became so.

A raggedy looking fella in line came up to me. "Hey. You know that comely young Joe, don't you?" he said.

I said, "What comely young Joe?"

"The comely one," the fella said. "The one wears the navy get up all the while."

"Mister," I said, "is you talking about a navy called Mattie Hakes?"

"Oh, I thought his name was Nelson. You know him too?"

"No, no, I ain't never heard of no Nelson. But, do you know where he's about? A navy called Mattie Hakes, that is?"

"Well," he said, spitting chew, "I heard tell him and another whitey are boarded up making strange bedfellows in a shanty south of the city. Not only that but they're wanted by the law. For robbing union property. And they own debts. Owe me $10 for my get up. Union navy registered, see. Got to be to wear the uniform." And he showed me a tattoo of an eagle and some words that must have meant what he said.

"I'd go and get it myself but I had to sell my horse. And as you can see I ain't got the means for long travel. Up hill and all."

I looked down and saw he had a leg missing.

"I lost my peg when them damn confeds tried blowing up the rail bridge with nitro glycerin. They never did get her, but they got my leg."

"Oh, that's a real shame," I said, "but look mister, can you tell me how to get to this cabin? I'll get your $10 back for you?"

"Why you want to be going up there? You seeking retribution?"

"I might be, yessir."

"Why boy, what them bandits do to you?"

Out the corner of my eye I saw a familiar looking horse. The kind Jinxy rode.

"Uh, what?" I said to Peg Leg. "Oh, yes, stole something, belonging to a brother."

"Well," he said, "if you come by getting my $10 back off them, I doubt I'd ever see the sight of you again. But seeing, as you want your own vengeance. I'll tell you where they're hid. Maybe the luck will be on your side. Say, where's your brother at?"

I saw the rider on the familiar horse. It was the Jinx. Heading down my way. Two of his long-coated cronies riding along side.

"He got a gun on him?" said Peg leg.

I looked at Jinx and saw that he did. Along with his hanging rope.

Peg Leg spit chew on the ground. "Well, your bro'll need a firearm if he's going up there, that's for sure. I owned a Colt .56, brand new it was. First weapon ever issued to a man of color in the whole of the state. Proud of it I was. Had the finest balance a gun ever had. But, I fell on hard times and sold it to a red-eyed Spaniard who couldn't hit a bull's ass with a handful of banjos. Could sure as hell fasten a lasso though."

Jinx was coming close, hanging onto his shot with one hand and the rein in the other. He was eyeballing every single individual on a horse, and looked madder than a peeled snake on a hot day in July.

"Oh mister," I said, hanging onto my hat, "Can you just tell me where's the place at? Please mister, please."

"What? Oh, let's see: you take the rode out the city, and head for the hills. Take the mule trail heading for the coast. Keep going until you find Old Dead Red. You can't miss him. He's about as old as Moses. Top half him's long gone. From there, look for a trail heading south. If you head out now, you should make Dead Red by sundown. Just don't mosey. And keep a lookout for wolves. Make sure your guns are loaded. You'll need them."

Chapter 35
Old dead Red

I'd been traveling for what felt like twenty miles on the mule trail. Up and down I rode, through the sun baked headland of the Lone Mountain, until I came to a forest of redwoods. I left the sun behind and rode into the wilderness, with trees as tall as Jacob's Ladder; ferns the size of a small body; gentle leaf bearing trees surrounded by their young, and a whole world smelling of green life and old death.

Somewhere in the forest, coyotes were howling. Crows left the cover of the treetops and cawed for the night to come. The horse began to grunt. She was sweating, and blowing hot. I figured with all this greenery, there had to be a creek around someplace. Just around the trail bend was a great tree stump the size of a shanty.

It was him.

Old Dead Red.

I hitched the horse to a nearby sapling and ran to him. I climbed up him, inside of him, through his decaying holes that made for fine lookouts, and back inside of him again. He smelled of everything that had ever lived and died in that forest, and crawled with the many-legged things that lived on what was left of him.

I clambered to the top of the great stump. Found a ledge of sorts that seemed safe for perching and balanced myself by holding to a piece of tree that stuck up like a ship's mast. From my crow's nest, I surveyed my surroundings. It was well into dusk now, and the green bushes cast dark shadows that made it hard for any path to show up. I heard soft rustling behind me. A deer was making its way through the slender line to the right of Dead Red.

"It's thataway," I said to myself. But then I saw another deer trailing in the opposite direction. So now there were two routes leading in either side of the compass.

"Shit," I said. "Which way am I supposed to go?"

Nearby in the forest, the coyotes were howling in harmony. Soon wolves joined in, barking deadly songs of their own. I held on tight to my tree-mast.

Joe's ghost climbed inside my head and stood there inside my mind's eye with his hands in his pockets. "I know exactly where we are," he said. "There's a Muwekma town about a mile and a half that away. Now, I reckon we head up there. We can trade that horse. Probably get two for what this one's worth easy."

"Look Joe," I said. "I ain't got time for stopping with Raccoon and his relations for nothing. He gone and run out on me same as you. Same as always happens. And I sure as hell ain't parting with Saul's horse. Once I done with my mission, I'm taking her back to him."

"Well, his brother will hang you. For horse thieving."

"I ain't stole his horse, I only borrowed him. And you're one to talk of stealing."

"I only borrowed what I could not afford. I'd have had that gold fortune if that Devil hadn't come a calling. And got me waylaid."

"Oh goddam it," I said, "Stop splitting hairs. You know damn well borrowing's same as stealing. It's all the same goddam thing."

"No, it ain't all the same goddam thing."

"Well so what if it ain't. I ain't selling Saul's horse, that's final."

"All right fine," said Joe, "we don't sell the horse. But boy, I don't know whether you noticed or not, but it's getting dark. And we don't have a lamp. We don't have food, and we don't have a gun. And what's more, I don't even know where the hell we're going, for you're jack shit at reading stars."

"South," I yelled at him, "we're going south."

"Well, I figured we were going south. Dumbass me reckoned on that part when we started going south. But why the hell are we going south?"

"To save Mr. Hakes."

"To save Mr. Hakes? To save Mr. Hakes from what?"

"From Jinx playing cat's cradle with his neck, that's what."

"Oh, to hell with Mr. Hakes," said Joe. "He can save his own neck. It's our necks you ought to be saving."

"Well I don't know what you're fretting for. You're already dead." Then I stopped fighting. I felt the blood run fast from my face down to my boots. I stood there cold.

"What is it?" said Joe.

"The horse," I said, my eyes looking about in the near darkness. "Where the hell is it?"

I looked over at the hitching tree.

No horse.

I looked all around me. Nothing. Not a hoof in sight.

I listened out. The wolves in the distance were growling and barking mad. I reckoned they were about a mile off. But when they called again, they sounded closer. Half a mile.

I slid down from the top of the stump and down into its belly. Climbed out and started looking all around for Saul's horse. I was surrounded by bushes, dense trees and ever closing darkness.

Close by, coyotes cried like beaten children. The wolf pack growled and could be heard fighting one another. I figured they must have got something. I called out for Joe. But that devil had abandoned me once again. I held myself together with my arms, and covered my mouth when I felt the itch to scream.

I heard a rustle in the bushes yonder. I climbed back inside Dead Red and climbed to the top of where his head used to be.

The night was falling, but the full moon was rising. It provided a road of heavenly blue light along the path ahead.

I prayed for Angel Gabriel to guide me. I felt him come over me with his wings on my shoulders, warm and strong. I left Dead Red. Pushed my way through thorny vines and ragged creepers. Deep, deeper into the blackening forest I moved. Carefully, carefully I followed the light. Soon I heard a noisy stream. Then I saw her.

Saul's priceless horse.

It seems she had led Gabriel and me down to the river.

I stood on the edge of fast moving, clear running water. Ankle deep Darling stood, her head drooping as she drank.

First thing I did was remove my hat and use it as a bowl to wash my head and drink.

Darling comes to me. Shining in the moonlight, nudges her pretty head against my own scraggy mane. I sat down on the gravel next to her, dipped my hat and sipped sweet cool heaven.

I looked beyond the wild down rush, toward a large rock sitting in the water that split the stream into two paths. "I know this place," I said to Gabriel and the horse. "I come here with Mr. Hakes all the time on a Sunday. We must a come by it a different way."

I took stock of my bearings. Reckoned we must be on the other side of the river. The horse and me drank more water. As soon as I'd quenched my thirst, the full weight of weariness fell upon me. My body burned and ached from riding so long as tense as a wire. The wolves had stopped yowling. Now there was only the occasional bark and snarl.

"Think they'll come this way?" I said.

Gabriel said nothing. For it turned out he was a mute.

"Doubt it," said the horse. She was digging her hooves in the gravel, showing up tiny shiny flecks of gold in the twilight. She stopped and turned her head back to the river, and listened for the sounds of the night. "Coyotes might," she said. "But they're a bunch of scared chickens. Probably stay clear of us."

I drew in a cool breath and lay down upon the riverbed. Put my arms behind my head and looked up at the darkening sky. There were still signs of sunset. Pink and purple brushed over night blue. Stars were beginning to peep out. I watched them being born before my very eyes. A moth with shaky wings hovered. It hung around a while, until another come. Together they fluttered up toward the stars. I turned my head and looked back toward El Dorado, and pictures of Sweet Virginia drifted inside my head. Soon my eyes closed, and slumber became my friend.

"What we really got to worry about is the bears," said the horse.

I opened my eyes. And dared not close them again.

There was a noise.

The creek was wide-awake. But there was another sound. I jumped up. "Did you hear that?" I said.

The horse kept quite and listened. "I hear it," she said. "It sounded like a familiar whistle."

"That ain't no whistle," I said. "Sounded more like a critter. A big one."

"It's coming from the river," she said, stepping into the water and looking out.

I waded into the water with her, and hung on to her saddle. I looked out across the rugged water. Cloud blinded out the moonshine. When the way became clear I saw Saul: on horseback. Knee deep in water, and not a hundred yards away.

Gonz was there also. And two others from the gang. But, there was no Jinx.

I knew that Devil and his noose had to be somewhere close by. Some branches behind me cracked. My heart beat hard against my chest. The hair on my neck stood up like a wolf's. I could hear every single sound as though it were coming from inside my ears. Wood snapped. Leaves rustled. But it was only a deer. Trying to rescue some leaves being held prisoner by a bunch of treacherous thorns.

I turned my attention back to the river. The water was black. The crows had stopped cawing. The night had finally come to call. I could see Saul's face lit like a corpse in the moonlight: the silhouette of his rifle resting on his lap.

I heard the cocking of a gun. I put my hands up and said a prayer to Jesus. Squeezed my eyes shut and waited.

I heard a loud crack and fell to my knees, hitting stones in the water.

I figured I'd been hit. But nothing hurt. Reckoned pain doesn't show straight away. I looked up. With both eyes wide I looked across the river for Saul.

But like the day, he was gone.

Chapter 36
The shack

I asked myself, "What just happened?" and told myself, "I don't know." Maybe Saul was going to try and cross the river further upstream.

I jumped on the horse and rode off back to Old Dead Red. It was dark and all I had regarding light was the glow of a full moon.

I headed south. The trail was narrow and bendy. I kept the North Star behind me and kept Sweet Virginia in my head to keep my pluck from running scared. Soon, I come to see a light shining through the leaves ahead. It was the yellow glow of a lamplight.

I kept the light in my eye, and my heart steady. Soon I made out the dark shape of a cabin. Closer to it still, I heard voices. Men. Two at least.

I hitched up the horse and headed for the shack.

The window was covered with a piece of pale leather that had been nailed from the inside. Shadows moved. But they told me nothing.

I tried looking in between the log walls but all I could see was pure blackness. I put my ear close to the wood and listened for goings on inside the cabin.

I heard fighting words. One of them swore to Jesus. The other started laughing. Then he stopped. And all was quiet.

Then one of the men started making awful sounds. Like you hear on the battlefield when the smokes clear and you go around searching for what they can't take with them anymore. And sometimes they ain't dead yet. They put their hand out and try grabbing hold of you, to drag you down into that crater grave of blown up bodies with them. With all those begging words. Pleading for your life words.

My heart was running fast. My body was hot but my skin was freezing over. For it was Sweet Virginia's voice I'd heard crying out. I knew it was him for I lived only for hearing his voice. And right now, he sounded like Floyd. Just before the noose got too tight for him to talk. Before the choking and the dying come. I heard it so. All the while, I stood outside doing nothing. Letting him die, die, die right in front of my ears.

Sweet Virginia was in trouble.

I had to make myself a man and do it fast.

I looked around. Two dead rabbits hung by the side of the hut. A musket rifle was propped up beneath them.

I removed my boots, then stole over and picked up the gun from its place against the timber wall.

The hares above my head began to swing and creak. I stopped them dancing with my hand. Their fur was soft and warm in my fingers. Their bodies stiff and cold in the night.

The musket weighed heavy in my arms. I held onto it with both hands and went to the door. I tried lifting the gun up to my shoulder first, but it wasn't going to work. I knew less than most about employing a firearm, but the thing I did know about a musket was that it could rip your arm straight out of its socket if you weren't careful. I'd seen it happen once, and remembered it well now. So I held it low down, tight against my hip, and set my finger on the trigger.

I stood by the door. I looked at the shadows moving on the skin window. I saw hands dancing and faces turning. Arms untangling and backs arching. It was then, an unwelcome thought made a nest inside my head. It had come flying to my mind before, but I'd chased it away and punished myself for listening to such lies. For Peg leg had talked of strange bedfellows up on the mountain, and I figured those words were nothing but poisonous feathers blowing fast and free in the wind, for Virginia loved me so, even though he never said the words to me, not once, not never. Now Peg leg's words come flapping back to me now. Like a gang of angry crows, picking inside my head, tearing out pieces of my brain. Making it burn. Setting my ears on fire. Making them a ring, ring, ring.

My finger stiffened on the trigger. I held my breath and opened the door just a crack with my shoulder. I stood still. My arms and legs were shaking. My eyes were wide and the hut was dark, all but for the flicking glow of a lamplight burning, which got through the crack of the open door.

The smell spoke to me first. The scent of the Dead Man: all sweat and liquor; shit and spunk. My eyes took a few moments to see into the shadow, and then all was revealed to me. There were two men: Matthew Hakes and another. A long, white bodied one going all out. Wild horses, howling coyotes, sweating pigs and all the rest. My blood ran hot. My body shook. They were too busy being friendly to see me. Kissing and holding on to one another like sly lovers in the Rose Park. My heart was beating in my chest to come out of my body. My soul called to the Devil to go on back to hell.

I moved from the door in silence. With the musket low down against my thigh, I aimed for the stranger's back.

I was sweating. The sweat spread to my fingers and the gun slipped from my hands. It did not drop but the effort of re-adjusting it against my hip again made noise and alerted them to me.

They untangled themselves fast, fast, fast.

I felt for the trigger.

The long-body turned to face me. His hair was stuck to his maw. He peeled it away with his hand. One side of his face bore the scar of a knife. Cut long ways down, starting from his forehead, and taking some of his eye along with it. The knife had then changed course and tore across his nose and cheek, before turning back down his neck. There was no mistaking who he was.

Him who used to be Violet: Little Brother Johnsie.

My mouth burned dry. I swung the musket from one man to the other. Mattie Hakes was crouched over on his knees, behind Little Brother like a coward. He wiped his mouth with the back of his hand, and I saw his hand was shaking. He fumbled around on the board for his shirt. I figured he might be up to tricky business so I stabbed the musket in his direction, saying, "Stay where you are or I'll shoot you."

Hakes left his shirt alone. His hand scampered back to his yellow-belly knees.

I ran my eyes back and forth between the two of them.

"Kid," Hakes said to me, putting his hands up.

I stabbed the air with the gun and said, "My name is not kid."

Neither of them moved. All eyes were on me.

Little Brother started to talk calling me, "Boy."

I raised the muzzle as high as I could, pointing it at his chest. "Shut up," I said, swinging the musket at him. "My name ain't boy neither. My name is Jones. Goldsmith Jones. And you wronged me," I said, turning the gun back to lying, cheating, Hakes.

"If you don't mind, " said the Little Brother. "I only wanted to ask you, how you found us here? Are you with people?"

I ran closer to him saying, "Shut your mouth. I don't want you speaking to me," and turned my attention back to Hakes.

He was naked. The glow of the lamplight shone on him, like angel Gabriel. His pretty eyes talked to me. I began to listen. He wanted to say precious words, but I refused him like he'd done me.

My tears were coming. Water ran down my cheeks and dripped onto my hand. The wolves outside were calling again. Coyotes were singing their deadly song.

"You said you were going take me with you, to San Marco," I said to him. "You were going to get the ranch and I was going to mind the horses, remember?"

"Well I don't exactly recall the conversation," he said, twiddling his fingers in the air. I caught him making sneaky glances with Little Brother.

"Stop looking at him," I said, holding the gun close to my hip, and aiming the muzzle at his head. "Why are you looking at him for? You're looking at me. I'm the one talking to you."

"I am looking at you," said Hakes, holding his hands higher in the air. "It's only I don't remember making such plans is all."

"No, of course you don't," I said. "You were too busy playing bitch and hound with me to recall nothing. And I risked my life to come here, to save your neck from Saul and his crazy headed brother Jinx. They're coming for you right now. Going string you up, Mattie Hakes, just like them rabbits out there."

I caught Little Brother out lowering his hands.

I swung my hip and held the musket toward him. "Put them back up," I said, "right now or I kill you dead."

He said, "No, I won't," and kept them down.

I wrestled with the musket in my arms, to stop it from slipping. "Then, Mister, I'm going kill you," I said, getting on target and feeling for the trigger.

Little Brother rose up. I took stock of him: a pale giant with a messed up face. His shirt was undone. He took the time to fasten up his belt. And then he comes for me.

I took aim. My whole body shook like a drunkard on a dry wagon. My eyes were blinking, my fingers trembling on the trigger.

Then he was on me. Picked the musket from my quaking hands, and in a single motion, twisted the gun around, and rammed the butt end into my face.

The force made my skull rattle and sent my body collapsing down onto the hard, dirty floor. I thought my face bones had been shattered and the shock of the blow caused me to shiver and scream, like a scorched cat.

Blood gushed from somewhere near my eye. I felt for the gash and tried holding back the bleeding. The wound was on my cheek. It burned hot and throbbed angry. Warmth ran between my fingers, down my chin making red puddles on my shirt. I spat out a couple of teeth and looked at them with one wide eye, crazily wiping the blood away to see the polished white, no longer living in my head.

Dirty metal stung my nose.

Something cold and hard was hurting my forehead. I looked up. Little Brother stood, steadily holding the musket with one hand, pressing the barrel into my thin skull.

"You, young sir," he said, "has been unnecessarily violent toward my gentleman friend and me."

I looked up, shaking, and blinking at what I heard was Violet's words.

"Now," he said quiet and slow, "I'm going to talk to the count of three, and you are going to tell me where Saul's at. And if you ain't done telling me by the time I get to the number three, I'm going to make a hole in your head, the size of my fist. In other words, I'm going to blow your brains out. Understand?"

Warm water ran down my legs and stung my thighs.

"One," he said.

"I don't know," I said, shaking, "I swear."

"Two."

"He's gone," I said. "I saw him but I lost him back at the river. About five miles back."

"Three."

"I swears to Jesus I ain't seen them since. I figured he's here already. I was coming for to do the rescue, of Mr. Hakes."

"Did you hear that?" said Virginia, getting dressed. "Here already, is what he said. Goddamn son of a bitch," he said to me, "you've gone and led that crazy black Spaniard straight to us." He took out a pistol of his own and began loading shot into it.

Little Brother lowered the musket from my head. He rested it against his shoulder like a military. "How did you get up here?" he said.

"Horse," I told him.

"Stolen from who?"

"Saul," I said, crying without tears. My face hurt so much I could no longer make words.

Mr. Hakes ran up to me and waved his pistol at my head.

"You stupid little cocksucker," he said. "What kind of dumbass would steal a horse from that crazy-headed nigger for?"

"I ain't stole it," I said holding onto my face. "He gave it me."

"Jesus Christ," he said, "I knew you were sweet on him but I didn't know you were so fool-headed full of romance you'd think he'd give you his goddam horse. What do you think he's going do? Go on the hunt of love for you? All that poetry going to your head? I knew it all along. You're his goddam fool. And you were gone and led him straight to us."

"Mr. Hakes," said Little Brother, "I do believe that scaring the boy is not helpful to our situation."

"Says the man who nearly blew his skull off a minute ago," said Hakes. He stuffed the pistol into his waist and spoke whispers into Little Brother's ear. When he was done talking to it, he kissed it.

I could only watch it all, with my one good eye, as I sat there bleeding and hurting like a cornered critter in a trap.

"We got to clear out," Virginia said, stroking Little Brother's back. "We can camp up by Two Crows and jump the 8:15 going north. I'll start loading the goods. You deal with him. But try not to kill him no more. And you," he said to me pointing, "keep your mouth shut unless you're told to answer, got it?"

I made a nod, then, with one eye blind, watched him carry on with his business.

My heart had sunk low. I was nothing to him. And had never been nothing to him. The truth of it came a slow, cold, bullet cutting through my chest. I wanted nothing but to lie there and let sleepy death come and get me.

"Get up on your feet," said Little Brother.

I pretended not to hear, but he took my arm and pulled me up anyhow.

My good eye had gone fuzzy. I held onto my face wound with one hand and staggered up off the floor, with him carrying me to my feet.

"Put your hand around my neck," he said.

I was woozy, so he did it for me.

My cheek was still bleeding. "Can I have something to bandage up my eye?" I said. "No," he said, "now move your legs with me."

Outside in the night, the Little Brother Johnsie bound me up. Tied my hands with rope and my ankles too. Set me on his horse. Then he and Mattie Hakes packed Saul's Darling with sacks of sweet smelling tobacco. Hakes was going to burn down the shack, but after Johnsie explained how setting the whole forest alight would probably attract unwelcome attention, he changed his mind. Together, with me hogtied over Johnsie's mare, we rode through the night, out of the forest, until we reached the railroad.

Chapter 39

Breakfast with Violet

They set up camp a short riding distance away from the train tracks. They kept me prisoner, laid down near the campfire. My bad eye was swollen shut, and my cheek was throbbing and making my skull ache with hot pain. Seeing the fire gave me comfort, but the glare pierced my brain like a knife.

I could hear Hakes saying to Johnsie, "I swear I don't know what he's talking about... I told you, he's one of Saul's Nancy boys... They'll say any old shit if they think it'll help them... Hell, I can't help it... they're always hustling me, chasing me down the street, following me everywhere I go... This one's gone sweet on me, that am all. So what if I did do dealing with Mr. P. I don't know why you're bitching so much. Where the hell you think I got the money for the horse? It ain't exactly growing on trees."

I was too tired and worn, and low in my heart to carry on listening. I dreamed up a time, before Jinx's slipknot, before the Gold Daddy full of shit, before traitor Mattie Hakes, before going down the dirty Dead Man, before setting eyes on Joe's swollen body beached up on the shore. Back and back I went, to a happy place I could barely remember. When a kind boy and me went rolling down a hill. Running up to the top panting and laughing, then roll, roll, rolling down again, smelling green grass, and flowers that only come along in the spring. And whatever happened to that kind boy? Whose name I could not at that time recall. My first friend. Who I cared for, with all my heart.

I woke up to the smell of coffee.

I'd been cut loose, and a horse blanket had been laid over me.

Crouched by the fire, Little Brother was stirring something up in a pan. He wore a black patch over his bad eye. He was giving me shifty looks from the side of his good one, the way Saul sometimes did.

I looked around for Hakes. He was pissing on a rock.

Little Brother brought me a tin mug of hot coffee and a bowl of boiled oats.

I watched him eating, savoring every spoonful myself. "What's in it?" I said to him.

He looked up and said, "Why? Don't you like it?"

I stopped eating, for that was surely Violet speaking words.

"Nossir, I do. It's just, I wondered how you make oats sweet." She swallowed and said, "It's called 'sugar'."

I nodded, took a sip of coffee, and kept eating. "Don't it makes your teeth black?" I said.

She shook her head and said, "Not if you brush them as a matter of habit. You never heard of a thing called a tooth brush, young man?"

"Nossir, I never heard of such of thing."

"Well, they ain't a new fangled thing. Been around a while." She went rustling through a bag and tossed it over.

I looked at it. Just a plain polished stick with some bristles on the end. "Can you give me a bandage for my eye now," I said, "sir?"

"You don't need one," she said. "Cleaner if you leave the wound to heal naturally. Put a cloth on it, it'll probably kill you," and she drank from her mug.

"Well I never knew that," I said.

She responded with a shrug.

She studied me and carried on eating. "So," she said. "You are acquainted with my brother."

"Brother?" I said.

"Saul," she said.

"Oh," I said.

"Never heard tell of me?"

"Oh yessir, I have. He talks of nothing else but you. I just don't recall him saying you were real brothers, that's all."

Violet nodded. "And how is he getting by?" she said.

I swallowed, and said, "Fine."

"You ever keep company with him?"

I nodded.

She looked at me sideways from her good eye, and said, "Anybody else?"

"Jinx and Gonz."

"No, I mean, the female sort."

"Women?" I said.

She nodded, and stopped eating while she waited for an answer.

"Reddie Mae," I said. "You know her? Red head. Wally-eyed…"

"Oh," she said, "oh, her."

"And Carlotta?"

She looked to the sky for her thoughts.

"Dark hair, curls. She goes in the cupboard a lot."

"Oh," she said. "That one. No, I never cared for her at all."

I nodded and we continued eating.

"How are his hands?" she said. "Does he suffer much?"

"No, they seem all right. George takes care of them."

"Oh yes. Well, at least, he can conceal the whole of his ugliness from staring eyes."

I thought it best not to say nothing. I began licking my bowl instead.

"Did no one ever teach you manners?" she said.

"Nossir," I said.

"Well, learn something now. You do not clean a bowl by licking it with your tongue like a dog."

I apologized, and she filled my bowl with more sweet food. "Mr. Jones," she said, "you made it your occupation to pursue my navy gentleman friend, when uninvited to do so."

"Nossir, I never did," I said, putting the bowl down.

"Are you calling Mr. Hakes a liar, sir?"

"Yessir, I am."

She eyeballed me with her unpatched eye, then looked down at her empty bowl, and began scratching it clean with her spoon.

Hakes come over. Crouches down to get himself fed. Starts talking on and on about train times and what he and Violet were going do when they got north.

I could have recited his words one by one. Get a paper partnership. Buy some land. Buy some horses. Get a couple of brides. Breed some children.

Violet nodded here and there as if she'd heard it all before too.

I decided to interrupt Hakes from his never-ending bullshit.

I got up, walked over to Violet, and pushed in front of Hakes, held out the toothbrush and said to her, "Thank you, sir, for your kindness."

She took it and said, "Thank you, Mr. Jones. I appreciate your courtesy."

I said, "You're most welcome, Mr—?"

"Violet."

"Mr. Violet, sir."

"You may address me as Johnson if it pleases."

"Johnson, you are most welcome." And I bowed like the Blue Boy, donning my hat and everything.

Then Johnson Violet took off her eye patch and said to me, "Do you, sir, think I am ugly?"

I looked at Violets face. A scar crossed the whole pretty landscape.

Hakes elbowed me on his way to putting his hand, uninvited,

onto Violet's shoulder. He began rubbing it saying, "Hell now, don't be crazy headed. You got a mean beauty, mister. A damn, mean beauty." He slid me snake eyes before kissing her full on the mouth and slipping her his tongue.

I went red hot. A fire boiled up in my chest. I blew out my nose like a young bull to let the steam out.

Violet pulled her face away from him before he was done. She turned to me and said, "Well, Mr. Jones? Do you think I'm ugly?"

"I ain't going to lie to you," I said. "The truth of it is, you ain't as comely as I figured you once were."

She stared at me with a blank expression.

Behind me, I heard Hakes snigger and say to me, "Jesus Mercy Christ. You are just all class."

I ignored him.

Violet comes back to me saying: "Thank you for your honesty, Mr. Jones. It's a welcome relief to my ears."

Mattie Hakes eyes went wide. "What?" he said to her. "I am being honest with you, mister. Why are you choosing to listen to that that little piece of shit for? I'm telling you, you are comelier than…"

Before he could say another word, Violet shot up off the ground and walked away fast, with her arms folded, to a place in the camp, far away from where he was.

Hakes took a pistol out of his boot and pointed it at me. "Goddam Nancy," he mumbled.

"My name ain't Nancy," I said, staring him dead in the eye.

He got ready to shoot words back at me then stopped himself. Lowered his gun. And gave me a sly, nasty look instead.

Chapter 40
The cockroach

Johnson put Violet to rest and returned to his manly other self again. Hakes and him were nearly ready to make tracks for the train. Johnson was kicking the fire out with his heavy boot when I heard something.

Johnson heard it too.

Horse hooves.

Galloping.

Three. Maybe five or six horses.

Johnson ran to his mount. "Mr. Hakes," he said.

Hakes weren't there.

The horses were getting closer. A train blew steam, its alarm whistled somewhere in the distance.

"Mr. Hakes," he said louder. "It's time to go."

Mr. Hakes came out of the bushes tying up his waistband. He quickly started loading sacks of tobacco onto Saul's horse.

"Leave it, Mr. Hakes," he said, "we ain't got time. C'mon, let's go."

I spun around wondering what the hell was going on. "What about me?" I said to him.

Johnson turned on his horse saying, "Boy, you ought to rid yourself of this great burden you carry, or it'll end up badly for you."

I said, "What?"

I followed after him. "What burden?" I cried. " What great burden you talking about?"

He ignored me, steadied his horse and called for Hakes to follow on, giving instructions on where to go and how to get there. Then he turned his steed around and rode off like hell fire towards the railroad.

Hakes grabbed the last sack of tobacco and went heading for Saul's horse.

I ran to her, and got there first. I pulled the musket they'd laid out from underneath the saddle.

I stood in front of the horse, guarding her. Held the musket low and pointed it at Hakes, carrying a bag of tobacco in his arms. "You ain't taking Saul's horse nowhere," I said.

"Look, kid," he said.

"It's Mr. Jones to you," I said.

He dropped the sack on the ground. "Alright. Jones," he said. "Look, I only need the horse to get to Two Crows. I jump the train; you get your horse back. It's simple."

I said, "It ain't about the horse."

"All right, all right," he said, " Look, I know you're sweet on me kid, and I'm sorry about that, truly I am. But, look; I tried doing you a favor. Now, if you hadn't tried robbing the old Daddy you would have been living the high life right now, and that's a fact. He told me so himself."

"What are you saying, 'you told him so yourself'? You set me up with that crazy-headed son of bitch, is that it? Is that what you're saying?"

"Now don't go blaming me for your misfortune, all you had to do was comply. Now move aside. And put the gun down, you ain't got the balls to use it anyhow."

I held the musket up against my shoulder and aimed for the ground next to Hakes' feet. My arm trembled and my eyes went blurry. I thought I saw Hakes move. I closed my eyes, took in a long breath and jerked the trigger.

It fired off. I flinched and the barrel shifted. The shot blast through the barrel out into the wide open space in front of me.

My shoulder shot back and pulled out from its socket. The bullet whistled as it went flying wild through the air.

Then, there was no sound at all. Just a dizzy ring-ring-ringing.

I tasted gunpowder on my lips. Grit was stinging my eyes. I was blinking, and looking around for Mattie Hakes.

He was flat on the ground, at first. He got himself up. Then, fell back down again. Did the same a second time.

On the third attempt, I watched him look down, to see what the problem standing was.

"My leg," he says. "What did you do to my goddam leg?"

I could barely breathe. I looked down and saw the bottom half of Hake's left leg was missing. All that remained was a string of red flesh hanging down like butcher's meat. Hakes went crazy-headed loon, looking around him for the rest of it.

And he found it. A couple of yards away, where Saul's horse had been standing. She'd run off some, when the shot was fired.

I watched him hop over to it, and picks up the stump from off the ground. Then I watched him sit down in the dirt with it, hanging on to it like a child. Laughing to his self as he tried putting it back onto his knee, which was also gone. The bullet had blown the whole thing off. All's I saw, from where I was standing, was a bunch of red-splintered pieces all over where he'd been when I took the shot.

I still had tight hold of the gun. My eyes kept going blurry. The whole world as I knows it, faded in and out. I heard my own breath getting loud. My heart went thumping and pumping: getting ready to explode.

A warm hand comes pressing down on my shoulder. I caught the scent of incense and the bitter smell of shot powder on my tongue.

Without even seeing his body, I knew it was him.

"Let go of the gun now, Little Brother," he said to me.

My fingers were clenched so tight hold of that musket, it was as though they were fused into one and could never be parted. Except for to cut away at my bones with a bowie knife, or a poker that's been resting on the red-hot coals.

"That's it," said Saul. "You're all done now. Ain't no more shot left. Just let your fingers go now, c'mon."

I dropped the weapon and Saul caught it and passed it through to air to Gonz, standing next to him. My legs lost all power for standing, and I fell to the ground.

The trees where they hung Mattie Hakes to finish him off were creaking. We were all sat around the campfire, the three Suarez brothers and me. They all thanked the Lord before dishing out the stew Gonz had made. I had nothing to say to Him. Or anyone again.

Gonz gave me a tinful and a spoon. I wouldn't take it. So he went and sat down next to me and walked back to his place by the fire.

When the brothers had done supping, they started drinking. But there was no getting pie-eyed. Saul forbids it. And Gonz and Jinx obeyed without protest.

Gonz began playing a familiar tune on a harmonica. Jinx kept a beat with the spoon on his tin can and sang the words. He wasn't bad at the singing neither. Which made me want to spit fire.

Saul took out a cigarillo from his jacket, lit it up, and then lay there watching his brothers make music. Tapping his foot to the beat.

I kept my eye on him. Once, he lifted his eyes to me. He searched my face and then fished around inside his coat pocket for something. Tossed me a whole cigarillo of my own to smoke. I thanked him with a nod. He did the same back. I staggered up, feeling beat up and bruised, and drew a light from the camp fire. I got the smoke going, and sat back down well away from singing Jinx but closer than I was before to Saul, who was smoking, and blowing rings up in the air.

He shook the whiskey jug at me.

I got up again. Had my cigar hanging out the side of my mouth just like him. I had blood everywhere; on my pants and on my new tailored shirt. And what I looked like with that swelled up black eye I do not know. For I did not have the pleasure of a looking glass.

I snatched the whiskey off of Saul. Stood there looking at him and taking my time with my swiggings. I shot a mean look at Jinx.

He stopped singing. And was staring at me with a pair of ugly snake eyes.

"All right," said Saul to me, "time to pass on the whiskey. Give it over."

I wasn't planning to obey at first. I stared at him and took a swig, making like I was going to drink it all. Dribbling whiskey down my neck instead.

"Come on," he said, "don't play the fool. I said give it to me, and sit down."

I thought about emptying that precious whiskey of his onto the dirt right in front of his eyes. For that would almost certainly get him going Jessie on me. Finally, get him punching at me. Then Jinx would join in. And Gonz. And one-legged him, swinging in the tree: creak, creak, creaking in the wind: he would have had his retribution on me.

Saul, with his hand outstretched to me, wearing hurt in his dark eyes, begged for me to be a good brother. So I gave the whiskey jug back. And sat nearer to him than I was before.

Some time later he got up, tapped his finger on my shoulder, and said, "Come walk with me a while, Little Brother."

The moon was almost full and it was clear and studded with stars. We looked up. Some were blue, some were red, and others were big and white. More went flying through the sky or falling to their death.

We took a stroll along the riverbed. The river was gentle and low. Every now and then a fish jumped up for air and splashed back down again. Some gentle critters were drinking from the stream and ran for cover as soon as we got close.

"How did you come by the name 'Jones'?" he said.

I said nothing.

We stepped over a dead tree that lay half buried in the river.
"Where's your people?"

I said nothing more.

"Well," he said. "You got people now." He found a rock he liked and told me to sit down next to him, so I did.

He took out his Chinese pipe and filled it up with black crumbs. He fired up a safety match and lit it up. When he drew, a cloud of perfume circled around him like a halo.

He gave me a smoke. My bad eye was beating sore. Within a few minutes of puffing, my head swam. My lips went numb. And then that feeling, of pure pleasure, coursed through my veins. Made me feel dizzy and sick and happy all at the same time.

"I didn't believe them when they came and told me you'd stole my horse," he said. "I was ready to bring out my whip a beat a boy for lying."

My head was too heavy to hold up so I let it rest in my hands, and then I let my hands rest on my lap.

"And you got your fine things all messed up," he said. " Fine things that I just spent a fortune on."

"I don't want nobody to die no more," I said.

"The only people who die are the people who don't deserve to live. Or, who are so good, that the Lord in heaven calls them up there with him, so they don't get to suffer no more."

"I just don't want anybody I love to die no more ever again."

I heard him relight his pipe. I turned my head in my hands and watched him. The moonlight showed his face. He wore a look of beautiful sadness. I took the pipe from him, and leaned my head against his shoulder, and smoked.

"I'm sorry," I said, and I leaned my head against him. He pulled me close, kissed the top of my head, and rubbed my shoulder and I did smile. I put my mouth to his neck. I could taste the salt on my tongue and it was good. But he pulled me off him saying, "Now looky here, it ain't like that with me."

"But, why?" I said. "I don't understand what it is you want?"

"For you to be my brother," he said. "To be part of my

family. You know, you are the true likeness of myself at your age, in many ways. And here you are. Proved yourself a grown man. I was 18 before I killed my first enemy. Jinx still has you beat, though. He was 12."

"Please don't say I killed Mr. Hakes," I said, holding onto his arm. "Please say it were the Jinx that done it."

"All right," he said, "if that's how you want the story to be told."

"It is," I said. "Oh, it is. I tell you it weren't me that stopped him breathing."

"Brother, he was already gone," said Saul. "You shoot a man's leg off, out here in the wilderness, and he ain't gonna live. Jinxy only hung him high so he could get to the other side quicker."

"But, why did he got to hang him so? Why not shoot him dead and be done?"

"Because you can't bury a body out here in the middle of a forest that's why. Look around you. There's only trees, trees and more goddam trees. So, where you gonna dig a goddam hole? The only way is to hang him up so as the wolves don't get him. Or they'll be pieces of him from here to San Marco. And that ain't gonna be a pretty sight to stumble on. Besides, Indian folks don't appreciate the likes of you and me leaving parts of human being all over their land, which is what this is. They say it brings out all kinds of strange spirits. And I got enough ghosts keeping me up all night with out their ghouls on my tail."

I buried my head in my hands saying, "It's all hopeless ain't it? I'm the one that killed him dead. That is the truth of it. Oh, why am I alive? Why ain't I dead with him and Joe? Why's everyone I love go dying on me?"

I pushed him away from me; I got up and stumbled into the river. I heard him behind me, calling. But I swore right then I was never going to hear him again. I was never going to hear nobody again. When I heard the splash of him coming to get me, I fell down on my knees and crawled through the water until I was swimming. I kept swimming toward El Dorado. Sometimes it was too shallow and I had to crawl again. Then the deep would take me down under, where I wanted to be. So as I could drown like Joe. But it was the cold that took hold of me. Soon my lip was shivering and I could feel no part of my body. Like smoking crumbs but there was no pleasure in it. Only a terror of being alone and drowning in the cold, unfriendly darkness.

Chapter 41
The white wolf

It was then I decided that I did not want to die. I wanted to live. The water was pushing me and pulling me downstream. Sometimes I was drowning, my head under the water holding my breath. Then I was in the air, and I caught what breath I could with what small time there was and went under living again. Then the water stopped beating me, and pushing me under. The river becomes gentle, and I saw a rock. I grabbed on to it with my good arm but it wasn't working, so I made my rescue with my right. And pulled my body up over it, hanging on tight to the slippy edge. I looked up and saw I was on the big rock with the flat top. The one Sweet Virginia and me took our pleasure on times and times before.

As I lay on the surface, a great pain comes to get me, making me cry out, many times.

The size of it—the splendor of it—made fear take hold of all my senses. I could not see, nor hear, nor feel nothing but its burny beating beneath my skin. Inside my bones. I was sure I was going to break apart, and shatter into the water. Like broke glass pieces of a window pane. I spewed up water and yellow bile. I prayed for strength and mercy. Reached out my working arm to the sky. Begging for help that would not, could not come. For I was all alone, with myself, in the wilderness.

In my burning bath of sorrow, my broke body laid low upon the hard rock. My head hanging, puking up nothing, but what was left of my life, that was living in my belly: I lifted up my good eye. I saw a shadowy figure up ahead. I blinked until I could see it with a clearer vision. White as new fallen snow it was. Eyes blue as the sky itself. Staring at me. Its nose was black, its body straight and still.

It was a wolf. A white wolf.

I kept my silence. My great pain beat inside my body, beating on me to cry out. But for my life's sake, I would not answer its relentless call. Instead, I kept my good eye peeled on the white wolf and listened to my pain's violent drum. It held its all-out hell-fire, and set steady aim on a single place. Told me now my good arm was broke. Throbbing inside and burning me with lashes of a fiery whip.

I kept my gaze on the wolf.

He kept his eyes on me and took a sideways step along the river bank. Stopped and considered me again.

Then he comes for me with slow, measured steps through the icy water.

He stopped again. And sniffed the air.

I reckoned he was coming to finish me off. My blood was baying for him to take me, for it was pouring out of the gashes caused by my turns in the rocky water.

But I turned fearless. My great pain was busy doing its work, but I would not concede. A precious feeling come, numbing my mind until I could barely care for pain at all. But, like the wolf, it was still there. Trying to possess me. I fought with it. Anger only made it fight harder. And punish me with its beating. Then I got my smarts. Made it become burning gold, forging my arm into a precious thing of pure beauty.

I thought about dying. How my wolf friend would come for me, and eat my flesh. Tearing at me, and what other pain that would be.

I was fearless now, but how fearless would I be when that time come? I reached into my back pocket. For, if I had any luck at all left in the world, it would be for my fingers to grasp hold of that knife—the white wolf—so I could cut my own throat with it, and save myself the torture of my inevitable end. And fortune was on my side, for how I do not know, save for some miracle of Jesus, it was still there.

With my working arm, I brought the knife to my lips, where I kissed the hilt. I looked at it. The white wolf carved into the ivory. I considered it against the real thing standing in the water in front of me. And how such beauty can never be created by human hands, no matter how skilled in the art.

I smiled at the golden day breaking through the trees. I welcomed my natural fate. I spoke to the white wolf. I said I did not mind being eaten by such a thing. For the idea that I would become part of he, not a man, not an object, but a critter living wild and free would be my deathly wishes if I could have chosen my own fate. For he was the Spirit Wolf, of Ohlone legend, as Raccoon had once told. And had living around his neck. Laying close to his beating heart. Whose blood now ran, pumping for life's sake in my veins. Soon I would be part of him. Part of the forest. Living for ever, unless mankind comes to shoot me down with deadly lead and explosive hell-fire.

But I was not a dumbass, and I did not care for being chewed to death while I was still awake to know about it, so I took my knife. And put it to my vein.

It was easy to find, for it was pounding hard inside my neck.

My right hand was weak, but I needed to use all my force to make it strong.

I held it there with the blade pressed close to its blue pumping cord. I waited for the white wolf to start a-coming. Timing it so that when he made his start I'd cut hard and quick. And keep cutting until I lost all conscientiousness of ever being alive.

The white wolf took his time. First, he comes a-creeping slowly toward me, traversing the water without a care for rocks or cold or broken down logs. He stood a little away from me and made a whining sound. Moved his head around and then turned his nose to the air, and barked like a stray dog.

Then he comes closer.

I moved my knife hand nearer to my flesh. The motion I made made him skittish. He turned quickly in the water. I figured he was going to run away, but he didn't. Only faced me again, and whined like he was the one hurting.

He moved slowly to me. My legs were numb, for they were naked and icy cold. I decided I'd wait for him to start on my bony flesh before I dig and cut my life away at the neck.

He comes a-creeping again, and sniffs at my feet. Then my knees and my thigh. He licked my skin, with a warm rough tongue. And kept licking me. But, not biting. Not yet.

He must have smelled blood for he was going crazy looking for it. Found my cuts and licked them clean. Then he heard something yonder. His ears pricked and he stopped doing and looked into the forest. He left my side and trotted over to the river bank. Began licking the front of his paws dry of my blood. Listened again.

Stopped.

Turned.

Took a lasting look at me, and then ran off, silent into the woods.

I relaxed my killing hand and let the White Wolf lay softly in my palm. Then I let it slide, and fall into the river below. Falling also, I drifted into deathly sleep.

Chapter 42
A new beginning

Something had a hold of my body, and I was lifted onto a horse and carried off back to someplace warm, smelling of wood smoke and dried fish. I heard the long, slow beat of a drum. I was laid next to a fire and wrapped in horse blankets. Soon sleep fell on me. Heavy, and deep.

I lay there shaking with chills. I rolled my hands over my belly; there was a puddle of sweat where it caved in. My chest was running wet. My heart was hot. I looked at my soaking arms all covered in gooseflesh. My throat burned, and I tried not to swallow. For the fiery pain of it caused my body to flinch. And that got my belly going mad-dog, tearing at my insides, beating them with little fists, and making me wretch. One time I puked up the Devil's black coals. And I knew I was done for. The Devil would be waiting for me, to take me to down to hell.

I cried out and thrashed around, begging for mercy. "Jesus," I cried out, "Jesus save me. Save me. Please."

I felt a soft cold cloth press against my forehead and wipe my face and burning cheeks. I looked but could only see the desert haze. A shape of somebody was there. I held out my hand to them. "Make Jesus take me with him," I said. I felt a body sit down on the board. I smelled the leather. And incense. The shadow of a calfskin hand took hold of mine.

"You're going to be with Jesus, Little Brother," he said. "The Padre's here. He's going to see you get there." Then he grasped my hand tight, and I feared he would leave me, so I held on.

"Don't go," I said, "please don't leave me to die alone. It's always been you. The first time I set eyes on you. I felt it. Hold me while I die." But he let me go like I knew he would. Somebody else took his place. Speaking strange Spanish and crazy English. I smelled Violet's frankincense. I called her name. She didn't answer.

A hard thumb dug oil on my forehead, my shoulders, and my heart—that was dying sore.

I saw a light in front of me. Flickering like a candle flame. There was a body. It was Joe returned from the grave.

I stretched out my hands to him and smiled. "Joe," I said, "Joe, you come back. You came back again. You Devil. Oh Joe, why'd you leave me so? I told you he weren't no angel. Why you never listen to me?"

"I told you to take no heed," he said. "All in God's plan like I said."

"You and God been planning things? Couldn't you tell me about it? Instead of letting me land in the shit?"

"I couldn't say nothing," he said. "Boy's got to learn to be a man on his own."

"I killed a man, Joe. I loved him, Joe."

"Oh, I saw the whole thing," he said. "Jesus and I watched it all from atop a cloud. I tell you that Devil had it coming for a long time. The Lord was pleased you got rid of that dark heart. Said he only ever causes him pain just to look at his pretty face."

"I know it," I said.

Then a shadow comes, and Joe was gone.

I was covered in the cold darkness of the river again.

I heard somebody say, "Jonesy."

I felt the air in front of me for a face.

"Jonesy," he said again. I knew it be Raccoon. He weren't a child no more. He were like a grown man.

I felt a hand go into my own, and clasp my fingers.

"Jonesy," he said, "please, don't go yet. Stay here. In the forest. You and me. We can roam together. Both of us. Like wolves in the night."

Then I saw Raccoon was not a body at all. He was a wolf. The white wolf. The spirit of the forest that come to lick my wounds on the river again. I had my hand on his paw. He licked my face. And I licked his. My body becomes a wolf. Covered in fur and full of hunger and energy. I ran off the bed, and he ran with me. We ran together, fast, fast, to the river. We stopped, panting, and drank the river cold. Then we were off again. Wagging our tails and stopping to bite and growl and clean each other's coats with our tongues. Rolling over in the pine needles and running off again. Running high to the top of the mountain. Looking down at nothing but fir trees and bustling critter life within. Howling with our noses in the air at the many stars that made the sky twinkle like specks of gold in the river bed.

I woke up the next morning to hear birds singing. I felt the warm sun on my face. I thought I must be in heaven now. I opened my eyes to see the place. It was Raccoon's new found home: the Rancheria, where all the Muwekma folks lived. I could smell it all, smoke wood and dried fish.

Raccoon caught my eye. Pointed and yelled at a woman sitting in a chair sleeping. She jumped and turned her attention to me. "Oh," she said. "Praise the Lord, he's alive." She was fussing over me, wiping me down and sitting me up, lying me down again.

Raccoon stood there, just staring at me like I was a spirit returned from the grave. I held up my brother hand to him. Showing him my scar. He held up his, showing off his own.

Next day he said, "I'm going to catch a fish for supper, you want to come?"

I was deathly tired but I said yes.

He wrapped a horse blanket across my shoulders. And put my boots on for me. Made sure they were tied on good so I didn't fall. Helped me walk down to the river.

Crows were cawing, horses were neighing. We passed by the stable and my precious Darling come to see me: trotting over with her white socks, and pressing her pretty head against mine.

I kissed her good morning, and then we carried on, along a deer trail shining in the sun, smelling of fresh green life.

Every now and then we stopped for me to catch my breath. One time we watched eagles nesting in the trees in the blue sky above. Next time we looked at a deer and fawn chewing blackberries from a prickly vine.

We got to the river and Raccoon made a fire. Sat me by it. Then he went and caught a fish.

He killed it quick and held it up for me to see.

It was a daddy. Enough for two suppers.

I clapped my good hand on my lap.

He smiled.

We sat together watching it cook.

We drank real Chinese tea. He smoked sweet Virginia from a pipe made of clay.

Took off his dead dog paw and fixed it around my neck.

When the fish was done, he tore into its belly and fed me some with his fingers.

I closed my eyes and tasted pure pleasure with my lips.

Opened them again and saw his face, looking at mine, with marvelous eyes.

And we smiled at one another.

And we smiled.

The End